MARISOL
ACTS THE PART

ALSO BY ELLE GONZALEZ ROSE

10 Things I Hate About Prom

Caught in a Bad Fauxmance

MARISOL
ACTS THE PART

ELLE GONZALEZ ROSE

Joy Revolution
An imprint of Random House Children's Books
A division of Penguin Random House LLC
1745 Broadway, New York, NY 10019
penguinrandomhouse.com
GetUnderlined.com

Text copyright © 2025 by Elle Gonzalez Rose
Jacket art copyright © 2025 by Natalie Shaw

Penguin Random House values and supports copyright. Copyright fuels creativity, encourages diverse voices, promotes free speech and creates a vibrant culture. Thank you for buying an authorized edition of this book and for complying with copyright laws by not reproducing, scanning, or distributing any part of it in any form without permission. You are supporting writers and allowing Penguin Random House to continue to publish books for every reader. Please note that no part of this book may be used or reproduced in any manner for the purpose of training artificial intelligence technologies or systems.

Joy Revolution and the colophon are trademarks of Penguin Random House LLC.

Editor: Bria Ragin
Cover Designer: Casey Moses
Interior Designer: Kenneth Crossland
Production Editor: Colleen Fellingham
Managing Editor: Tamar Schwartz
Production Manager: Shameiza Ally

Library of Congress Cataloging-in-Publication Data is available upon request.
ISBN 978-0-593-90052-9 (hardcover) — ISBN 978-0-593-90051-2 (trade pbk.) —
ISBN 978-0-593-90053-6 (ebook)

The text of this book is set in 12-point Baskerville MT Pro.

Manufactured in the United States of America
10 9 8 7 6 5 4 3 2 1

The authorized representative in the EU for product safety and compliance is
Penguin Random House Ireland, Morrison Chambers, 32 Nassau Street,
Dublin D02 YH68, Ireland, https://eu-contact.penguin.ie.

Random House Children's Books supports the First Amendment
and celebrates the right to read.

Para Abuela,
la mejor cocinera
en todo el mundo.

CHAPTER 1

Paparazzi get a bad rap. Sure, the shouting and talking over each other can be overwhelming at first. But after a couple of months, it becomes background noise. Like flies buzzing in your ear.

Which, yes, is usually annoying, but this is the good kind of buzz. Not the "sneaking sips of champagne" type of buzz, but something way more exhilarating. The buzz of people clamoring to get closer to you, to hear your voice, to get a single photo of you. The buzz of *attention*—the most powerful drug in Hollywood.

"Ready?" I readjust my purse in the car, making sure the designer's emblem is prominently featured and visible from all potential angles—a lesson I learned the hard way during my last brand ambassadorship. Getting chewed out in rapid Italian by a sixteen-year-old designer who thinks they're Versace reincarnated because you covered up their logo with your "sweaty American armpit" is very humbling.

Camera-ready, I turn my attention to Miles. For someone who's the star of this celebratory dinner, he's not looking very celebratory. Sweat droplets bead along his forehead, smudges of foundation stain the napkin he used to blot himself dry.

"I told you that you have to use setting spray!" I scold before reaching into my bag. Luckily for him, I never leave the house without a bottle. You'd think after four years of crack-of-dawn hair and makeup calls, he'd actually listen to the makeup artists we spent most of our mornings with.

Miles grimaces when I spray a light mist across his face, breaking out into a coughing fit when he accidentally inhales some of it.

"Sorry, sorry, sorry!" I apologize quickly, tossing the bottle back into my bag before I fan his face while he hacks like an eighty-year-old smoker.

Our driver and self-appointed bodyguard, Luis, throws the car into park and arms himself with an umbrella before exiting and heading straight for the crowd of men holding cameras and swarming the backseat door.

"Back it up!" Luis shouts into the crowd, wielding his umbrella like a sword until he's made a narrow path for us to get to the entrance.

I grab Miles's hand, giving it a "look alive" squeeze, and put on my best picture-perfect smile before Luis opens the door and we're met with a flurry of heat, voices, and flashing lights.

Miles shies away from the sudden brightness, shielding himself like a vampire from the sun. I'd ask him if he was okay if we had any time, but the camera firestorm has already begun, meaning the longer we sit here, the better the chances they'll get an unflattering shot.

And there's nothing the internet loves more than an unflattering photo of a hot young celebrity.

I tighten my grip on Miles's hand, tugging him along as I gracefully step out of the car. He doesn't follow like he usually does, dragging behind me like a dog on a leash instead. His hand is tense, uncomfortably stiff and clammy. To save him from the paparazzi getting a shot of him mid-grimace, I position myself in front of him as he exits the car. The crowd focuses on me and the way the hot pink sequins on my minidress gleam in the flash of their cameras. Thank God I went with the Louboutin pumps, or else there's no way I would've been able to cover up six feet of Miles with barely five foot two of me.

"Marisol!" the crowd cries out in unsynchronized chaos. They throw out questions and comments, their voices piled on top of each other until the noise morphs into the static I'm used to. Too jumbled for me to do anything but ignore it, smile, and wave.

Miles takes the lead, ducking his head away from the flashes and ushering me forward so quickly I almost trip.

"Slow down," I hiss once I've caught my balance, making sure to keep my smile in place as we make our way through the crowd toward the restaurant, Capri. But Miles either doesn't hear me or doesn't care, and picks up our pace instead. I let out a quiet *humph* and begrudgingly follow. I spent more than an hour putting together this ensemble; it deserves a moment in the spotlight.

The crowd parts for Miles. At this pace, it's a miracle I make it to Capri without breaking my neck. I can already see the headlines: TEEN STARLET DEAD BY DESIGN: IS THE PRICE OF FASHION WORTH IT?

(Yes, it is. These pumps make my legs look phenomenal.)

A valet in a white tux holds open the door and gestures for us to head inside. Miles leans against the coat-check stand and rubs his left temple, looking like he's fighting off a migraine. I reach for him, prepared to ask what's wrong, when the maître d' appears beside us, red leather menus in hand.

"Right this way, Mr. Zhao," she says with a prim smile, not even bothering to look at me. An annoying yet sadly not unusual new aspect of Miles's and my relationship.

It makes sense, I tell myself as we follow the maître d' to the dining room. As of last week, Miles has officially landed the lead role in season two of *The Limit,* an anthology series that swept both the Emmys and Golden Globes last year.

Not that anyone knows that yet.

The show's director, Rune, is weird about spoilers. So much so he's even keeping the cast announcement on lockdown until they start production. But still, Hollywood thrives on SoulCycle, matcha lattes, and gossip. People were bound to find out, lockdown or not. Especially with the sudden shift in Miles's image ever since we wrapped the series finale of *Avalon Grove,* the teen drama that brought us together. The shaggy-haired fourteen-year-old I met at a callback four years ago has blossomed into a full-on leading man, complete with a six-hundred-dollar haircut and abs so defined you'd think they were photoshopped.

Meanwhile, my career has been a bit . . . stagnant. A

slew of auditions came rushing in when *Avalon Grove* wrapped two months ago—studios eager to try to book me now that I wasn't tied up with my usual shooting schedule—but none of them have panned out. Not the high-concept A24 dystopian rom-com, or the Paramount+ paranormal romance about a headstrong huntress falling for a fledgling vampire, or the young adult Netflix series about a group of college friends studying abroad. I was so sure I nailed that last one.

The market's tough right now, my agent has assured me about a dozen times. Mostly to keep me from spiraling about whether launching my career with a teen drama has ended it prematurely instead of igniting it. Especially considering the only feedback we've gotten is that I wasn't the "image" they were going for. Which definitely seems like code for "We don't cast a teeny-bopper actress for our highbrow show" to me.

At least it's not just me. A few of my other friends from the *Avalon Grove* cast have been in a lull too. The most I've done so far has been a shoot for a new antiaging skincare brand—which feels a little odd for me, an eighteen-year-old, to be the face of, but hey, I won't ask questions as long as I get paid.

So, yeah, it definitely makes sense that people care more about Miles and his career right now. Totally. One hundred percent. The pinched expression still hasn't left Miles's face even after we're seated, sparkling water and fresh bread waiting for us on the table. They were even able to seat us beside the window with stunning views of the sunset. From this high up, you can't even see the traffic clogging the I-5. Los Angeles has never looked better.

The crowd is thinner on a Wednesday night, but not any less star-studded. I quickly scan the room from behind my menu, spotting a group of girls from a Netflix dating show, a few familiar faces I can't quite place, and a couple in a discreet shadowy corner—the star of the latest Marvel movie cuddled up with a pretty young brunette I'm 98 percent sure is *not* his wife.

Can't blame the paparazzi for camping outside of Capri like they're waiting to get into a concert. Hundreds of actors, musicians, and influencers pass through every day like clockwork thanks to their strict "know someone who knows someone" reservation policy. And everyone knows there's nothing we Hollywood elite love more than exclusivity.

If the waiters weren't forced to sign NDAs, they'd make a killing leaking stories to the press.

The completely-in-Italian menu still throws me off as much as it did the first time Miles and I came here, for our first anniversary. Last time, I accidentally ordered what I quickly learned was a whole braised fish. As in head-on, soulless-eyes-blinking-up-at-you whole. The night was so traumatizing, I've been a vegetarian ever since. Well . . . except for In-N-Out. There are some sacrifices I'll never be willing to make.

God, I could go for a Flying Dutchman.

My stomach rumbles in agreement. I set down my menu and lean across the table, prepared to ask Miles if we can swing by the drive-through on our way home, when I notice that he's staring into space, frowning. His menu is still unopened.

"Hey," I whisper as I shift my chair closer to him. "Are you okay? You've been . . . weird tonight."

He's been more than a little weird, but calling him out on

it won't make the situation any better. Miles has always been a terrible texter, but he's reached new levels of terribleness lately. He didn't even respond when I sent him a video of my French bulldog, Bruiser, chasing her nub of a tail. And he *always* responds to Bruiser content. The whole reason I even have her is because he adopted her for me on my birthday last year after I, while high on Novocain from a root canal, spent three hours crying to him about how I didn't book the lead in the *Legally Blonde* reboot. Seriously, who else in Hollywood has a wardrobe as pink as I do? No one.

Not to mention that we've barely seen each other this month. If I can get Miles to reply to my texts or answer my FaceTime calls, he usually only has time to brush me off by saying he has "to go to the gym" or has "a meeting in ten." Who goes to the gym at five in the morning?

Scratch that. I know: soulless people.

Next week, he'll be moving to New York to settle in before filming *The Limit* for the entire summer, and who knows how many times I'll get to see him then. Or if I'll even get to see him. Showmances aren't built to last, but we had something different.

Have, I mean. *Have* something different.

While millions of viewers watched our characters, Celia and Joe, play the will-they-won't-they game for four seasons, our own love story unfolded with a lot less drama. From the moment he came ambling up to me on our first shoot day, offering me a muffin from crafty and a handshake, I knew I was done for. His smile was like a bolt of lightning—sharp and magnetic, leaving me breathless. The brush of his skin against mine when we hugged at the end of the day made my stomach twist into a thousand knots. On the drive home, when Mom asked how the first day went, all I'd been able to say was that I felt like I'd eaten an entire bag of Halloween candy.

And I still feel that way sometimes. Especially since we wrapped the show. But that strange fluttering in my gut doesn't feel giddy anymore—it feels . . . nerve-racking.

Sometimes I wish we could be more like Joe and Celia—or, as the fans dubbed them, Jolia. Childhood best friends turned high school sweethearts who braved new relationships, cheating scandals, and a very dramatic senior year breakup before ultimately finding their way back to one another ahead of prom. A love story trapped in time, sealed with the perfect kiss-in-the-rain ending.

In real life, we don't get the luxury of a season finale.

"Sorry. M'fine." Miles shakes himself off before turning back to me with a smile, reaching for my hand across the table. And just like that, with nothing but a grin and the brush of his thumb across my knuckles, I'm that fourteen-year-old girl again. Smitten and helpless to resist the boy in front of her.

I slide back into my seat with a new sense of comfort as our eyes meet—his a vibrant forest green that reeled me in four years ago. Our futures as actors (or *artists*, as Miles insists) may still be up in the air—well, mine more than his since I'm still very unemployed at the moment—but maybe this doesn't have to be. Maybe Milesol, another fan-generated nickname, doesn't have to end because Jolia's story is over. Maybe I'm overthinking things now that I don't have anything else to occupy my time aside from teaching Bruiser to sit (pointless) and filming self-tapes (not pointless, but it sure as hell feels like it when you're not landing any jobs).

Maybe we can have a happy ending too.

"I think we should break up."

I choke on my water.

Miles leans over to pat my back as I work through a coughing fit, but I push his arm away, suffering alone. Our waiter eyes us warily as my coughs echo through the dining room. Miles turns to give him a thumbs-up and a reassuring smile.

"W-what do you mean we should break up?" I ask once I've caught my breath, finishing off my water before taking his and finishing that too.

Despite the rocky start, dinner had been going perfectly. Miles ranted about the price of short-term rentals in New York, I carefully avoided any discussion of my latest round of auditions, and just when I thought he was going to ask me if I wanted dessert, he springs this on me instead.

I did *not* put myself through the torture of wearing shapewear *and* a push-up bra to get dumped at Capri.

"Well . . ." Miles begins. He runs a hand along his modeled-after-the-gods jawline. It's hard not to be distracted by it even when I'm pissed off and confused. No wonder there are several fan accounts dedicated to posting photos of his jaw.

"Well?" I parrot back when my patience runs out. My voice comes out worn, scratchy. As if I didn't down enough water to keep three camels going for a year.

"I think we're going in different directions," he finally blurts out, avoiding my eyes by focusing his attention on something behind me. "I'm going to be in New York soon for *The Limit,* and you'll be . . ."

"I'll be . . . ?" I prompt, because I'd love to know what I'm going to be doing for the foreseeable future.

Please enlighten me, Miles.

He bites his lip, clearly weighing what he wants to say as he keeps his gaze fixed somewhere in the distance. "This is a big opportunity for me," he says, pivoting after what feels like a hundred years of silence. "Working on this show could completely change my career, and I want to make sure I'm giving it the attention it deserves."

"And you can't do that while dating me?" I question, crossing my arms.

I'd like to think I'm not a needy girlfriend. Yes, we used to spend almost every day together on set, so distance would be something new for us, but I know how important this new show is to him. I know I can't pop up in New York whenever I want—and, quite frankly, I don't want to. Planes are terrifying—humans should not be allowed to go thousands of feet in the air in a metal tube—so I was planning to save my sanity and wait for him to come home for breaks, with one or two visits to the city in between. I know he's going to throw himself fully into this role, but is it too much to ask that he save a sliver of himself for me?

"It's . . . you're . . ." Once again, Miles trails off, and in the silence, I hear a piece of me break.

"I'm what?" I ask, and I hate how small my voice sounds. How I immediately start combing through years' worth of memories to understand what could've led to this. A time when I let him down, or said something wrong, but all I can see are the good moments. The nights talking on the phone until we both fell asleep. The trips to the beach in oversized hoodies and ball caps so we could avoid being noticed. The stolen kisses between interviews and subtle brush of our hands beneath tables.

Miles groans, as if my feelings are a chore. "C'mon, you know what I mean."

"No, Miles, I don't," I snap.

He sighs and runs a hand through his hair. For once I don't marvel at the ways he's changed—from his fashion to his hair to his now flawless, acne-free skin. Instead, I hope his thick, dark hair gets tangled in one of the dozens of silver rings he only started wearing because his publicist told him it was "edgy."

"We did the whole teen-drama thing together, and that was fun, but I'm ready to start taking myself more seriously. My agent thinks *The Limit* could get me some major award nominations."

Okay? Last time I checked I'm as serious as anyone else in this room.

"And I'm not serious enough for you . . ." I say.

His silence speaks volumes.

"You're . . . y'know. You love those Lifetime movies and stuff," he says finally. "Those type of roles."

Wow. Okay. My lips part but no sound comes out, and all I can do is stare out the window because I might lose my cool if I have to look at Miles. Just because I've done one guest role in a Christmas movie and gravitate toward romance scripts doesn't mean I'm not "serious" about my literal job. Does that mean all he can do is Marvel movies because he's obsessed with comic books? And since when does that dictate who is and isn't "serious"? What does it matter if I wind up making my living playing roles that I like—roles that are fun and flirty and swoony? It's *my* career. Not his.

"Why don't you pivot and try reality TV instead?" he suggests, as if that absolves him of basically trashing my career. "You loved that dancing competition you did."

"Because I'm an actress," I reply through gritted teeth. *Dancing Divas* was fun, sure, but I obviously can't make a living on celebrity competition shows. And I don't *want* to. Contrary to what Miles might think, I'm good at my job. My Teen Choice Award confirms that. My millions of followers too. *Avalon Grove* isn't the type of show that wins awards like *The Limit* does, but that doesn't mean I didn't crush my performances season after season.

My hot pink nails dig hard enough into my bare arms that pain shoots through me, but all I can do is glare at the boy in front of me, and hope my stare is hot enough to burn.

A server in a crisp white button-down and red silk vest approaches us, speaking in the same heavy Italian accent as the rest of the staff, which we know is for show. Most of the staff here are aspiring actors who wanted a day job that lets them practice their accent work.

"Are you ready to—"

"Not yet," I interject before the server can finish, the man doing a complete one-eighty the second I interrupt him and walking away before I can finish.

My stomach clenches at the thought of how many other

epic celebrity breakups may have gone down right where we're sitting. What better place to end things than at a restaurant with an ironclad NDA?

"You're an amazing person, Mari. For real," Miles continues, finally meeting my eyes, once the server is out of earshot. I don't fall for the allure of his gaze this time—if anything, being forced to stare at his full lashes makes me that much angrier. I hope he goes bald in his thirties.

"And I'm grateful we got to spend our teenage years together. But we're adults now. We need to evolve. Things are going to change for the both of us."

"Nothing's changed for me," I reply, voice wavering but steadier than before. Other than now having the most free time I've had since I was in middle school, everything has stayed the same for me. Brand deals, self-tapes, my team pushing me to bite the bullet and finally go blond. My feelings for him.

And maybe my feelings for him will never change.

Miles winces, and I kind of relish watching him squirm. But the vindictive thrill is short-lived, quickly replaced by an overwhelming need to sob. I press my balled fist against my mouth, focusing on the pain of my nails digging into my palm instead of the urge to cry. Thank God I wore ultra-strength lashes tonight. The last thing I need is an eyelash strip dangling like a rogue caterpillar. Even a category five hurricane couldn't knock these bad boys off.

What hurts the most is how formal this all feels. Like we're severing a business contract instead of a multiyear relationship. I spent most of my teenagerhood falling for him. There are entire blogs dedicated to us—to our relationship outside of the show—posting photos of us walking red carpets and sharing knowing glances from across rooms. We were more than our characters. We were *real*.

"Mari . . ." Miles begins, reaching for me again.

"I want to go home."

I want to go back in time, to the stupid, beautiful moment when I fell in love with this stupid, beautiful boy and warn my younger self that it'll all go up in flames. I want to crawl into bed. I want to scream. I want to eat my weight in peanut butter.

He stops, his hand lingering in midair above my shoulder. It falls limply back down onto the table, his fingers a few inches from mine. He's close enough that I feel heat radiating off him.

"C'mon, Mari," Miles tries again, but keeps his distance this time. "We can go after dessert."

"Seriously?" I snap.

He shrugs, his cheeks pink as he settles back in his seat. "I really like the tiramisu here."

The groan that comes out of me sounds more like an animalistic growl. His brow furrows as I grab my purse off the empty chair beside me. He's watching me all wide-eyed and Bambi-like as if he doesn't think he's done anything wrong.

The server suddenly reappears beside me, cautiously leaning toward our table. "Is everything—"

"I'M FINE!" I shout so loudly it startles the rest of the dining room into total silence.

Socialites and award-winning actors blink up at me from their overpriced penne vodka, strangers witnessing my lowest moment. Their eyes follow me as I storm out of the dining room, but Miles doesn't. That hurts more than a plea to come back, that he doesn't even think I'm worth chasing.

I quickly text Luis.

> Dinner wrapped up sooner than expected. Can you pick me up now?

> Had to run some errands—still about thirty minutes away. Everything okay?

The rational thing to do would be to go back to the dining room and suffer through dessert with Miles until Luis gets here. I wouldn't have to say anything, but the thought of that makes my blood boil. I've already made the dramatic exit. I can't turn back around with my tail between my legs. If I'd brought a less expensive purse, I might even consider hitchhiking.

I decide to take refuge in the bathroom, tipping the attendant by the sinks a twenty for extra privacy as I lock myself into the closest stall and open up my phone. Views as spectacular as the one we had at our table come with a price, and in this case, it's any type of reception. If my phone wasn't a glorified camera in here, I'd call my mom and ask her to come pick me up—but just sending a text back to Luis, letting him know I'm fine, takes two tries before the message gets delivered. Plus, there's no way she'd be able to make it through the traffic in less than an hour. After another ten minutes attempting to open a rideshare app, and another five to confirm my ride, I rush out of the bathroom to meet the driver and put this nightmare of a day behind me.

Mentally, I'm already deciding which rom-com to binge once I'm home. The thought of changing into my favorite pajamas and curling up with Bruiser on the couch is the only thing stopping me from breaking down. Every time I let my mind drift back to Miles—to any of the hundreds of memories I have of him—feels like a punch to the gut. I wipe at my damp cheeks, eternally grateful for the setting spray keeping my foundation and concealer in place, as my legs carry me on pure instinct. Until a flurry of flashing lights knocks me back.

"Marisol!" the same voices from earlier shout again. Without Luis to break up the crowd, the paparazzi surround me like sharks to blood in the water. Their questions overlap one another, all of their voices melding together into one suffocating wave of noise.

"Where's Miles?"

"Why are you two leaving separately?"

"Do you have anything lined up now that you've wrapped on *Avalon Grove*?"

"What's next for you?"

"How was dinner?"

"Did you two have a fight?"

"Leave me alone!" I shout, and for the first time, the paparazzi quiet. Their cameras fall to their sides, mouths open in quiet shock as I struggle to breathe. I don't even realize I've started crying again until the tears drip down to my chin, one falling onto my Tiffany charm bracelet.

The peace doesn't last long. A balding man with two cameras around his neck takes a photo so close to my face the flash makes stars cloud my vision. That whips me back to reality, and I use the small window of time I still have to rush out of the swarm. With the spell broken, the rest of the photographers join back in, scrambling for "the shot" and calling my name as I push and shove my way through the sweaty, packed crowd.

When I finally emerge on the other side, my ponytail extension is hanging on for dear life, and I'm seconds away from having a meltdown. Miraculously, my Lyft driver awaits in his Honda Civic chariot only a few feet away from the curb. I dash into the backseat, holding my breath until the door has closed behind me and the paparazzi's shouts have dulled to white noise. The driver slams down on the gas, pulling back onto the road so fast I'm pressed against the leather seats. Five stars, for sure. Both he and the staff at Capri will be getting a generous tip tonight for dealing with my post-breakup drama.

In the rearview mirror, I spot some of the photographers chasing after the car, others eyeing their own cars on the opposite side of the curb before ultimately returning to their posts by the entrance. I can hear the one closest to the car shouting out to me, even over the smooth jazz the driver has playing on the radio.

"Did something happen between you and Miles?! Did he dump you?! Is he cheating?!" he shouts so frantically you'd think he was drowning and begging for a lifeboat. All while still taking dozens—probably even hundreds—of photos of me until he's nothing but a speck on the horizon.

Okay, fine, I was wrong. Paparazzi are the absolute worst.

STARS WEEKLY

BREAKING: *AVALON GROVE* SWEETHEARTS CALL IT QUITS AS SHOW COMES TO A CLOSE

BY NORA MURPHY

Social media was abuzz last night when photos emerged of *Avalon Grove* star Marisol Polly-Rodriguez storming out of A-list hot spot Capri in tears after arriving with longtime boyfriend and former *Avalon Grove* costar Miles Zhao. Rumors quickly swirled as it became clear that the starlet was leaving—in a hurry, at that—without her beau. Fans began to speculate that the adorable couple had abruptly split—something that perhaps Polly-Rodriguez should've seen coming, according to an insider. "Those two have been on the rocks for months," our source said.

Stars Weekly can officially confirm, in an exclusive statement from Zhao's team, that the couple has split after nearly four years together.

"Adjusting to this new, exciting phase of my career has meant evolving both personally and professionally. I'm so grateful to have met Marisol and the years we got to spend together. She's an amazing person, and I wish nothing but the best for her moving forward."

COMMENTS

WTFFFFFFFFFF HOW IS THIS HAPPENING

LOL who didn't see this coming? She's a massive airhead, obviously he was going to dump her eventually

im a child of divorce

this makes sense tbh. he was always a waaaaaaaaay better actor than her lmao

omg wait does this confirm he's officially in season two of the limit?????

idk the two of them never made sense to me

HOW AM I SUPPOSED TO BELIEVE IN TRUE LOVE NOW

CHAPTER 2

"Americone Dream or Half Baked?" Lily asks in lieu of a greeting as I open my front door. She and her twin sister, Posie, arrived a record-breaking twenty minutes after my SOS text to them about the breakup.

My stomach rumbles as I consider my ice cream options. "Both?"

"Both, it is," Posie replies, pulling two spoons out of thin air.

Opening the front door for them was the first time I've left the nest I built in the living room last night. After forty-five minutes of alternating between sobbing on the couch and sobbing in the reclining chair, I was too wiped to climb up the stairs to my room. My mom came to the rescue with a pair of pajamas fresh out of the dryer, a blanket, and so much hot chocolate my teeth have started to ache.

By morning, I'd stopped crying long enough to send an SOS signal to Lily and Posie. *Avalon Grove* may have been the start and end of Miles and my epic love story, but at least it gave me my best friends. It's a miracle that we're as close as we are, considering they played my character's bitter archenemies. We may've hated each other on-screen for four seasons, but we've been inseparable off-screen ever since we bonded over our shared love for glitter eye shadow and rom-coms.

Bruiser perks up at the arrival of the twins and fresh snacks, tongue lapping out of her mouth happily and a dribble of snot running down her mouth as she curls up on my lap.

"Gross, Bruise." I groan when some of her snot gets onto my pajama pants. As wonderful company as she is, she's definitely not my most hygienic friend.

Lily saves me from another snot attack by lifting Bruiser into her arms, and they settle down beside me. The girls watch me pop the lids off both pints and help myself to a spoonful of each. My stomach will hate me for this tomorrow, but I can't find it in me to care today.

The combination of the chunks of chocolate-covered waffle cone and caramel from Americone Dream and the brownie and cookie dough from Half Baked creates a euphoric taste explosion in my mouth, making my entire body shiver. All I've been able to have for dessert publicly for the past three months is the sugar-free-dairy-free-low-calorie-no-fun sorbet I did a brand deal with. Thankfully, I'm not bound to Berry Delicious Sorbet now that they've declared bankruptcy. Heartbreak calls for full-calorie goodness.

"How're you feeling?" Posie asks after I've handed her the Half Baked to focus my attention on Americone Dream.

"Like garbage." I gesture down to my stained pajama pants. "And I look like it too."

"Well, I thi—"

"Please don't tell me I look beautiful."

Both Lily and Posie pout. It'd be impossible to tell them apart if it wasn't for the diamond initial necklaces they always wear. They don't make it any easier with their wardrobes, either. Today they're decked out in matching baby-blue tracksuits with their blond hair pulled into sleek high ponies, their usually pale skin glowing with the subtle radiance of a fresh spray tan. "But you do!" Posie protests.

I glare, and she immediately backs off. Posie has enough energy and enthusiasm to power a ten-story building, but I'm not ready to be recharged.

"Sorry," I apologize quickly, not meaning to take my anger out on the people who drove all the way from Santa Monica to be with me. I punctuate the statement by offering both of them spoons and holding the pint of Americone Dream toward them. "Thank you for being here."

"Of course," Posie says, my earlier snap rolling right off her back as she helps herself to a bite of Americone Dream first, then Half Baked. "Miles is such a dick."

"Seriously," Lily agrees, leaning her head against my shoulder. "Anyone who dumps someone as amazing as you needs to seriously rethink their life choices."

I snort around my ice cream, and as unattractive as the sound is, it feels good to laugh. My lips and throat still ache—as if I haven't used the muscles to laugh in years instead of a few hours—but I'll take the pain to feel something other than self-pity.

Happily digging into our ice cream, we all turn our attention to the final moments of the latest Hallmark Original I'd been watching before they got here. I wrinkle my nose as the heroine seals her happily-ever-after with a kiss, her handsome leading man promising to love her forevermore.

"Liar," I mumble under my breath.

If there's one thing I've learned in the past twenty-four hours, it's that happily-ever-afters are 100 percent bullshit.

Lily and Posie each give me worried glances. I can't blame them for looking at me like some kind of subterranean monster has taken over their best friend's body—because that's exactly what I am. An unholy creature. Leaving my hair in a bun overnight has left it so tangled I couldn't pull out the pen that accidentally got trapped in the mess, so I've decided to just leave it in and deal with the consequences later. I popped off all my acrylics in a fit of rage last night, leaving my chewed-to-nubs nails on full display. I skipped seven of the ten steps in my usual nightly cleansing routine, which means I woke up with a zit the size of Texas on my chin and enough whiteheads on my forehead to grate cheese. And I'm pretty sure there's still mascara smudged into the creases of my eye bags.

Needless to say, I'm a hot mess. And not even the fun kind.

Something beneath my cocoon of blankets and takeout containers begins to buzz, along with a notification on my Apple Watch informing me that my agent, Delia, is calling.

Suddenly, Mom appears in the doorway of her office, holding up her own phone.

"Are you going to answer?"

I sigh and sink into the comfort of my hoodie like an ostrich shoving their head in the sand. "Do I have to?" I reply, my voice muffled by the fabric.

Lily and Posie exchange frowns while Mom gives me a

glare that makes it clear I don't really have a choice in the matter.

"Fine," I mumble, digging for my phone in the crumb-littered couch cushions while Mom switches into Manager Mode as she slides in her AirPods, accepts the call, and heads back to her office.

Most days, I'm grateful to have my mom as my manager. If it weren't for Mom knowing how terrible I look in cool tones, I might have let Delia hound me into going platinum blond by now. Nobody stands up for you like the person who spent seventeen hours in labor birthing you. But today, I wish she would just be my mom and let business calls wait until I don't feel like I've been run over by a semitruck.

"Hey, sorry," I mutter when I answer my phone, brushing chip crumbs off the screen and throwing it on speaker so Lily and Posie can hear too. "Couldn't find my phone."

"No problem," Delia's assistant chirps. "Grabbing Delia, Joanna, and Blake now."

"O-oh," I stammer, leaving us to listen to the agency's signature funky hold music. Immediately, I regret putting the call on speaker.

The full Marisol Polly-Rodriguez team is almost never on the same call together. It would take a year and a day to coordinate my lawyer, Joanna's, and publicist, Blake's, schedules with Delia's and my own, and probably another hour to wrangle us all onto one conference line. The last time the three of them called me at the same time was to tell me *Avalon Grove* was nominated for a Teen Choice Award *and* the MTV Movie & TV Award for Best Kiss—the highest honors a show like ours could be bestowed.

This is either really, really great or, more likely, really, really, *really* bad.

Isn't it bad enough that I had to get unexpectedly dumped? Why is the universe trying to torture me?

The music comes to an abrupt stop as a *bloop* announces Delia's assistant's return. "Everyone is on," she says before the members of my team start talking at once.

Delia takes charge, shushing the others with an intensity that I can feel even through the phone. She holds a beat, waiting until the line is fully quiet, before speaking. "How are you, Marisol?"

Oh God, something is definitely wrong.

Delia Lane is one of the best agents in the business for a reason. She has an encyclopedic knowledge of every single actor, representative, and who's who in the entertainment industry, and has a client list that I'm *still* amazed I'm on. Which means she's always running a mile a minute from meetings to sets to premieres in Europe or some exotic island. I wouldn't be surprised if Delia's assistant has to schedule time in her calendar for her to sleep.

Delia's time is precious. And across our three years together, she's never once greeted me during a call. As soon as she's on the line, we get right down to business. Someone like her doesn't have time to waste on pleasantries when she's calling to tell you she booked you an audition for the next major fantasy franchise.

Unless she needs to soften some kind of blow . . .

"Fine," I answer reluctantly.

I'm sure the paparazzi photos of my less-than-graceful exit from Capri are splashed across the internet by now, but they barely paint the full picture. For all the public knows I just got a migraine and took my frustration out on the unsuspecting public in a moment of weakness. We should have a couple weeks to figure out how to navigate my new Miles-less life—assuming they're not firing me right now.

The thought of it—both me being fired and having to treat my breakup as a business move—makes my head throb as I hold back yet another wave of oncoming tears. And here I thought last night's ugly cry had wiped me out.

"Some photos of you went up on *Stars Weekly* last night—"

"Miles broke up with me," I explain before Delia can even finish. Might as well rip off the Band-Aid now and work out our damage control plan later. Again, assuming they're not kicking me to the curb.

"We know," Blake replies in his usual flat monotone.

"W-what?"

"We drafted up a response to the piece," he continues as if he hadn't heard me. I can hear the muffled sound of typing, followed by a ping as an email titled **STARS WEEKLY BREAK UP RESPONSE (Draft 1)** comes through on my phone. "If we get your sign-off now, we could have this up within the hour."

My head spins as I struggle to put together what they've thrown at me. "Response to what?" I ask, opening up the email Blake sent me.

"To Miles's statement about the breakup."

Miles's *what?*

I'm frozen by the shock of what Blake said, as casually as if he'd been going over the details for an interview. It hasn't even been twenty-four hours yet, and Miles has already talked to the press? Sure, my dramatic exit didn't leave us with any time to sort out the logistical details of our breakup, but I didn't think he'd go spilling to the media immediately.

To think I'd spent most of last night checking my phone, hoping with what little optimism I had left that he would text, or call, or show up on my doorstep with a dozen roses and an *I screwed up* balloon. Honestly, I would've let him back in. I would've given him hell first—unless he brought chocolate, because chocolate heals all wounds—but at the end of the day, I would've forgotten the way I felt at Capri and kissed him because it wasn't the last time anymore.

But he didn't even have the decency to warn me before he told the entire world that he'd broken my heart.

"Miles told them?" I ask, my voice cracking as I struggle to choke back a sob.

On either side of me, Lily and Posie tap away at their phones—probably searching for the article. Before I can ask my team to send it to me, Lily does the honors herself, handing me her phone.

At the top of the page is a high-definition photo of me in all of my tearstained, smudged-mascara, nose-running glory at Capri. With the exception of Mom's lock screen photo of me eating dirt when I was two years old, it's the most unflattering photo of me that's ever existed. And that's saying a lot—there are many pictures of me eating pizza on the internet. No one looks dignified while trying to manage a cheese pull.

And there's more than one photo. The reporter was sure to include as many shots of my now-infamous exit as they could cram into one article. You can watch in real time as I reach my breaking point, starting from my shock as I realize the paparazzi didn't conveniently leave the second I wanted them gone, leading up to an image of me mid-shout as I yell at them to leave me alone.

"We think it's important to position you as hopeful about the future," Blake says, but the words go right over my head as I scan the article as quickly as I can, scanning for Miles's official statement.

I scoff at the claim halfway through the article that Miles and I have been on the rocks "for months." I'm sure their "insider source" is someone who worked on the show for a day and wanted a quick fifty bucks. It wouldn't be the first time someone I barely know has tried to use talking to me for less than a minute as a one-way ticket to quick profit or fifteen minutes of fame.

After scanning past the unfounded source, an eerie sense of déjà vu washes over me as I read Miles's statement.

The exact same things Miles said to me last night. Almost word for word. I'm an "amazing person." Evolving "personally and professionally." Yadda yadda. So spot-on I can hear his voice reading each word, breaking my heart all over again.

Was he reading off a script last night? Did he send his speech to his reps beforehand? Did they rehearse like breaking my heart was another scene he had to memorize?

Before I can stop myself, I scroll down to the bottom of the article. Straight to the comment section. In a moment of weakness, I seek validation. Something you should never look for from outside sources. I look for someone who can see the truth, that Miles is a dirtbag who let me think I was his endgame when I was actually a subplot in the story of his career.

Most of the responses are run-of-the-mill. "Who are these

people" and "Why is this considered news?" types. After wading through the top comments, I stop.

Accounts with photos of me, or Miles, or both of us as their icons flood the comments with heartbreak, devastation, and support. For a few seconds, I let myself revel in it. Taking comfort in the fact that the world was as shocked by my dumping as I was. But, as always, I let myself linger too long. Long enough to see the comments people like me are meant to avoid.

Dozens of them. More than I expected. The replies are a warzone. M&Ms—the die-hard Milesol shippers—come to my defense while even more faceless accounts come out of the woodwork to tear me and my relationship apart.

It's not the first time I've been exposed to hate. Anyone in our industry has, even if you try your best to avoid it. No matter what I post, there'll be people spamming the replies with the worst kind of hatred. Some are easier to ignore—the ones accusing me of getting lip filler or photoshopping my acne away. Others hit harder. Especially the ones who insult my intelligence, as if they can make that kind of judgment about me from a selfie I took on the beach with a coconut emoji caption. Those have always been the ones that feel the loudest—the comments calling me dumb, or an airhead, or worse. Either because they need to make themselves feel better or because I'm an attractive woman on the internet, and that means people think they're entitled to tear me down.

It hurts even more now, though. Seeing people praise Miles, speculating about his new lead role and his sudden need to dump me, like that makes it okay. Like I'm not a person with feelings too. That's not surprising, though. Miles has never had to deal with the level of hate I get for something as innocent as a photo of my morning iced coffee. None of the boys in the cast has.

The supportive comments brush right past me because my cruel brain's only able to focus on the negativity. All the horrible things anonymous strangers have to say about me, my relationship, and my career. Echoing what Miles implied last night—that I'm not serious enough for him. That he's destined to be a star, and I'm not. Dread bubbles in my stomach and crawls up my throat. The pounds of sugar I've consumed since last night betray me in the form of heartburn and the urge to throw up on my laptop.

Et tu, Ben and Jerry?

"Marisol?" Blake asks, snapping me out of my self-deprecating spiral.

"Y-yeah, sounds good," I mumble as I shake myself off, assuming he was talking about the statement he drafted. Lily takes back her phone and runs a soothing hand down my arm. "Approved."

Probably not the best move to approve a public statement without reading it first, but I don't think my uneasy stomach could handle having to read through a clinical summary of my relationship. That can be filed away into the "things to regret tomorrow" folder, which is getting concerningly full.

"This could be a great opportunity to get you into more rooms!" Delia says brightly, shifting the conversation into a more positive light. "I know the last few auditions haven't worked out, but your name's back in the media circuit again, and that never hurts." I wouldn't think the details of my breakup being splashed across the internet would be a good thing, but I guess it's true that all publicity is good publicity. "There's a new teen drama in development at the CW. Casting hasn't started yet, but I can set up something for you and the showrunner?"

Last week, maybe even yesterday, I would've jumped at the chance. Another shot at a role in something I'm used to. *Avalon Grove* was rare in its decision to cast actual teenagers, but I can still bank on my baby face for another five years at least. Still, even though I'm trying to ignore it, Miles's voice haunts me. Like the world's most annoyingly handsome poltergeist.

"What about something different?" I suggest delicately.

"Like daytime?" Delia asks in pure terror. "Please don't tell me you want to do daytime."

Absolutely not. *No one* looks good in daytime lighting. "I was thinking something with more . . . prestige."

Delia hums in thought. "Did you have something in mind?"

I bite my lip, pushing away my doubts and hesitations before I can let them stop me. "What about *The Limit*?"

"Yes!" Blake exclaims at the same time that Delia lets out a tentative "Well . . ." Lily and Posie each let out a quiet gasp, immediately covering their mouths.

The room goes totally silent.

Delia then picks up the torch.

"They *are* looking to fill a few more roles that you might be good for. No promises, but I can try to get you a self-tape at least. Or maybe even in the room if I can pull the right strings."

"Absolutely not!" Mom interjects, suddenly appearing in the doorway to her office again, staring directly at me as she speaks. "You can't go out for the same show that Miles will be on."

"Why not?" I reply indignantly, ignoring the echo of her words through the phone a few seconds after I watch her say them. Why should the guy who dumped me get to dictate what I can and can't audition for?

"Because . . ." Mom trails off, sighing and pinching the bridge of her nose. The line stays quiet except for a muffled cough from Blake. Lily's and Posie's heads go back and forth between me and Mom like they're watching an intense tennis match as she walks toward us.

Mom mutes her phone before setting it aside on the coffee table, then leaning down to kneel next to us on the couch. "Don't put yourself through this, Mari," she whispers, resting her hand on my knee.

The softness of her touch threatens to break me. I could end the call now. Tell Delia I'll call her back and cuddle up with my mom and best friends and cry like I want to. But for a flash of a second, I felt something close to hope, to *excitement*. And I don't want to let that go. Not yet.

"Legally, it's not a problem," Joanna interrupts, startling both Mom and me out of our staring contest. "Unless you think he has any reason to file a restraining order against you."

I tear my gaze away from Mom's, shifting my attention back to my phone. "I think I'll be fine." Miles may be an ass, but he doesn't run Hollywood. I'm just as entitled to a part on *The Limit* as he is.

"Are you sure this is something you want to do?" Delia asks warily. "There's this great Netflix rom-com that you'd be perfect for. Or a comedy about—"

"I'm sure," I say before she can finish. "Time for something different, right?"

"Right . . ." Delia's tone remains hesitant, and the silence that follows her reply isn't promising, but she at least feigns enthusiasm when she promises to send me updates and details once she has them.

When the call ends with the promise of more to come soon, Mom gives me a disapproving eye. Even Bruiser seems intrigued when I sit up straighter than I have in the last twenty-four hours and pull my hair out of its wreck of a bun for a more presentable, slicked-back ponytail instead. I smile as I turn off the TV, dust the crumbs off my hoodie, and gesture for Lily and Posie to follow me up to my room.

"Let's start laying out some potential audition outfits."

They exchange a confused look, their frowns loosening and turning into smiles as they lunge off the couch. As we head upstairs, we're already brainstorming what top would look best with my hot pink pleated skirt, Bruiser in tow. Mom sighs and goes to clean up our abandoned ice cream.

Who says I can't take myself more seriously too?

CHAPTER 3

Not for the first time, I curse my weakness for caffeine.

"Fill this out, please," a harried casting assistant says as he hands me a clipboard that I almost drop thanks to my shaking hands.

If I actually had the ability to drive past a Starbucks drive-through without getting myself a little treat, I wouldn't be sitting here, panic through the roof with a desperate need to pee at what is possibly the most important audition of my career. It's bad enough that I had to drive two hours out of the city to this sketchy warehouse because Rune insists on keeping things under wraps. I'd made the foolish decision to wait until I got to the audition to use the bathroom only to find out they don't have one. What kind of monster holds auditions in a bathroom-less abandoned pencil factory?

I did *not* cut the tags off this Dior skirt to risk peeing myself the first time I wear it.

To get my mind off thoughts of completely bombing this audition and getting permanently blacklisted from Hollywood, I quickly scan the list of questions on the clipboard.

> Approximately how long are you able to go without food?
> Have you ever experienced lucid dreaming?
> On a scale of 1–10, how comfortable are you with liminal spaces?
> Would you feel comfortable being locked in an enclosed space for up to ten minutes?
> If you spotted a dangerous creature in the woods, would you stand your ground or run? Explain your choice.

"Uh—"

"Just approximate," the casting assistant replies as if I'd asked a question aloud. He disappears back into the room off the hall before I can get another word out, locking the door behind him.

Well. This is definitely the most interesting audition I've ever been to.

I should've seen this coming when the initial self-tape asked that I "emulate an animal that speaks to me." It took almost three hours of shooting and four scrapped animals before I finally settled on a take where I genuinely felt like a cow. Delia had praised my performance when I sent her the final clip, but it's impossible to tell if my moos were any good. Bruiser started to growl at me during the last few takes, so I must've been somewhat convincing, at least.

And lo and behold, it got me here. To what is gearing up to be the weirdest experience of my life.

Filling out the questionnaire at least gives me something to concentrate on. I fudge my answers a bit. Tight spaces have always made me feel uneasy, but there's no way I drove all the way out to this creepy warehouse only to have my claustrophobia get me written off before I can even get into the audition room.

I'm so focused on rating my comfort level with liminal spaces that I don't notice another person sitting across from me until the casting assistant reappears, handing her a clipboard and the same terse "just approximate" instruction before leaving again.

Carefully, I peek at the girl with bouncy curls on the other end of the room. I'm instantly relieved that I saw the light and booked a keratin treatment last week. A gift to my poor, neglected hair after leaving it in my postbreakup messy bun for over eighteen hours. The pin-straight curtain falling delicately over my shoulder gives me the perfect cover for scoping out the competition.

The girl doesn't fit the typical LA actress mold. And she clearly doesn't know about the weather. My nose wrinkles as I take in her black long-sleeve shirt and jeans. It's not a bad outfit—it actually really suits her. But the thought of wearing long sleeves—and black, at that—makes my skin clammy. The temperature here is higher than in the city, clocking in somewhere in the mid-eighties, according to my car's dashboard. Along with not having bathrooms, this warehouse doesn't have AC either. We're both trapped in a torture dungeon. Yet there's not so much as a single bead of sweat anywhere on her.

Meanwhile, I'm here struggling not to sweat through the three layers of deodorant I applied after I parked my G-Wagon in the lot out back.

But it's not the too-warm outfit that draws my attention. It's the unfairly perfect curve of her lips as she reads the questions on the sheet to herself, and the glossy shine in her thick spiral curls that would put any conditioner model to shame. And her dark, arched brows that probably never need to be shaded in, and the soft, natural glow of her warm brown skin.

She's so pretty that looking at her makes my heart pound like I just ran a marathon.

"Marisol?" the casting assistant calls out from the doorway.

I pry my eyes away from the girl, cheeks flushed from the suddenly too-hot room and the fear of almost getting caught acting like a total creep. I fan myself with the clipboard and follow the casting assistant, making sure to keep my gaze fully averted from Ridiculously Beautiful Girl. Now is *really* not the time to get hit by bisexual panic.

The door closes behind me with a menacing *thunk*, the casting assistant sliding behind me to lock it before ushering me down a dimly lit hallway. The sketchy vibes are through the roof. If I wasn't already sharing my phone location with my mom, Delia, and Lily and Posie, I would've immediately turned back around and gotten the hell out of here. At least if something suspicious goes down, my people will know where to find my body.

We step into a room painted a blinding shade of white with nothing inside it except for a camera on a tripod, a black fold-out table, three chairs, and two vaguely familiar faces.

"Hi, Marisol," Marie Williams, the casting director, says

with a warm smile. I've read for her a couple of times over the years, and even if I've never landed any of the roles she's called me back for, seeing someone I know and (kind of) trust eases my nerves.

Beside her, hunched and scribbling furiously in a notebook, is who I can only assume is the infamous Rune. There aren't many photos of him online, but from what little I found, he seems to fit the bill. Hair so blonde it's almost white with pale skin to match. His blue cotton sweater is mussed, wrinkled as though it's never seen an iron. Various splotches stain his black skinny jeans.

Suddenly, I feel overdressed in my pink leather miniskirt, matching ankle boots, and white silk blouse. I'll admit the pussy bow on my top might be a bit much, but if I want to take myself more seriously, I've got to dress the part.

Clearly, Rune doesn't feel the same way.

When he finally picks his head up, the intensity of his gaze nearly knocks the wind out of me. There's a strange, wild look to his eyes—like he's a starving predator on the hunt, and I'm his latest meal, served up on a silver platter.

"H-hi," I manage to choke out, pulling my attention away from Rune's piercing blue eyes and focusing on Marie instead.

The casting assistant bustles around me, muttering to himself as he fiddles with the camera. I readjust the pink bow fastened at the crown of my head, searching for something to keep my hands busy. While Rune whispers to Marie, mouth covered by his hand, I quickly glance down at the notebook he was writing in earlier. Coffee stains litter the worn pages of the Moleskine. Notes and drawings cover every inch of it, going beyond the laid-out margins and across the binding between the pages. Some of it has even made its way off the page, pen marks littering the slips of paper beneath his notebook.

"Stand here," the casting assistant says, not waiting for me to respond before physically moving me himself onto a black duct-taped mark in front of the camera.

I swallow hard and toy with my nameplate necklace while he adjusts the camera, then returns to the foldout table beside Marie and Rune.

"How are you?" Marie asks, her expression sympathetic when I jump at the sound of her voice.

"Good. Great," I reply with my best attempt at a smile. The sweat pooling beneath my arms and across my face is getting harder to ignore. Obviously, my makeup will stay in place, but knowing my eyeliner will stay as flawless as ever doesn't do anything to soothe the anxiety coursing through me like the venti extra dirty chai latte I downed on the way here.

In retrospect, five shots of espresso was definitely a bad call.

But in my defense, I barely got any sleep last night. Ever since Delia emailed me about this audition, I've been plagued by nightmares about forgetting my lines and completely blanking in front of Rune. I'm no stranger to auditions, and normally I'm able to calm my nerves with a morning run, but this has higher stakes than any of my other ones. Even the *Legally Blonde* reboot.

All the fears that have been piling up for months—that I'm being written off because of *Avalon Grove*, that no one wants to take a chance on me because they don't think of me as anything more than a "teen starlet"—bubble to the surface. Then there's the breakup. The growing mountain of ghosted auditions and callbacks. The lack of any calls to my agent except for brand deals and the occasional commercial. If I didn't have the right image for a Netflix rom-com, then how the hell am I going to fit the bill for a gritty prestige drama series?

After we wrapped *Avalon Grove*, Delia told me my career was only beginning, but it sure as hell doesn't feel that way when everyone's decided that one character is all I'll ever be able to do. And it doesn't matter that I think that's absolute bullshit. That I loved playing Celia, or that I loved working on *Avalon Grove* even more. It gave me and Mom financial security for the first time in years. It gave me my best friends. It gave me Miles, and as much as it might hurt to think about him now, I still can't find it in me to regret falling in love with him.

Was it the most groundbreaking and original show? No. Was it the greatest performance of my career? I hope not. But that doesn't change that it was still something important to people. An opportunity for teenagers to see themselves represented on-screen—not downplaying the emotional intensity of how it feels to fall in love at our age or brushing off our feelings. That show meant something—to me, to my friends, to the world. And I'm really freaking tired of people trying to make me feel like there's something wrong with that.

Needless to say, with those thoughts swirling, I got about two hours of actual rest. I either needed to hop myself up on caffeine and sugar, or risk falling asleep mid-monologue.

That is, assuming they'll have me read a monologue. No one has actually told me *what* I'm supposed to be doing yet. All I'd been told was to come as "open to the energy of the world" as possible. I did twenty minutes of yoga this morning, which means I'm more open to the energy of the world than usual, right?

Did Miles have to go through this? Because I can't imagine

Miles "Studies his lines until he can say them forward, backward, and in Mandarin" Zhao wouldn't have been panicking. He'd been intentionally vague about his auditions, thanks to the NDA he, and now I, had to sign before our in-person auditions. An NDA so long it may have demanded I sacrifice my firstborn if I ever talk publicly about the casting process, and I would have no idea—my eyes started to glaze over by page three. Of nine.

Still, the thought of Miles makes me hold myself with more pride. I may feel out of my depth, but that doesn't mean that I am. Something the world seems to have forgotten is that Miles started in the same place as me. Sure, he took a few extra acting classes during the summers, but that doesn't mean he's automatically leading man material while my career withers into dust. If Miles can pivot his career, I can too.

Rune whispers something to the casting assistant this time, careful to keep his mouth covered. Once Rune pulls away, the casting assistant nods and leafs through his clipboard before handing a half sheet to me.

"Please read this into the camera whenever you're ready."

It's a short, typed passage. Barely three lines. I scan them over and over, trying to memorize them as quickly as I can. Remembering lines has never been one of my strong suits. Miles used to joke that I wouldn't remember my own name if I didn't wear it around my neck every day. These are even harder to nail down—none of the sentences flow together to create a cohesive narrative.

```
I am the goddess of the death. Tomorrow
I'll see what the world has in store
for me. You mean nothing to me.
```

Definitely more intense than what I'm used to.

I inhale deeply, following the instructions from the yoga video I'd watched this morning to center myself and clear my mind. I can do this. I can be the goddess of death.

When I finish reading the lines to the camera, my panel of judges are completely stone-faced. It's not unusual for the people you're auditioning for to keep their reactions to themselves, but it does feel especially unnerving this time.

"That was great," Marie says suddenly, as if she sensed my panic, while Rune turns back to his notebook. "Can you try it again, but a little bit slower?"

I nod, give her a shy smile, and walk myself through a round of breathing exercises before reading the passage again. There's no immediate response to my second read-through. Marie looks warily over at Rune, who's still writing in his notebook, while the casting assistant taps away at his laptop. What feels like hours go by when Rune abruptly sits up, seemingly struck by a bolt of lightning, and stares me down with those electric blue eyes.

"Try it again, but with a more primal energy," he says, his voice low and gruff.

When he stands up, I expect him to be close to seven feet tall, but he's smaller than his aura projects. His rumpled sweater hangs loosely around his willowy frame, his clavicle on full display where the collar dips. With heels on, I'm only an inch or two shorter than him. He comes to the other side of the table, crosses his arms, and keeps his attention so set on me, it could drill a hole between my eyes. A jarring switch-up from him pretending that I don't exist for the past several minutes. He leans past the camera, so close I can smell the coffee and cigarettes on his breath when he whispers, "Harness your power."

I nod, averting my eyes away from Rune's invasive gaze and concentrating on the camera instead. Instead of launching right into the lines again, I close my eyes. Let myself stew in the emotions that have been stirring through me the past two weeks. Anger, resentment, guilt.

Fear.

Fear that I'll never be enough. Fear that I'm *too much*. Fear that I don't know who I am anymore, even though my millions of followers think they get me.

A rumble in my chest powers each word when I finally recite the lines again, my shoulders trembling from the force of my short performance. Tears blur the corners of my eyes as Miles's voice swims in and out of my ears again and again. *I'm ready to start taking myself more seriously.*

I'll show him serious.

When I finish, I will myself to stop shaking.

I don't apologize, even though my gut tells me to. It's the most vulnerable I've ever let myself be in front of a camera— something my past roles never demanded of me. If this is what makes me a "serious" actor, I'll prove that I can do it, tears and all. Carefully, I angle myself away from the camera to wipe beneath my eyes. I didn't think I'd need the water- proof mascara today, and the last thing I need is raccoon eyes documented on film.

The room goes silent. Not even the scratch of pens on paper. I can't muster the strength to look at Rune, who's still so close I can feel an uneasy prickle beneath my skin.

"Bring in the other," he says before returning to his seat. I didn't realize I'd been holding my breath until I let out a quiet exhale when he speaks again, my body finally relaxing as the room fills with quiet noise again.

The casting assistant bustles out of the room while Marie flips through a binder in front of her. I shuffle awkwardly off my assigned mark, composing myself in a corner while I wait for the casting assistant to return. Moments later, he's back with Ridiculously Beautiful Girl in tow, looking as confused as I was when I first stepped into the room.

"Marisol, this is Jamila El Amrani," Marie pipes up, putting a name to the Ridiculously Beautiful face.

"Hi!" I say, sounding totally chill and not nervous to see her.

The last time I had a callback with another person was when Miles and I read together for our final *Avalon Grove* audition, and I'm not any less awkward at the big age of eighteen than I was at fourteen.

I stick one of my hands out for her to shake, then immediately regret it when I realize how clammy it's become in the few seconds since she walked in. And it's probably obvious that I was crying minutes ago. Fantastic first impression.

Jamila takes my hand, and I try not to dwell on the softness of hers. Or the way the thin rose gold rings on her fingers slot perfectly against the silver ones on my own. Or how good she smells. Because she smells *really* good. Like cinnamon and oranges and honey. Fall in the middle of summer.

"Hi," Jamila replies so quietly I wouldn't have thought she'd said anything at all if I hadn't seen the slight part of her lips. Maybe I'm not the only one who's nervous out of their mind, which is a comforting thought.

The casting assistant hands both of us a new slip of paper. An actual scene this time, pulled from a script. It's only a handful of lines—three each. But it at least has a setting and a couple of stage directions and context to help ground us in the scene.

"Jamila will be reading for Character A, and Marisol will read for Character B," Marie instructs as the casting assistant hands her and Rune their own copies of the scene. Rune doesn't bother to glance up from his notebook.

We settle on opposite ends of the room to study the scene. Out of the corner of my eye, I can see Jamila mouthing the lines like she did earlier.

I pry my eyes away from her and go back to my own paper.

Even with the additional context, I struggle to get a grasp on the scene. We don't have names, or even character descriptions. For all I know I'm playing a middle-aged Italian man.

According to the stage directions, we're in a living room, in the middle of a heated argument that starts with Character A bursting into tears. I breathe a subtle sigh of relief—at least I don't have to pull out any more tears today. From what I can tell, something I said is what made her cry in the first place. What we're fighting about is vague. So, I make up a quick backstory for myself—a jilted businesswoman confronting her husband's lover—to help find my footing. I can't imagine Jamila is older than me, so chances that we're auditioning for any wife and mistress roles are slim, but hey. Whatever helps me harness my power.

"Whenever you're ready," I say to Jamila once I've got a decent handle on the lines, already hardening my stance and tensing my muscles, preparing to morph myself into a woman scorned.

Jamila nods, tucks the paper into her back pocket, and fixes her eyes on me. I don't have time to be thrown off by the jolt that runs through me when her dark brown eyes meet mine.

Like the flick of a switch, her completely emotionless expression transforms into one of heartbreak. Her lower lip quivers, her shoulders hunch until she's only barely holding herself upright, and tears stream down her cheeks. As in tears. Plural.

"Why are you doing this to me?" she pleads, her voice so choked and desperate I completely forget we're supposed to be acting out a scene.

"Y-you . . . you deserved this," I stammer out far later than I should. The backstory I created goes out the window as all the confidence I mustered leaks out of me like a popped balloon.

"I didn't mean for this to happen," Jamila continues without missing a beat, almost choking on a sob as she takes a trembling step toward me.

I stumble backward, ripping my arm away from her grip, which, while accidental, is still in character. "But it did," I snap, attempting to use my frazzled energy to my advantage.

Jamila shakes her head, her hands trembling as she curls them around herself and lowers her chin to her chest. Thick teardrops roll down her cheeks and splatter against the white tile floor. "I promise it won't happen again."

"Your promises don't mean anything to me." I use the opportunity to turn away from her, focusing on a chip in the white brick wall across from me instead. I cross my arms tightly in a display of control. Power.

"Please, don't."

Rune claps as soon as Jamila utters her last line. "Beautiful. Now take it one more time from the top. Marisol, don't turn away from her this time," he says as he writes something in his notebook so furiously it splits the page down the middle. He doesn't let that stop him, flipping instead to the next page, which is already stained with black, blue, and red pen marks.

We do as he says, resetting to our original positions. Jamila quickly dabs at the tears streaking her cheeks and swipes the mascara smudged beneath her eyes. I do my best to shake off my nerves, reharnessing all my power as the casting assistant counts us down.

Once again, Jamila and I run through the handful of lines. Like before, she bursts into tears the second she says her first line, but I don't have the option of turning away this time. Instead, I gaze directly into her wide, watery brown eyes as I step farther into her space.

"Your promises don't mean anything to me," I sneer, using the little bit of extra height I have from my heels to look down on her with as much contempt as I possibly can. I don't need to watch the footage back to know my glare is hot enough to burn.

She doesn't back away from me either, though. She stares straight into me, shoulders trembling as she comes close enough that I can hear her racing heartbeat—or is that mine?

"Please, don't," she whimpers, and for a second, I think she's going to reach out and touch me, but the casting assistant calls cut, and like the flip of a switch, she wipes the sorrow off her face.

Rune doesn't give us any praise when we wrap this time. "Jamila, stay," he grunts, caveman-like, not turning away from his notes.

Marie glances cautiously from him to us, a tight-lipped smile on her face when she turns to me. "Thank you so much for coming in, Marisol. We'll be in touch."

Everything happens so quickly I don't even realize what Marie said until the casting assistant heads for the door, unlocks it, and gestures for me to find my way out. That's it. A two-hour drive and possible bladder infection for nothing. Ten, maybe fifteen minutes in front of a director who didn't even look at me half the time.

"O-oh," I say without thinking, immediately wishing I could take it back. Wipe the shock off my face before they can notice. "Thank you so much," I tack on quickly, hoping it'll cover up my first blunder.

My body locks as I nearly walk right into Jamila when I head for the door. Besides the dampness of her cheeks, you'd never be able to tell she was practically bent in half, begging for forgiveness and fighting back sobs barely a minute earlier.

"It was nice meeting you," she says.

"You too," I reply with a stiff smile. It would've been nicer if we'd met anywhere else. A coffee shop. A hair salon. Walking our dogs down the same street. Anywhere but here, in this room where we're competition.

And she's clearly the winner.

With one last wave to Marie and the others, I rush out of the bathroom-less warehouse. Four texts are waiting for me

when I get back in the car and grab my phone off the dashboard.

Mama

Text me how it goes. Love you munchkin x

Miles Zhao

Did I leave my headphones at your place?

GROUPCHAT: avalon girlies <3

Posie

Break a leg today!!!!

Lily

You're going to crush it!!!!!!

And for what feels like the millionth time this week, I burst
into tears, ignoring the stabbing pain in my bladder as I collapse against the wheel and sob myself dry yet again.

I am so *not* crushing it.

CHAPTER 4

I'd like to think I'm taking my flop era in stride.

I've only watched Miles's story twice this week. Well . . . three times. But that was only because my finger slipped and I forgot to skip over it while doomscrolling at two a.m. It's the closest thing we've had to communication since he texted me after my audition last week. A text I promptly ignored. Yes, he did leave his five-hundred-dollar headphones at my place, and yes, I am keeping them for myself. Call it collateral damage.

My walls may still be up, but, admittedly, I did linger on the story he posted last night of the view from his first-class American Airlines window seat. An appropriately moody clip of the gray clouds storming over the distant city horizon. By now he'll have touched down in New York and moved into the 550-square-foot studio in the West Village I found for him. The place has panoramic views of the city, a recently refurbished kitchen he'll never use because he can barely boil water, and in-unit laundry he probably won't even notice because he insists on sending everything to the dry cleaners. On Monday, he'll be on set, reading lines and preparing to stage-kiss Ridiculously Beautiful Girl because there's no way she didn't get cast, and no world in which a director turns down the chance to put two wildly attractive young actors together on-screen.

I'm fine with that. And not seething with jealousy whatsoever. I've made my peace. He gets to live his high-profile actor dreams in New York, and I get to stay here in LA, watching TikToks with Bruiser for six to eight hours a day while casting directors toss my headshot in the trash.

My career isn't officially over, but it's hard not to feel like it is. I've had enough time since my audition to pull apart all the reasons I'm not landing any new roles. From my acting abilities to my attitude to the outfits I wore—I dissect every detail, but still can't find an answer. With another one of our *Avalon Grove* castmates—who played Miles's best friend, Brody—landing the lead in a new Hulu drama about a student having an affair with his professor, my sadness turns to bitterness. Why does it seem like the boys from the cast are the only people who are allowed to reinvent themselves while Lily, Posie, and I are typecast as lovestruck teens based off a single role?

I'm not surprised. But I *am* annoyed.

"Hey, Munch . . ." Mom knocks quietly on the doorframe to my room, and I pause the two-and-a-half-hour-long video dissecting *The Vampire Diaries* I'd been watching. "How about we go out for dinner tonight? Anywhere you want."

Guilt tugs at my heartstrings as I give her a small, sympathetic smile. The only thing I hate more than Miles right now is turning Mom down. She's proposed everything from trips to the Grove to weekends in Lake Tahoe to try to get me to go outside. And she's not the only one.

My group chat with Lily and Posie has mostly been turned-down invitations for brunch and mani/pedis—which, if I didn't lie and tell them I was getting over the flu, would normally be taken as a signal that I've been kidnapped and am currently in distress.

While my skin could definitely use some sun, I haven't worked up the courage to ignore the dread that washes over me like an ice bath every time I think about leaving my safe space.

Because I *can't* just go outside. Mom gave an earful to the paparazzi who were camped on our block, but all that did was get them to move their operation to the end of the street. And even if I can make it out of here without being bombarded, there aren't many places in this city where they won't find you. From the grocery store, to the In-N-Out drive-through, to the dentist's office, they're always there, lurking around a corner. Waiting to snap a photo of me that proves to the world what everyone's speculating: I've been a total wreck since Miles dumped me.

And I'm not going to prove them right.

"I'm good, thanks. Maybe next week?" I suggest to soften the blow. Mom's usual frown is replaced by an elated grin— a little too elated, I worry. Hopefully, by then, the paparazzi will have moved on to the latest celebrity breakup and left me to wallow in peace. If not, I'll have to disappoint my mom over and over again until I can leave my house without feeling like I'm on the run for murder.

"It's a date," Mom replies, even though I haven't *really* agreed to anything, but she's always been an optimist. She takes her wins where she can get them. "I was thinking we could—"

Mom trails off when both of our phones go off. I glance over at where Bruiser is curled up in the crook of my arm, her paws resting on top of my phone. She's still fast asleep, despite the buzzing.

"It's Delia," Mom says, her brows furrowed.

"Probably calling to tell me I didn't get *The Limit*. Big surprise." Maybe she's delivering a personal message from Rune himself, letting me know that my audition was so bad it offended him.

"Hey, Delia," I answer halfheartedly, bracing myself for the inevitable rejection. Bruiser, now awake, licks my arm in solidarity.

I'm reciting Delia's usual spiel in my head, still fresh in my mind from the rejection I got last week—*Sorry, M, this one didn't go our way*—only to be greeted by a chorus of voices instead. Delia, Joanna, and Blake all talking over one another.

Oh God, this is it. They're firing me. For real this time.

Delia clears her throat, asserting her dominance over the others and waiting until they've quieted down to continue. "How fast do you think you can pack your stuff, Marisol?"

What would I need to pack for? They can't fire me and evict me from my apartment, right? But Joanna did help us find this place. Oh God. I can't be single, jobless, *and* homeless. I'll have to crash on Posie and Lily's couch. Wait—their mom is allergic to dogs. I can't leave Bruiser with anyone, she's a nasty little goblin to people she doesn't know. But boarding long-term is so expensive and—

"Because you're going to need to get to New York ASAP!"

Everyone around me bursts into celebration. Clapping and cheering and what sounds like champagne popping while Mom rushes up to hug me.

"Wh-what?" I choke out.

"You booked *The Limit!*" Delia explains, the most excited I've heard her since I landed *Avalon Grove.* "Not a series regular role, but a pretty hefty guest star role. Six episodes at least. Maybe even the full eight. I'll send you all the details in an email, but they're on a tight schedule. This is big, Marisol. I'm talking potential award-season-nom big. Do you think you can make it to New York by next week?"

Holy shit. I did it. I'd written off my chances so quickly I never thought to consider what it might feel like to *actually* get a part.

And it feels pretty freakin' amazing.

"Yeah, for sure!" I reply without thinking. Hell, I'll buy the plane ticket right now. Finding a place to stay this late in the game won't be cheap, but I'll sleep in a cardboard box if I have to.

Well, maybe a hotel.

"You can stay with your dad until you get settled," Mom suggests excitedly before pulling me in for a bone-crushing hug.

Bruiser joins in on the celebration, barking as loud as her little lungs allow as Mom and I hold each other close and squeal and dance around the room like we've won the lottery. For the first time in almost two weeks, I feel hope. Joy. *Excitement.*

Because I'm going to prove Miles, those anonymous commenters, the casting directors who passed on me, *everyone,* wrong.

CHAPTER 5

I'm going to die. Any minute now the engine is going to bust, and this plane is going to go spiraling to the ground. Or we'll run out of gas and start plummeting out of nowhere. Or—

"Pretzels before we land?" a flight attendant asks, snapping me out of my panic bubble.

I take the packet she offers me with a queasy smile, grateful to have something to occupy my attention. Even my ultimate comfort movie—*The Devil Wears Prada*—couldn't soothe my nerves. Attempting to sleep left me alone with my thoughts, staring out the window, and preparing for disaster. The "ultrasoundproof" headphones Miles left at my place didn't do much to help either. Honestly, the sound quality isn't even that great. For half a grand, I should be able to hear the music in my bones. These could barely muffle the sound of Bruiser's snores.

According to the screen in front of me, there are only thirty minutes left until we touch down at JFK. Excited as I am to finally get the hell off this plane, my stomach is still uneasy at the thought of what's waiting for me when we land.

Well, *who*.

My dad had a more enthusiastic response to Mom suggesting I stay with him and his partner at their place for the summer than I'd originally thought. At most, we text once every couple months. Last year I don't think I communicated with him at all outside of the occasional Instagram like. I wouldn't blame him for not wanting to house a teenage starlet who gets stalked by paparazzi on the regular, genetics be damned. But according to Mom, he's waiting for me with open arms.

It's not that I don't like my dad. Or that he doesn't like me. Things are . . . weird between us. Granted, our family situation has been sort of weird since the moment Mom decided she was tired of waiting for the right guy to come along to start a family. She hadn't even finished her spiel when my dad, her platonic bestie since kindergarten, agreed to help her. Nine months and several long-winded explanations to their friends and family later, they were blessed with the ultimate early Christmas gift: me.

There was a time when we lived together in a cramped two-bedroom in Inwood, but all I have from that period of my life are the photos in the baby book Mom keeps in the living room. Shortly after my second birthday, Mom packed up our stuff to pursue her own acting passions in California, while my dad stayed in New York, the place he's called home his entire life.

It's not like something shifted between us as I got older. There was never any romantic tension between my parents since my dad is extremely gay (his words, not mine). There was no huge explosion. No massive fight that tore our family apart. It didn't take long for me to realize my origin story was unusual. Even as I looked around at my classmates' different families—single moms and dads and grandparents or uncles as parents and blended families full of half siblings and stepsiblings—I never saw one that mirrored ours. It wasn't that my dad left or didn't care about me. He's always sent gifts or cards for my birthday and messages around the holidays. We've had dinner a handful of times when I've had to go to New York for press or shoots. He even sent me a gif of the Minions holding a glitter banner reading **I'M SO PROUD OF YOU** after I came out as bi on my Instagram. Which, while cringy as hell, was very sweet.

We feel like . . . friends. And not even good friends. The type of friend you keep in touch with after you moved away, but it never feels the same because you'll never have the good ol' days back. Except I don't even remember the good ol' days.

Mom shot down my hesitance at staying with him over the summer, insisting that it would be fun and he would love to see me. I gave in eventually because, well, I don't really have anywhere else to go. All the apartments I reached out about were snatched off the market before I could even ask about putting in an application. Miles always talked about how cutthroat the NYC rental market is, but I can barely even finish swiping through photos of a listing before it's been rented by someone else. And I really don't want to spend over five hundred dollars a night on a hotel room that Bruiser will probably destroy because she hates new spaces (which I sympathize with).

Thanks to *Avalon Grove,* I have more than enough in my savings account to get by, but I've never really felt comfortable shelling out that kind of money for something so temporary. Not when Mom and I spent pretty much my entire childhood living paycheck to paycheck. You never shake off that kind of frugality.

It doesn't matter that I don't even know what to call my dad because "Dad" seems too intimate and "Carlos" feels too formal. I won't say (aloud) that I'm still pretty pissed at how he's never really been *there* for us, even when Mom was working two jobs and doing an online gig on weekends to make ends meet. I can't care about sharing a space with someone who barely knows me, even though he helped create me. He and Mom may still be best friends, but that doesn't mean the same applies to me and him. None of this is relevant, I know, because I'm getting to live out my dream. My latest one, anyway.

"You two can bond!" Mom said before throwing a parka into my suitcase because "it can get cold in June."

At best, I come back home in three months with a dozen casting agents knocking on my door and a renewed relationship with my estranged dad. At worst, I come back with nothing to show for my cross-country adventure except an agitated dog and some dry skin. Cross-country flights are horrendous for my acne.

While the plane starts its final decent, I do my best to distract myself by playing word games on my phone. The flight attendant gives me a sympathetic smile as I grip the armrest of my seat for dear life while she does her final walk-through. The attention has thankfully been off me for most of the flight thanks to the K-pop boy group—who are as handsome in person as they are in their music videos—seated in the rows behind me.

I hold my breath, recite the alphabet in my head, and tap my foot so hard it goes numb until the plane finally touches down on the sweet, sweet ground. Bruiser lets out a quiet bark in celebration as we slow to a stop. Gravity has never felt so amazing.

A flurry of notifications pops up as soon as I switch my phone off airplane mode. Responses to my Insta story—a shot of my legs folded on my suitcase at the airport lounge with the caption *see ya later LA* 😌—asking where I am or wishing me a safe flight. Multiple texts from Mom, Lily, and Posie wishing me luck and smooth travels. And one from my dad.

> Waiting for you on the other side! Welcome to New York 😊

I do my best to swallow my nerves as I text back Mom, Lily, and Posie, like a few of the fan messages, and walk myself and Bruiser's carrier off the plane. I'm not sure what to expect at the end of the hallway leading to baggage claim. My dad in his favorite Mets cap, most likely, with his partner, Jerome, maybe. But, in a nightmarish twist of events, it's none of those things.

It's a swarm of paparazzi.

High-pitched screams drown out the photographers' questions, and I'm left frozen in place by the sudden onslaught of attention. White spots cloud my vision, the crowd barely visible as the camera flashes pick up with every step I take.

I can't make out faces, only shapes. Young girls huddled in packs holding up signs and banners written in . . . Korean?

Oh.

Several burly men in crisp black suits push past me, rushing to the real center of attention. The K-pop boys move quickly through the crowd, bowing politely and giving a few waves as their security guards guide them toward the exit. The fans move with them, following at a borderline inappropriate distance, the guards barking orders at them to stay back.

"What brings you to New York, Marisol?" someone asks before snapping a photo so close to my face it blinds me for several seconds. Just my luck: one singular paparazzo decided to stick around.

Before I can give him a vague nonanswer, a familiar voice cuts in.

"Mari, over here!"

We both turn and find my dad is holding a sign of his own. **WELCOME TO NEW YORK, MUCHKIN!** is written in black marker, complete with several of my baby photos adorning the message like a frame. Including the one of me eating dirt.

The paparazzo jumps into action like a dog after a bone, racing up to my dad and snapping as many photos of the sign as he can.

"Are you her dad? Is she here to visit you?" the paparazzo asks, the questions coming out a mile a minute.

I swoop in before my dad can respond, loop my arm through his, and tug him toward the exit. "No comment!" I shout over my shoulder, hustling us onto the sidewalk in record time.

Anyone else who might've cared about my presence is too wrapped up in following the boy group to their black Escalades, but I still lower the brim of my ball cap until I can barely see what's in front of me.

"Quite an entrance," my dad says once we're outside. He scratches his head in confusion as someone runs straight into oncoming traffic to catch up to the boy group.

My reply is swallowed by a car horn and shout of "Are you outta your mind?!"

"Is that all you brought?" he asks with a raised brow, jutting his chin toward Bruiser's carrier.

In my rush to get the hell away from that paparazzo, I completely forgot about my luggage. I whip around and peer through the glass double doors at the carousel we ran away from. Even from several feet away, I spot one of my hot pink suitcases. Mom says they will attract too much unnecessary attention, but that's the *point*. Everyone's luggage looks the same, so you've gotta stand out unless you want to go home with someone else's underwear. Duh.

"I didn't get a chance to grab my stuff," I say with a sigh. Out of the corner of my eye, I can see the lone paparazzo lurking near the entrance to baggage claim, searching for any other notable faces who he can harass.

My dad follows my eye line, humming in thought once he spots the photographer. He snaps his fingers, a smirk playing at his lips as he races over to a maroon car double-parked beside the curb. He pops the trunk and roots through bags of fabrics, sequins, and several rolls of tulle before finding what he's looking for: an NYU Drama hoodie and matching hat. He quickly pulls them on despite the criminal ninety-degree heat—seriously, the air is so thick it feels like I'm inside of someone's mouth—and throws on a pair of sunglasses for good measure.

"Radio's busted, but the AC should work," he says as he tosses me the keys to the car. "If it doesn't, slap the dashboard a couple times. And if a cop comes and tells you to move, sniffle and tell 'em you're here to pick up your estranged sister. Works every time," he says so quickly I've barely processed any of it before he's gone.

New York is certainly eventful so far.

I set Bruiser's carrier in the backseat, rewarding her for her patience with a couple of chin scratches and one of those dried bacon strips that make dogs lose their minds. She goes to town on her well-earned prize while I shift my attention to getting some much-needed airflow going. The inside of the car is as cluttered as the trunk—receipts and notepads littering the floor, boxes of shoes stacked in the backseat. Very fitting, considering my dad is an Off-Broadway costume designer. It takes several slaps and a well-placed kick to the dashboard to get the AC switched on. The air is dry and a little musty, but anything is better than roasting like a Christmas ham.

By the time my dad returns, his slicked-back hair has fully broken free from its pomade shell. That's one thing we both have in common: our hair *hates* heat. Though the similarities don't end at our hair. There's no denying that we're father and daughter, with our matching dark brown hair, eyes, and lightly tanned skin. Thankfully, I also inherited his flair for fashion. No offense to Mom, but she barely knows the difference between silk and satin.

Sweat lines the collar of my dad's hoodie as he lugs my

three oversized suitcases toward the curb, collapsing against the car with a groan.

"What've you got in here?" he asks as he struggles to catch his breath. "Bricks?"

"Shoes, mainly," I reply, pulling my cap down enough to shield me from any lurking photographers before getting out of the car and helping him load my bags, which is a two-person job. "You never know when you'll need a three-inch, five-inch, or six-inch heel. So I brought options," I explain as I grip the other end of a suitcase, count down to three, and heave it into the trunk.

"At least you're prepared," he mumbles, more to himself than to me, as he eyes my remaining two suitcases with dread.

Thankfully, my sundress-and-makeup-essentials suitcase and sensible-crop-tops-and-shorts suitcases are easier to manage. It takes a surprising amount of brain power to figure out how to get the trunk to close, but after a few minutes of Tetrising my bags, we're taking off onto the JFK exit ramp.

The hour-long drive to upper Manhattan is . . . awkward. Not made any easier by me choosing to sit in the backseat so I can keep an eye on Bruiser's carrier. There's nothing she loves more than a car-ride vomit session.

"How was the flight?" my dad asks.

"Not bad," I reply. "I'm not great at flying, but I managed."

"Your mom always hated flying," he says with a wistful smile, peeking at me in the rearview mirror, but he doesn't say anything else.

"You excited to start filming?" he asks twenty minutes later.

"Yeah," I say with a smile that's as stiff as my back after that five-and-a-half-hour flight. "Lot of lines to learn, though."

"Better more lines than less."

"Right."

"Yeah."

It's like a terrible first date, but we don't even have a movie or dinner to distract us. We sit in silence. My stomach gurgles from a dangerous combination of motion sickness and hunger as we cross the bridge from Queens to Manhattan. I'm tempted to ask him to pull over as we drive along the East River so I can hurl directly into the unusually green water, but no need to publicly embarrass myself five minutes into my NYC residency.

Traffic thins the farther uptown we go. The bustling crowds and towering skyscrapers I've come to expect from New York City are replaced by worn brick buildings and kids perched on stoops, trading bags of chips and candy. There's even actual greenery, much to my surprise. Large trees cast shadows across the block my dad pulls onto, all of them perfectly spaced apart. At the tree in front of his building, stones painted with names like Manny and Zhaniya are gathered along the trunk next to a sign reading **DON'T EVEN THINK ABOUT LETTING YOUR DOG SHIT HERE.** Fire trucks whiz past us as we park in front of a gray prewar building. Even through the piercing screech of ambulance sirens, I can hear more commotion coming from the city—the rumble of the subway, two men arguing on the corner about who owes the other a round of drinks, a delivery driver shouting into his phone that an order was packed incorrectly. "It said *no* beef, not *extra* beef!"

It's chaotic, and messy, and absolutely beautiful.

"Home sweet home," my dad announces as he parallel-parks so smoothly it should be shown in driver's ed classes.

I don't know what to say as I take in the street I'll be living on for the next three months. Should I ask if the pierogis at the Ukrainian place across the street are any good, or if the fire hydrant outside of it is supposed to be spewing water like that, or where that incredible smell of fried meat, spices, and something I can't quite place is coming from? My stomach answers for me, rumbling so loud it could probably be heard back in LA.

My dad lets out a quiet laugh, nodding his head toward the building. "Head in. Jerome made lunch."

"Don't you need help?" I cast a wary glance at the trunk.

He shakes his head, tossing me a ring of keys. "I've got it. Go get settled. We're in five-E."

While he heads for the trunk, stopping to make small talk with the women playing dominos across the street, I carefully pull Bruiser's carrier out and head for the building—the biggest on the block. It's not one of the picturesque brownstones I'd been picturing when Mom told me he lived in upper Manhattan. There's no plant-covered stoop, or bay windows facing Central Park. But it's close to public transportation, doesn't cost four figures a night, and accepts Bruiser, so it has everything I need.

Over my shoulder, notes of my dad's conversation trickle over to me on a breeze. Their Spanish is too rapid for me to follow, some words clipped short and others spread out, the meaning behind it muffled like a song playing in the next room. I'm able to catch a couple of familiar words as I fumble with the keys to find one that fits into the lock. Hija. Visitando. Un ratito. It's not a secret that they're talking about me, but it feels odd not to be able to put together the pieces. Not for the first time, I bristle and try to shake off that nagging, uncomfortable feeling that I'm not a part of something I should be.

My worries go straight to the back burner once I throw the door open. A mix of intoxicating smells hits me like a tidal wave as I step into the entryway. Smoked meats, fresh bread, and the sharp tang of garlic. My nose pulls me in a dozen different directions, but I ignore my senses and stay on course, scanning the hallway for an elevator.

Except there isn't one.

Okay. No problem. I should've seen that coming. New York is notorious for its walk-ups. LA may have spoiled me when it comes to in-unit laundry and elevators, but a couple flights of stairs won't kill me. Plus, it's free cardio. Five fewer minutes on the elliptical every day.

I head up to the second floor, scanning the hallway for any sign of 5E. Nothing. Not on the third floor either. It's not until I get to the fourth floor that I realize why I haven't found their apartment yet.

It's on the fifth floor.

"Jesus," I mutter under my breath as I start the trek up to the next floor, my calves burning and shoulder aching from having to carry Bruiser too. She wriggles in her carrier, as upset about the climb as I am. Stars dot my vision as I heave for breath on the fifth-floor landing, my tank top soaked in sweat, the baby hairs at my temples curled tight as springs. So much for that keratin treatment.

The door to 5E bursts open before I spot it, Jerome stepping into the hallway followed by a deep-fried scented cloud.

"Welcome, bebesita!" he announces, a spatula in one hand and an oven mitt in the other. His tight coils are hidden beneath a plain black ball cap, and his dark brown skin glistens with sweat and a few subtle traces of glitter. I set down Bruiser's carrier and launch straight into his embrace, letting him pull me slightly off the ground and twirl me in a circle. I'd linger on the irony that I had a more heartfelt reunion with my dad's partner than with my *actual* dad, but I'm too excited about seeing Jerome again to care.

Across the seven years since I first met him, Jerome and I have interacted way more than my dad and I ever have. Maybe it's because he's eight years younger than my dad—something they tease each other about constantly—or that he actually knows how to DM someone without sending the same message five times. Or maybe it's that Jerome is cool as hell. A production manager at a fashion magazine by day and a drag queen with a weekly show in the West Village by night, Jerome is the type of person I instantly knew I'd get along with. He's the only person in our strange little family who understands my hatred for kitten heels and knows the difference between a blow dryer and a diffuser.

"How did you—"

"Heard you huffing and puffing up the steps," he answers before I can finish, nodding his head toward the stairwell. "It gets easier, promise."

It'd better. I don't think my body can take that kind of physical anguish multiple times a day. Not to mention that I'll have to carry Bruiser back and forth whenever I take her out. She can barely handle a thirty-minute walk—tackling these stairs would be her Mount Everest.

Once I've picked up the carrier, Jerome sweeps me into the apartment with a dramatic wave of his arm and a trill of "Welcome to Chateau Rodriguez-Morales-Avila!"

I'm too distracted by the spread of food laid out on the

kitchen table to question why they have three last names between two people. Or why there's a framed photo of J. Lo photoshopped as Jesus hanging on the door.

"Eat, eat," Jerome urges, thrusting a plate into my hand and nudging me toward the elaborate spread. "As your abuela would say, eres muy flaquita," he says, pinching my "too-thin" waist for emphasis.

I don't linger on the fact that he's doing an impression of my own grandma, and I have no idea if it's accurate. The last time I saw my abuela in person was probably when my parents were still living together. We've FaceTimed a few times when my dad was over at her place during the holidays. All I really know about her is that she hates Judge Judy, and I'm named after her mother—Marisol Emilia de la Cruz Burgos, "the most headstrong woman I've ever met," according to my dad.

Well, at least that's one thing I inherited from my dad's side of the family. I'm nothing if not stubborn as hell.

I listen to Jerome and my growling stomach and reach for the closest item to me—a bowl of thinly sliced fried plantains. The first bite is so hot it burns the roof my mouth, the simmering oil clinging to my fingertips.

"Rookie mistake," Jerome chides as I drop the plantain back onto the plate and fan my mouth and let out short spurts of cooling breath. He ladles a spoonful of what looks (and smells) like a combo of ketchup and mayo onto my half-eaten plantain. "Tostones *need* sauce," he explains like it's common sense.

Which, to be fair, it probably is to anyone who has a basic understanding of their cultures' cuisines. Mom tried to incorporate Puerto Rican dishes into our dinner rotation growing up, but she can barely handle microwaving a Lean Cuisine without risking third-degree burns. Hamburger Helper was as fancy as it ever got until *Avalon Grove* came along and I finally made enough money to splurge on twenty-dollar salads every other night.

Jerome is right: the sauce blend brings the plantain—*tostone*—to new heights. The mayo-ketchup blend soothes my burnt tongue, letting me appreciate the salty, deep-fried goodness. Perfectly crunchy on the outside, with a fluffy potato-like center.

How have I gone eighteen years without these?

"Knew you'd like it," Jerome says with a grin. The foodgasm must be written all over my face.

I help myself to a second and a third tostone, along with a spoonful of yellow rice and beans and something wrapped in a green leaf after he assures me everything is vegetarian-friendly. While eating, I subtly take in the apartment. The room—a combined kitchen, living, and dining area—is definitely cramped, but they've made the most of the space. Family photos, signed Broadway posters, and costume props, like fans and decorative masks, adorn the walls. Two large flags from their respective cultures hang at the center of it all— Puerto Rico for my dad, Panama for Jerome.

The brown leather couch is clearly well-loved, but well-maintained too, with a multitude of plush throw blankets to cover up the scuffs and tears in the leather. There's only room for one person to fit comfortably in the kitchen at a time, but they at least keep their lone counter free of clutter. Pots, pans, and woks hang from a rack above the stove, with various appliances, from air fryers to blenders, carefully sitting atop the fridge.

"Better, right?" Jerome asks, snapping me back to reality.

I nod as I swipe my last tostone through the sauce. Normally, I don't allow myself this many carbs in a single meal, but screw it, I deserve it. There's no way I'm depriving myself of all the food New York City has to offer.

"Much better," I say around another blissful bite, and nod in agreement.

An exasperated groan pops our little foodie bubble. My dad collapses through the door completely drenched in sweat, crumpling into a heap on the floor surrounded by my hot pink suitcases.

"Jerome makes the best tostones in the city," he wheezes. His face has gone as red as the fire trucks that zoomed past the block when we arrived. "Just don't tell your abuela," he adds in between heaves for breath.

Dad looking like he's on the brink of a heart attack must be a regular occurrence since Jerome saunters right past him to admire the largest of my bags. "You came prepared," he praises as he takes in my modest—seriously, I left at least half of my shoe collection at home—army of luggage.

"We're gonna need a second apartment to store all this," my dad says with a sigh as he picks himself up and wipes the dust off his hoodie.

Jerome rolls his eyes, brushes him off with a wave, and gestures for me to follow him, pulling two of my bags along for the ride. "Ignore the drama queen."

If I thought the kitchen/living/dining area was cramped, it's nothing compared to the hall off it. I can barely squeeze Bruiser's carrier through without feeling claustrophobic.

Off to the left is a bathroom with a toilet, sink, and shower all crammed together. Beside the bathroom is a less horrifyingly small room that must be their bedroom. They've done a lot with the space—squeezing a king-sized bed and a vanity in without making the room feel too cramped—but it still pales in comparison to my place back in LA.

I'm so distracted by the size of the bedroom that I almost walk into Jerome. He opens a door at the end of the hall, revealing a closet with a couple of mounted shelves on one wall and a window overlooking the community garden across the street on the other.

"It'll be a tight squeeze, but I think we can make it work."

I perk up as I observe the closet from the hallway. I didn't think I'd have the luxury of a walk-in closet in New York when the rooms are already the size of shoeboxes, but I'm pleasantly surprised. The additional shoe rack is a nice touch, but any moisture that comes in through that open window will be hell on my sensitive fabrics. This'll do nicely for storage, though.

"I can definitely make this work," I say before helping Jerome wheel in my remaining two suitcases. Having all three pieces of luggage in here takes up most of the closet, but if we can shove them underneath a bed or something, I should be fine.

"Now, *that's* the right attitude," he says with a snap of his fingers and a pointed look at the kitchen/dining/living room, where my dad is still panting for dear life. When my dad ignores him, Jerome heads toward their room. "I'll grab the air mattress."

I freeze after setting Bruiser's carrier on the ground. "Air mattress?"

"Ugh, I know, I'm sorry." Jerome stops in the hall to whip around and give me a pout. "We tried to see if we could get a regular twin mattress to fit but couldn't get it through the doorway. This isn't one of those terrible air mattresses, though!" To prove his point, he pulls a box out from his bedroom, **LIKE SLEEPING ON AIR** written in bold along the side. "Only top of the line for our bebesita."

My body is still too hungry and rattled from the plane ride to put these pieces together quickly. In slow motion, it clicks into place. I turn back to the room behind me, the one I can barely stand in without risking stepping on Bruiser's carrier. No other doors off the hall. Nowhere else to go from the kitchen/dining/living room either.

This isn't my closet. This is my *room*.

"O-oh," I stammer, unsure what to say without sounding like I'm on the brink of a meltdown.

Which, to be clear, I absolutely am.

I kneel beside Bruiser's carrier and open the flap so she can stretch her legs. She walks in an aimless circle, as if to say, "Uh, is there anywhere else I can go?" No, babes, there isn't.

With my bags shoved against the wall there's barely enough space for me to shimmy into and out of the room. Bruiser gives up on trying to find a place to settle and heads out to explore the rest of the apartment. I try to hide my panic as I take in the room—*my* room—properly this time. If I stretch my arms, I can touch both walls with my fingertips. There's the smallest closet known to interior design in the corner that looks like it can barely hold two pairs of jeans, so unless I want to leave designer tops and dresses scattered on the floor, I'll have to keep most of my stuff in my suitcases. There'd better be an iron around somewhere—I can*not* be seen out in public in wrinkled clothing. With a sigh, I sit down on my largest suitcase because the brainpower it's taking to figure out how I'll unpack has zapped me dry. I have no idea where Bruiser's dog bed'll go, let alone where mine will.

Thankfully, I don't have to figure that out yet, since Jerome lets out an ear-piercing screech.

"What is that?!" he shrieks, pointing at where Bruiser is attempting to nuzzle her head on the end of a Persian carpet runner.

I rush into the hallway, scooping Bruiser into my arms and nuzzling her until she finally stops trying to escape from my grip. Jerome must have thought her carrier was a regular purse—happens all the time, ever since I customized mine to a much more eye-catching hot pink fabric. If I ever decide to quit acting, I bet I could make a killing working in dog carrier design. There's no reason dogs shouldn't be able to travel in style too.

"This is Bruiser."

As if on cue, a snot bubble dribbles out of Bruiser's left nostril. Great first impression, Bruise. "She's cute most of the time," I reassure him, carefully adjusting my grip so her bodily fluids don't rub off on my shirt. "Well, some of the time," I mutter, more to myself than to her. She's kind of a walking disaster—but who am I to talk?

Any protests Jerome may have had are swallowed when my dad, finally recharged from his harrowing journey up the stairs, reappears in the entryway to the hall. "What a cutie," he says with a grin before petting Bruiser on the head, grimacing when his hand—somehow—comes back wet. "Well, what do you think?" he asks after wiping his hand on his jeans and giving me an eager smile.

"It's . . ."

Too small. Up five flights of stairs. Not the Manhattan paradise I thought it would be. "Amazing," I finish. Because even though my dad and I barely know each other, I don't have it in me to break his heart.

He lets out a clap of excitement, urging us all to step out of the cramped hallway and back into the also-cramped kitchen/dining/living room. "We're so excited to have you here, munchkin. I know your mom said you might be looking into finding a new place to stay once you're settled, but you're welcome here for as long as you want."

Jerome gives me a vigorous nod of agreement.

"Thanks . . ." I hesitate, unsure how to actually address my dad now that I have to. "Dad," I say, going with the least controversial option even though it still doesn't feel quite right.

Well, better late than never, I guess. My dad is now officially . . . Dad.

His expression shifts subtly, something I can't quite read. Before I can tell if he's upset or elated, he puts his more neutral smile back on and hands me back the plate of food I'd abandoned in favor of exploring my new closet—room.

"We'll give you some space to get unpacked and settle in. We're in here if you need anything."

I give him a weak smile, struggling to keep Bruiser from wriggling her way out of my arms. Once I set her back on the ground, she follows close behind me as I head back to my room. I sit on the ground, taking up the last stretch of available space, and try to distract myself from another panic spiral by grabbing my plate from where I left it on the windowsill and shoveling rice into my mouth. As expected, it's delicious.

Light and fluffy with flecks of cilantro and cut-up chunks of avocado so creamy I wouldn't be surprised if they were scientifically engineered in a lab, all perfectly blended together with a mix of spices I don't think I've ever experienced before.

Well, my room may be a literal closet, but at least the food is top-tier.

Beyond my tiny window, a flock of pigeons perched on an AC unit battle over an abandoned pizza crust. A woman pushes a cart of sliced mangos dusted with chili powder down the block. Kids race onto the playground between two apartment buildings, tossing their backpacks aside as they swing themselves onto the monkey bars.

Without thinking, I pull my phone out of my pocket and take a photo of the view, strategically setting up the angle. No visible street signs or murals. I've learned the hard way that when you have over three million followers, even the most minute details can land you in hot water. Definitely don't want an overeager fan standing outside the building—because it's happened before. More than once.

Instead, I keep the photo focused on the way the sky is painted soft orange and pink as the sun sets behind the jagged skyline of office buildings, apartments, and skyscrapers. First I send it to Mom and Lily and Posie with an assurance that I made it to Dad's, and then I post it on my socials, complete with a subtle but effective filter and a simple caption.

Please be nice to me, NYC ♥

CHAPTER 6

Everyone knows the first table read sets the tone for the rest of the season. Whether the cast will get along. If any castmates might turn into something more. Who the troublemakers and divas are, and who'll play by the rules.

And, most importantly, who the MVP will be.

Not to brag—okay, maybe a little—but I was *Avalon Grove*'s MVP for all four seasons. The only person who didn't immediately tell everyone if you shared a secret? Me. Need a shoulder to cry on? Moi. Or a backup outfit after one of the infamous crafty ketchup packets exploded all over yours? I've got you.

Taking my career in a new direction doesn't mean I have to change everything about who I am. I can still be a consistent, reliable, and friendly castmate even if I'm spending most of my days tearing people down and crying on camera instead of falling in love with them and worrying about a chem test.

And what better way to start things off than with cupcakes?

Doughnuts are my one true weakness, but Dad and Jerome insisted that Magnolia Bakery is the way to go, promising me that they have the best dessert in the city. So far, I definitely don't disagree. The red velvet cupcake I had before dinner—because obviously I had to taste-test them myself first—might be the best cupcake I've ever had. Still doesn't beat a doughnut, but it gave Krispy Kreme a run for its money. Light, fluffy chocolate cake with the perfect amount of rich cream cheese frosting. If that was the last bite of food I ever had in my life, I wouldn't complain. I even sent a text to Mom with a photo of the cupcake and a message reading *when I die bury me with this,* which got me a very prompt phone call warning me not to joke about dying.

But seriously, they're that good.

My precious cargo of two dozen cupcakes is strapped into the seat beside me in the car production sent to pick me up from home. The driver beams when I offer him one on my way out, happily accepting a double chocolate one for himself along with a promise to meet me out front once the table read is over.

The studio production rented for the table read is one of a dozen on the same block. I don't know much about Brooklyn, or Red Hook specifically, but the brief impression I get after I step out of the car lines up with everything I've been told. The street we turn down is entirely refurbished warehouses, faded paint commemorating them as former factories and canneries. A few restaurants and breweries take up the first floor of several of the buildings—sectioned-off picnic tables and umbrellas lining the streets. Around the corner, bikes go whizzing down the path along the water. My heart leaps when I spot a glimpse of the Statue of Liberty, her torch rising above a large brown brick building.

Sadly, the interior of Greenbelt Studios isn't as exciting as the exterior of the block. Production assistants and producers go whipping past me carrying scripts, clipboards, and precariously stacked to-go trays of coffee. I move through the madness with practiced ease, keeping my elbows tucked close to my chest and dodging a few close calls with the people whose eyes are glued to their phones.

I may feel out of my element when it comes to acting in a serious drama, but the chaos feels comforting. Almost like home. The rule book for being on set is one I know like the back of my hand. Beginning with Rule Number 1: Stay out of everyone's way. Navigating a film set is a fine art that can take years to perfect.

And based on the crashing sound on the other end of the room, someone has *not* mastered it yet.

A girl in a headset, holding an empty Styrofoam drink container, is flat on the ground in a puddle of spilled lattes. Her A24 hat has been knocked askew, but her blond pony is still perfectly in place. I'll have to ask what hair spray she uses. At least her all-black ensemble, while damp, is saved from any potential staining. Rule Number 2 of being on set: Don't wear anything you don't want to risk ruining permanently. Hence my choice of an outfit so last season it's practically vintage.

The muscles in her jaw clench as she glares up at whoever ran into her, ignoring the coffee spreading across the floor, dangerously close to a stack of scripts sitting haphazardly on the floor.

The seamless flow of the room comes to a crashing halt,

everyone frozen for a fraction of a second before recalibrating. Someone dives for the scripts and pulls them out of harm's way. Another starts mopping the coffee puddle.

"I'm so sorry," the person at fault says, kneeling down to pat the spill with a stack of tiny napkins.

My breath catches in my throat, my heart suddenly beating at double speed.

Because the chaos bringer is Ridiculously Beautiful Girl.

I shouldn't be surprised to see her. I said myself that she was pretty much guaranteed a part on the show after that audition. A quick search for her on IMDb revealed that she either hasn't been in anything before or hasn't been in anything big enough to warrant her own page. Yet, anyway. The sight of her knocks something loose inside of me. Unlike last time, I don't lose my confidence when her eyes meet mine, hers as wide as the buttons on her cardigan. Because this time, I'm in my element.

Carefully, I cross the room toward her, setting my boxes on a nearby folding table to kneel down in front of her. "Hi."

"Hey," Jamila replies with a shy smile, abandoning her fruitless attempts to mop up the coffee.

We hold there, eyes locked on one another, unsure what to say next, until the production assistant breaks the spell. "I can handle it," she mutters bitterly, clearly trying to get us to move.

Cheeks on fire, I give her a polite smile and jump back up and grab my cupcake boxes. Before I can offer a cupcake to Jamila, the all-too-familiar scent of Jo Malone's wood sage and sea salt cologne washes over me. In a Pavlovian response, my body shivers, the blood in my cheeks creeping down to my neck as I whip around and find myself face to face with none other than Miles "Heartbreaker" Zhao.

I wish I could say he looks terrible since the breakup. That the acne he fought so hard to cure finally cropped back up because he drowned his post-dumping-me sorrows in takeout and ice cream like I did. But his skin is as flawless as ever. He's tanner too—artificially or naturally, I'm not sure, but it's unfair that I can't even tell. Normally he doesn't let his hair get this long, the ends of it falling gracefully in front of his face, but the length suits him. The natural swoop framing his face shows off how genetically blessed he is. He's swapped out his usual shorts and linen shirt to match the New York aesthetic: simple black jeans paired with a tucked-in designer white T-shirt and combat boots. He's even got the classic blue-and-white *We are happy to serve you* coffee cup, even though I know for a fact that he hates coffee.

"Marisol?" he asks in confusion, taking a step back like he's worried I might be a ghost.

"Oh, hey," I reply as casually as possible, ignoring the fact that I'm sweating in places I didn't even think it was possible to sweat. The baby-pink bodycon maxidress I picked out for the day seemed like the perfect choice at the time. A subtle, summer-appropriate cherry pattern that complements the natural blush in my cheeks, with a skintight fit that hugs the curves I inherited from Mom. Now, though, I'm realizing that there's no way I'll get away with hiding any sweat stains.

And there could be a lot of them.

"What're you doing here?" Miles continues, thankfully not detecting my nervousness.

I carefully balance my boxes in one hand to reach into my Telfar bag and pull out a script. "I'm part of the cast. Duh."

He takes the script from me to examine it more closely, needing to see the proof with his own eyes. I'd be offended by the shock written all over his face if it wasn't so amusing watching him try to puzzle this out like it's a physics equation.

"You got a part," Miles echoes, gesturing toward the bustling production around us. "On *this* show?"

I give him a delightfully puzzled look. "What, like it's hard?"

The way his mouth parts in a silent gasp would be enough to make me cackle if I wasn't so focused on my performance. After I've snatched my script back, I flip open the box on the top of the stack and hold it up to his nose. "Cupcake?"

He's still too shocked to do anything other than numbly shake his head. I flip the box shut, give him a too-sweet smile, and head toward the conference room at the end of the hall.

"See you in a few," I call over my shoulder, seamlessly avoiding a boom operator before turning a corner and disappearing from view.

The second I'm out of Miles's sight, I press myself up against a wall and bite back a scream of excitement. I knew Miles's reaction to seeing me would be priceless. Getting the call that I was on the show was incredible, sure, but seeing the gears turning in his brain was well worth the effort it took to get here.

Guess I'm not as unserious *as you thought, Miles.*

With a triumphant smirk, I hold my head up high and waltz into the room where several tables and chairs are set up for the read-through. I set down my bag on the seat marked with my name—at Miles's left, with Jamila on his right.

Beside a counter laid out with protein bars, muffins, and fruit, I spot Rune. He's even more disheveled than I remembered. His royal blue sweater—a terrible choice given it's almost eighty degrees out—is rumpled and stained. The edges of his sleeves are frayed, stray threads tangled all the way down to his rough, dry knuckles. He clearly hasn't shaved since the audition, his few days of stubble now grown out into a full dark-blond beard, in harsh contrast to his unruly ice-blond hair and brows.

"Hi!" I say brightly, resisting the urge to tap him on the shoulder to get his attention. Something tells me he's not the type to take kindly to unprovoked physical contact.

He blinks up at me from his script with wide, owlish eyes. His thick brows furrow; his chapped lips press into a thin line as if he's trying to place who I am and why the hell I'm here.

"I'm Marisol," I offer, doing the work for him. *He probably didn't recognize you,* I tell myself as I hold my smile in place. Directors must see hundreds of actors a day, and it's been almost two weeks since my audition. Plus, I have caramel highlights now. Totally different look.

Even with my name, he still doesn't seem to be able to place me. His expression doesn't soften, no shine of recognition in his piercing blue eyes.

"Polly-Rodriguez?" I add, hoping that'll bridge the gap. But no dice. Just an empty thousand-yard stare.

Well, he'll definitely know who I am in the next hour.

Before my brain can go down a panic spiral of wondering if he never meant to cast me in the first place and whether this was all either a massive mistake or a horrendous prank my team is pulling on me, I flip open the box in my hand and hold it out toward him.

"I brought cupcakes!" I say as brightly as I can even though I'm definitely starting to panic. I can't let him see the holes in my armor this soon into the game. "For the first day of production."

The cupcakes do the trick. Rune finally stops staring at me and focuses his attention on the box instead. The stern line of his mouth twitches slightly—into a smile, I hope. But of course, it's a frown.

"Are any of these gluten-free?" he asks, his voice hoarse like he's getting over a cold.

"Oh." My heart drops into the pit of my stomach. "N-no. I'm so sorry."

I've spent the past ten years living in Los Angeles—how the hell did I forget to make sure I had gluten-free, vegan, *and* keto options?

"But I can—" I'm not even sure what I'm offering when Rune holds a hand up and cuts me off before I can finish.

"You can take your seat," he says, the timbre of his voice so low I'm not sure if he means it as a threatening command or a gentle suggestion.

Either way, I follow orders.

Confidence shaken, I rush back to my seat at the table, setting my box down and trying to control the heat in my cheeks.

Other members of the cast slowly begin to trickle into the room. My grasp of this season's plot is limited—pun intended— at best. Rune's overzealousness when it comes to leaks applies to the script too. Last week, Delia sent me a heavily redacted script for the first episode of the season, edited down to include only the scenes I'm in.

Confusion about the plot of the show aside, I was pleasantly surprised by the size of my role. Delia said it was a substantial guest star role, but based on the number of pages I have, I'm in at least 75 percent of the first episode, with a guarantee that I'll be in six of the total eight episodes of the season.

No surprise, Miles's character, Will, takes up the biggest chunk of the pages I'm able to read. A troubled, but privileged, teen boy who battles the allure of drugs and alcohol when he has to grapple with the loss of both his dad and his younger brother in a car crash he may or may not have caused.

Definitely a far cry from *Avalon Grove*.

My character, Zoe, is a step out of my own comfort zone. Once again, I'm tied to Miles but in a very different way than Joe and Celia were. While Celia was the shy wallflower with a passion for gardening, Zoe is an oil heiress with a platinum credit card and a grudge against anyone who's ever gotten in her way. Which now includes Will, ever since he dumped her days after his dad and brother's funeral. Did Rune know about us, or is the breakup parallel a coincidence? In any case, from what I can tell, Zoe is mean, ruthless, and an absolute bombshell.

Our scenes together are charged, fraught with a spark that's either hatred or unresolved sexual tension. I've gone from the sweetheart, the girl who gets the happy ending, to the girl everyone is supposed to hate. Part of me is intimidated by the thought of playing someone so outside of my usual range— and what it'll mean to play someone designed for people to hate. But a bigger part of me is pumped. What better way to break out of my lovestruck-teen typecast than by playing someone who sounds like she'd happily run a boy over with her Prius if he so much as breathed in her direction?

While everyone else trickles in, I sneak a few peeks at the rest of the cast. From what I can see, we're the youngest members of the cast. The men huddled at the end of the table, laughing and slapping each other on the shoulders as they flip through their scripts, have faces I vaguely recognize but can't quite place. Opposite the men are several women reading quietly to themselves, wearing crisp button-downs and pencil skirts or slacks that wouldn't be out of place in an office.

Beside the group of women is a surprisingly familiar face.

Dawn Greene is one of the few young actresses of my generation who didn't get her start on a show like *Avalon Grove*. Though, fun fact, I did see her in the waiting room of one of my final callbacks. Of course, she wasn't *the* Dawn Greene at the time, but I knew she looked familiar when I saw her plastered on posters across Hollywood Boulevard a few months later. I've always wondered if we were going out for the same part, since there wasn't anyone else in the waiting room that day. If she was, I wish I could've added that to my acting résumé—*potentially beat out Dawn Greene for her first major part*. That's got to count for something.

Dawn's career started off with a bang—playing daughter to the lead in a prestige drama series called *Coldhearted*, about an average man turned serial killer that lasted six seasons. While her role didn't earn her any major awards, she did win the country's heart—becoming Hollywood's sweetheart with her gold ringlet curls, rosy cheeks, and bright ocean-blue eyes.

Things didn't slow down for Dawn after that show wrapped, either. She's had a handful of lead roles since then in smaller budget, but still highbrow, coming-of-age films, and a few horror films that were duds script-wise but huge smashes at the box office. The last show she did—about a girl who starts a burglary ring at her college—was canceled after a single season but earned her plenty of praise, along with several award nominations. Her loss at the Emmys last year sparked a sizable outcry online.

In short, she's exactly the type of person I should befriend on my journey to evolve my career.

I lean over toward Dawn, her white-blond hair held back in a sleek bun with a few well-placed curls framing her face. She doesn't look up from her phone until I clear my throat, jumping as if I startled her.

"I'm Marisol, nice to meet you!" I say, careful to avoid letting my voice get *too* high-pitched, the way it always does when I'm nervous or excited—and today I happen to be both.

Dawn gives me a tight smile. "Pleasure," she replies, her posh British accent clipped and to the point, so different from the American one she often has on-screen.

I consider offering my hand to shake, or telling her I'm a big fan even though, honestly, I fell asleep during the pilot of her last series, but I decide against it. The last thing I want is to seem like an overeager fangirl. Or risk her asking me what I liked about the show.

Her brows furrow suddenly, scrutinizing my face so intensely it makes my cheeks hot. "Aren't you an influencer?"

"O-oh, no," I say quickly, though I *have* done my fair

share of brand deals. Who am I to turn down getting paid in exchange for trying new skincare and makeup, which I was probably going to do anyway? "I was on *Avalon Grove*. And a couple of smaller-budget movies," I explain, resisting the urge to list the rest of my filmography. Besides *Avalon*, not much from my résumé is a standout.

Dawn hums and nods, but I'm not sure if that means she knows what show I'm talking about. Instead of offering up any insight, she turns back to her script, ending the conversation abruptly.

"Cupcake?" I offer, going for a last-ditch attempt at saving this awkward interaction.

Dawn seems straight-up annoyed this time, grimacing at the box I push toward her like I'm offering her a platter of live squid. "No, thank you," she says without a hint of a smile, and turns back to her script again.

Well, all right, then.

A few of the women seated to her left peek up from their scripts or phones, giving me and my cupcakes a glance before deciding I'm not worth engaging with. One even wrinkles her nose.

Since when are cupcakes considered so horribly offensive? I knew I should've stuck with doughnuts.

Before I can lick my wounds, gather my courage, and try again with someone who hopefully won't shoot me down, the rest of the cast files in and Rune steps into the center of the ring of tables. Miles and Jamila quickly take their seats beside me, their cheeks flushed like they sprinted across the street to make it in time. Something churns in my gut as I watch them share a knowing glance, shy smiles tugging at the corners of their lips as they set their scripts down on the table, Miles hiding his grin behind his coffee cup.

Seems like they've hit it off already. Which is good—great, even. Everyone's life is easier when the cast gets along. The three months Lily and Posie were fighting with another one of our castmates about some misunderstanding involving a borrowed dress were torturous. I spent weeks running messages between them because they refused to actually speak face to face and had already blocked each other on their socials. Absolute nightmare. I'm still not sure what role Jamila will be playing in the show, but she's bound to have a good chunk of it with Miles, considering he's the lead. We'll also probably have a couple scenes together.

So, yeah. This is totally cool and normal and I'm definitely not feeling weird about the way Miles is peeking at Jamila right now instead of paying attention to Rune.

Guess I'm one to talk. Continuing with my hypocrisy, I lean back slightly and linger on Jamila while Rune scans something on his phone and calls out to a PA to bring him his tea.

Jamila is more in her element here than she was in LA, I notice. Definitely more appropriately dressed for the weather, in a flowy white linen top tucked into a pair of wide-leg beige trousers. Her so-dark-brown-they're-almost-black curls are neatly held up in a tortoise hair clip. Seems I'm not the only one who got highlights: ribbons of gold and mahogany run through the tongs of the clip, a mirror of her honey-colored eyes. Like at the audition, her lips part slightly as she reads quietly to herself. They're glossy this time—her lips. Not that I'm looking at them. Just admiring the shade she went with, a soft, barely-there red that makes her brown skin pop. I linger on them for a moment longer than I should, gazing at the Cupid's bow above her full upper lip and the plump natural curve of her lower.

Because I want to ask her what lip product she uses. That's all.

"Welcome, everyone," Rune announces with perfect timing, snapping me back to reality in time for me to turn away before Jamila can catch me staring. "It's an honor to have you all on board for season two of *The Limit*," he says with more enthusiasm than I would've thought he was capable of. "A few ground rules before we get started. As I'm sure you already know, we're doing everything we can to prevent leaks. You'll receive your scripts no more than forty-eight hours before filming, in a password-protected file that only *you* should be accessing. And if anyone else does, we'll know. Don't worry."

A couple of people let out quiet chuckles while my heart rockets into my throat. We only have two days to learn our lines? We moved fast sometimes on *Avalon Grove*, but they always gave us at least a week to go over our scripts. I know we don't have a ton of time to shoot the entire season to stay within budget constraints, but if I'm as heavily featured in the rest of the episodes as I am in the first one, I'll definitely need more than two days to memorize everything.

Don't panic, I tell myself and throw on a smile and nod along like everyone else. The whole reason I'm here is to push myself—to become a more well-rounded actor. If I don't want this to be my last role in a true prestige drama, if I want to be respected in this industry, I'll have to learn to adapt.

Rune runs through the rest of his unusually long list of

ground rules. Some make sense: no removing props from set, keep phones on silent at all times, and no microwaving fish in the crafty microwave. Others are . . . unique. Like no helium balloons within fifty feet of set, or live animals of any variety—there goes any chance of bringing Bruiser to set with me.

"And one last thing," Rune says after instructing the production coordinators to have pasta served only on Thursdays. "No brightly colored clothing on set, please. Neutrals or black. Bright colors trigger my migraines."

His gaze flickers to me for the briefest flash of a second, his lips curling into a disgruntled frown. A jolt shoots through me like he's stabbed me in the chest. It's a subtle enough moment that no one except me should notice, the comment broad enough that it should be meant for everyone. But I'm the hot pink sore thumb in a sea of grays, blacks, and browns. I can feel the burn of a dozen eyes glancing over at me, my pink cardigan blaring as a fire engine's siren. I'm not sure if the snickers to my right are real or if my brain is playing a cruel trick on me, but I hear them nonetheless.

Immediately, I regret letting Jerome talk me into wearing this bolder ensemble instead of the simple black tunic dress from Anthropologie I'd considered.

"Be yourself, bebesita," he'd said as he brushed my hair over my shoulder, showing off the gold-plated *Marisol* necklace Mom got me for my thirteenth birthday that I refuse to take off, even if it clashes with the rest of my ensemble. We spun around to gaze at our reflections in the vanity mirror in his bedroom, my cheeks rosy from the bit of blush I'd applied earlier. He held the cherry dress up against my collar, the color bringing a warmth to my lightly tanned skin where the tunic had washed me out. "They'll have no choice but to love you."

I should've known better. Should've insisted that I should wear something more unassuming than my usual bold style.

At least Rune puts me out of my misery. "Let's get started," he says with a clap of his hands and a stiff smile that feels like a belly laugh coming from someone like him.

The room is a flurry of chairs scraping on the stone floor, pages flipping, and final sips of coffee. Rune does the honors of reading the stage directions, grounding us in a teen boy's messy bedroom, before Miles takes it away.

"It's my fault," he says, not full-on sobbing like the script calls for but layering his voice with a deep, wallowing sorrow.

"I promise it's not," Jamila assures him, her voice soft and sweet as she rests a hand on his back. "You know how much we all love you, right?"

They meet each other's eyes, Rune's voice a distant hum as the world melts away. So easily convincing the rest of us that they're in love already. Honestly, I'd think this was real if I wasn't at a table read.

I stiffen in my seat, squaring my shoulders and fixing my attention on my own script as I prepare for my first line.

"Are you done? Your mom's asking for you," I almost shout, adding a feigned knock on the door, interrupting Jamila's and Miles's characters' intimate moment.

Miles clears his throat, turning back to his page while Jamila's hand retreats back to her lap. "Y-yeah. Coming."

I bite back a smirk, letting pride wash over me as Rune continues on to the next set of stage directions. Being a bitch doesn't feel so bad.

Looks like Jamila and Miles aren't the only ones who can act the part.

I'm able to come out on the other side of the read-through unscathed. Reading the rest of the script with the full cast helps me put the last remaining pieces of this puzzle of a show together. Based on the first episode, the narrative is split between the teens and the adults—Miles taking the lead on the teen side, with me, Jamila, and Dawn in supporting roles.

Not at all surprising is the amount of scenes Jamila and Miles have together. The bulk of the first episode is the two of them together—either in her room, or his, or at a diner they love. What *is* surprising is the role she's playing. Adina, Miles's character's best friend since childhood. The first person he went to after the accident that killed his family, the girl he always searches for when things go sideways. The girl with a smile that feels like the sun. The girl who's more than small-town beautiful but refuses to accept it. The girl he loves more than anything, even though he doesn't know it yet.

The girl *I* was on *Avalon Grove*.

Our approaches to the cliché "girl next door" role aren't similar by any means. Jamila is softer spoken, gentle, and kind. The glimmer in her eyes tells the story for her—that she loves him as much as he loves her and she *does* know it. Where Miles and my on-screen story was more about lingering touches and smiles and glances held too long, theirs is a subtler dance around their feelings. There's something deeply moving about it, even when they're reading words on a page, not putting their full force behind each line. Maybe it's because of the writing. Weird as he is, I gotta hand it to Rune, he knows how to write a captivating scene. Or maybe it's the difference in the stories Jamila and I are trying to tell—one soft and light as cotton candy and the other born out of turmoil, like a rose from a crack in the street.

Or maybe it's because she's that good.

I don't let myself linger on that thought for long. Comparison is the thief of joy, or whatever that cliché says. Especially in a field like ours. If I compared myself to every single "girl next door" type, I'd drive myself nuts. I've seen plenty of talented performers lose their confidence by letting the fear that there's someone else who can do the role better manifest itself into reality. Jamila is clearly as talented as she is stunning, and while that's amazing for her, it shouldn't mean anything to me.

Eyes on your own script.

I *am* puzzled by the lack of scenes with Dawn, though. She's by far the most experienced of the teen cast, but she hardly has any presence in the pilot episode. From what I can tell, her character is Jamila's more outgoing best friend, but there's not much depth outside of her pressuring Jamila to sneak out to a party. I'm sure her character will have more to do in later episodes, though. Dawn Greene isn't meant for background parts. With a résumé like hers, I'm honestly surprised she's not playing Jamila's role, or at the very least, mine.

Someone starts up a polite round of applause as we finish the last line of the episode, ending on a cliffhanger where Miles's character is alone near some train tracks in the middle of the night after an argument with his grieving mother. Miles gives the most vigorous applause, going so far as to give Rune a standing ovation. We all follow suit out of politeness.

Rune preens under the attention, giving a modest bow before waving off the applause. "I'll see you all bright and early tomorrow, all right?"

He's met with a chorus of "all rights," "yeahs," and "cheerses." For a moment, I even forget about my less-than-stellar start to the day, letting myself get swept up in the excitement of the room. After one last round of applause, the buzz and bustle from earlier returns. The production crew darts across the room, collecting our scripts to shred them in the back office (again, to prevent spoilers), while several producers race to Rune's side, barraging him with questions and logistics for tomorrow's first day of shooting.

The rest of the cast files out in the same cliques they arrived with, some of them chatting about the show or plans for the night while others are glued to their phones and leave quickly. Dawn doesn't even bother saying goodbye before bolting out of the room. Miles's thick brows shoot up as he scans the several notifications on his phone.

"I've gotta run, but it was nice meeting you," he says to Jamila, giving her a friendly smile before turning toward me, said smile morphing into something unreadable. Somewhere between a grin and a frown.

"It's great to see you, Mari." His voice is soft, gentle, one might say. I can't tell if he means it or if he's trying to convince himself that he does, but it doesn't change the way my heart flutters when our eyes meet. Whether that's with longing, pride, or heartburn, I don't know.

"It's great to see you too," I reply, knocking my fist against his shoulder. "Castmate."

He lets out a short chuckle, eyes lingering on my necklace for what feels like a beat too long before he finally walks away, my skin prickling from this new, more welcome form of attention.

Glancing around, I realize Jamila and I are the only members of the cast left in the room. She packs her things into a *New Yorker* tote bag and slides on a pair of oversized sunglasses that, paired with her subtle red lip, perfectly capture the Old Hollywood glamour vibe.

"It's nice to see you again," she says, and I have to double-check over my shoulder that she's actually talking to me.

"Oh. You too!" I respond a bit too loudly—even for me. So much for not letting on about how much she intimidates me. "Cupcake?" I ask to cover up my nerves, though considering my track record with these, this probably isn't my best bet.

Jamila seems startled by the offer. Even through her dark tinted glasses I can see the way her eyes widen as she takes in the mostly untouched spread in the box.

"That's so sweet of you," she says, and maybe it's because she's the first person who hasn't looked confused by my presence, but it's the nicest thing I've heard this entire week.

She hums to herself as she runs her hand along the top of the box, pondering which one to take. It gives me time to admire her elegant slender fingers and the thin gold rings adorning them. A rose gold band with her initials in cursive on her pointer, and a laurel wreath on her ring finger, perfect complements to the glossy nude polish on her nails.

"My older sister's obsessed with Magnolia," she says after

selecting a vanilla cupcake with yellow buttercream frosting. The smell is so tempting I wind up grabbing one for myself too. "If we dare get her a regular cake instead of a dozen of these for her birthday, all hell breaks loose."

I watch in confusion and horror as she carefully pulls off the wrapping, breaks off the bottom of the cupcake, and places it on top of the frosting until she's created a mini cake-and-frosting sandwich without getting a single crumb on her clothes.

"And she never told you how to properly eat a cupcake?" I question without thinking. The uncanniness of it was too overwhelming for me to remember that criticizing someone during your first conversation doesn't set you up for a long and meaningful friendship.

Jamila instantly rolls her eyes, but thankfully she doesn't seem upset. "This is the superior way to eat a cupcake. Equal distribution of cake. Easy to bite into. And you don't wind up with a glob of frosting on your nose."

"But it's deeply unsettling," I add before taking a *normal* bite of my cupcake to prove my point.

Instead of replying, she bites back a laugh as her shoulders tremble slightly. Before I can ask her what's so funny, she reaches into her tote bag and hands me her phone, opened up to the camera in selfie view. "Point proven."

Sure enough, there's an enormous dollop of frosting on the tip of my nose.

"You got me there," I grumble, swiping the frosting only for it to smear down the bridge of my nose *and* somehow get tangled in my hair.

I can't win today, can I?

While I groan and struggle to wipe the yellow smudge off my face, she leans forward and pinches the bit that's stuck to the end of my hair. My body stiffens as her fingers gently brush against the bare skin of my shoulder, and I pray to every deity I know that she doesn't see the goose bumps that blossom beneath her touch.

"Do you want the rest of these?" I ask, eager to get attention off me. I push the box toward her. "So your sister can show you the error of your ways."

Jamila snorts, an unusually lovely sound. "You sure?" she asks with a raised brow. "Because it looks like you could still use some practice eating these correctly." She swipes her thumb against her nose and does me the favor of holding back her laugh again.

I swallow another groan, holding up my phone and wiping furiously until my reflection is finally free of any rogue frosting. "Yes, I'm sure," I insist once I've cleaned myself off and tucked my phone away. "You'd be doing me a favor," I insist, eyeing the box warily. "I can't be trusted alone in an apartment with two dozen cupcakes."

Jamila nods, tapping her finger against the strap of her tote bag. "If my sister found out someone offered me a box of Magnolia cupcakes and I turned it down, she'd kill me."

"Well, then consider this a humanitarian effort," I argue, closing the box and pressing it directly into her hands. "I'm saving your life."

This time, Jamila doesn't hold back her laugh. "Well, when you put it that way."

Over her shoulder, a PA orders everyone out of the room so they can reset for shooting tomorrow. I quickly grab my own bag and remaining box of cupcakes seconds before another PA swoops by and hoists the table we were sitting at into the air, moving it to the opposite end of the room.

"I'll see you tomorrow?" Jamila calls out in the shuffle of the crew and lingering cast members.

"See you tomorrow," I echo, too frazzled by trying to balance my cardigan, bag, and box in one hand to find her in the crowd.

Once I've collected myself and my stuff, I head outside to meet my driver and head back to Dad's apartment. As we cross the Brooklyn Bridge, I let myself process this mad dash of a day. It's easy to feel disappointed—over my not-so-great first impression, Rune's passive-aggressive comment about my wardrobe, and the overall lack of openness from the cast. Especially Dawn. But there were bright spots too. Nailing my performance, even though it was only a read-through. The face Miles made when he saw me. Jamila's smile, and the jolt of her fingers brushing against my skin.

Actually . . . maybe today wasn't so bad after all.

CHAPTER 7

Any hopes I had that Rune and I would hit it off after our less-than-stellar interaction at the read-through go out the window within five minutes of me stepping onto set for my first scene of the season.

"One second!" Rune shouts as I get settled on my mark, a black X taped on the floor of what's meant to be Miles's bedroom. He jogs over to us, pulls the pencil from behind his ear, and starts scribbling something in the margins of his script. "Let's adjust these," he says, holding the script out toward me and Miles once he's done.

It's hard to make out what his chicken scratch says. Panic quickly settles in once I realize that he's rewritten almost every single line I have.

"Can I—"

"Quiet on set!" someone calls out, Rune heading back to

his director's chair before I've even finished reading all the line adjustments.

Before I can protest, the lights beyond the set dim, while the lights on set crank up to full brightness, blinding me until I can't make out anything outside of the makeshift bedroom except shapes and shadows. The usual chatter goes completely silent except for the slap of the clapboard, marking the start of our first take.

"You can't just show up here whenever you want, Zoe," Miles says without missing a beat, despite the slight adjustment to his line.

I do my best to ground myself, focusing on the character and letting the words I'd studied last night with Jerome come naturally. "I was worried about you," I reply, slipping into my scorned ex-girlfriend role.

Miles scoffs, crossing the room to get away from me. "You've never been worried about me."

"I'm not a villain." Following the script, I reach out to grab Miles's arm and pull him back toward me, but Rune's voice disrupts the scene.

"Cut!" he shouts, the lights dimming enough that I can see him getting out of his chair. Sweat has broken out along my forehead by the time he makes it over to us. "Marisol, can you read the revised line?"

"Y-yeah, totally," I reply with as much enthusiasm as I can muster. One of the makeup artists appears beside me, brushing aside my hair to touch up the foundation on my damp forehead. "Can I see the script again? I didn't get a good look at the revisions."

Rune bristles, tightening his grip on the rolled-up script

before begrudgingly handing it over to me. "We'll take a five-minute break."

The noise and bustle return as a bell rings out, signaling the start of our break. Rune heads off to crafty, while Miles collapses onto the prop bed behind him, keeping himself occupied with his phone.

No one seems especially bothered by the need for an immediate break, but I still feel the pressure weighing down on me like a thousand-ton backpack. Dread creeps down my spine as I scan Rune's marked-up script as quickly as I can, repeating the edited lines to myself until they start to lose their meaning. The only thing that makes learning lines harder for me is nerves, and I have plenty of those right now. Unless I want to completely bomb my first scene on the show, I need to calm the hell down.

When I finally glance up from my script, my eyes instantly find Jamila, standing off to the edge of the crowd surrounding the set. She gives me a wide smile and a double thumbs-up once she catches sight of me. The tension in my chest loosens as I meet her smile with one of my own. My hands are still trembling as I give her a thumbs-up back, but the world around us doesn't feel like it's spinning off its axis anymore.

"I thought you said you've done this before?" Dawn pipes up from her seat beside Jamila.

My stomach drops, all of the nerves Jamila's vote of encouragement quashed rushing back. Dawn's expression is bored, and her own script hangs limply in her hand. Most people I've met in this industry aren't nearly as intimidating as they seem on-screen. Dawn, however, is the exception.

"I—I have," I stammer out, wishing she didn't throw me off my game. "I'm just . . ."

Terrible at memorizing lines?

"Let's take it from the top," Rune announces after what feels like barely any time, saving me from having to finish that thought.

Dawn's lips twitch into a smile that doesn't feel kind, while Jamila shoots her a look that isn't very nice either. I hand back Rune's script and take as many deep breaths as I can while everyone gets back into position. *You can do this,* I tell myself, screwing my eyes shut and blocking out the world for a few more seconds. In the darkness, I hold on to the warmth that spread through me when I smiled back at Jamila. The same way I'd felt whenever I met Miles's gaze from across set on *Avalon Grove,* knowing he was watching me. The comfort of knowing someone wants to see you shine.

It's not perfect. I make it through most of the scene without issue but stumble on my last few lines, combining the edited version and the original version into an unintelligible mess. We do another take, and another, and another, until the lines come to me as naturally as breathing. If you'd told me three weeks ago that I'd be able to perfectly recite my lines after having them changed seconds before filming started, I never would've believed you.

I guess anonymous commenters weren't the only ones downplaying my acting abilities.

We've done well over a dozen takes of the scene before Rune finally calls cut for good, giving us a "great job" before the crew gets to work setting up for the next scene. I'm able to sit the next one out while Jamila takes my place in Miles's bedroom. I breathe a sigh of relief when Dawn stalks off toward crafty as soon as I sit down beside her.

Jamila's outfit for the scene—a pair of sunflower-patterned overalls and a white crop top—is a stark contrast to my own devil-red bodycon minidress. It's odd, watching someone play the role I've played for years. The sweet, bubbly girl who wants the best for people. And Jamila plays it well, her posture morphing as soon as she steps onto the set. She holds herself with a certain lightness, a new bounce in her step as she twirls a finger through one of her curls. Part of me wonders if this would feel easier if I were playing her part instead. Something that feels more familiar, even if the tone of the show is a far cry from what I'm used to. But that defeats the purpose of why I'm here: to try something new.

Like earlier, Rune approaches Jamila and Miles with his crumpled script in hand, briefly showing them the tweaks he made before returning back to his chair. *Unlike* earlier, Jamila and Miles fly through the scene without a single hitch. It's such a flawless first run that Rune even gives them a round of applause in congratulations.

"Fantastic, you two. Let's run it a few more times." He murmurs excitedly to the executive producer on his left, unable to hide his excitement like a giddy toddler.

I can't even be mad at myself for my stumbling performance while watching Jamila and Miles on-screen. They're so captivating together, they pull the entire focus of the room. The usual subtle shuffling and clacking of laptop keyboards dies down completely, so silent you could hear a pin drop as everyone cranes their necks and stands on their toes to get a peek at Jamila and Miles.

It's one of the first few scenes of the pilot, focusing on Miles's character in the hours after his family's funeral. One that'll be sure to reel viewers in—especially when it comes to setting up the blossoming love story between Miles's and Jamila's characters.

"I don't know. It feels like everyone hates me," Miles says, nearly on the verge of tears, wiping at the corners of his eyes as he gazes at the tastefully photoshopped photo of him with his "family" on the nightstand.

Jamila tentatively reaches for him, her hand hovering in midair for a moment before finally resting on his arm—and like during the read-through, I can hear sparks ignite when he turns to face her. "I could never hate you."

The two of them have a natural chemistry, not afraid to get closer than they need to, or let their touches linger. They fit together like puzzle pieces, communicating with their eyes like they've known each other for years.

I can already see the flurry of tweets, comments, and posts fans will make about them as they wrap their second run-through of the scene. There's no world in which the internet doesn't latch onto them—both the characters, and the people behind the roles. I'd seen it for myself with Jolia, then again with the M&Ms shipping me and Miles. He and Jamila are the type of couple people will instantly fall for—on- and off-screen. They even have plenty of adorable ship name options. Jamiles, or, the better option, in my opinion: Mila.

The smart thing to do would be to go over my remaining scenes while the two of them film, but much like a car crash or a terrible reality TV show, I can't look away. The tension between their characters burns hotter and hotter with every take, building until it feels like they're moments from throwing the past aside and *finally* kissing when Rune calls cut one last time.

"That's the one!" Rune exclaims, giving the two of them *another* round of applause that the crowd—myself included—eagerly joins.

Both of their cheeks flush as they humbly wave down the applause, thanking Rune before stepping off the set and letting the crew reset for the next scene.

"You were incredible," I say to Jamila as she passes me. Shyly, I glance over at Miles. "Both of you," I add when his eyes meet mine.

Angry as I am with Miles for not giving me the respect of a private breakup, that doesn't erase the almost four years I spent loving him. I still care for him now, and maybe I always will. And today, I'm really damn proud of him. No one knows how hard he worked for this role like I do, and even if this show is what ultimately led to him dumping me in the first place, I can't shake off the pride of seeing him absolutely crush it the way I always told him he would.

"Thanks, Mari," he replies with a smile that brings me back to the early days of our relationship. The bashful compliments after every scene, the cautious hugs, our arms around each other. Something shifts in his eyes, his lips parting slightly, and I wonder if he feels it too. The pull of our shared past.

"You were great too," Jamila adds, disrupting my nostalgic fantasy.

Which is definitely for the best. I'm not here for Miles, I tell myself as I clear my throat and straighten out the hem of my dress. I'm here for me. This isn't about rekindling what we had on *Avalon Grove*—this is about proving myself to him, to the world, to myself.

Rune calls out for quiet on set again before I can reply to Jamila's compliment. The two of them take their seats in the chairs beside me, their names monogrammed on the backs, and let the adults playing our parents take the lead for a bit. We spend the morning knocking out a dozen more scenes— capturing several takes of each until Rune is satisfied.

Before beginning each scene, Rune, without fail, makes his line adjustments. It's comforting that not everyone adapts to the sudden changes as easily as Miles and Jamila did. Even some of the more seasoned actors stumble, Dawn included, easing my worries that I'm the lone disaster of the cast.

"Dawn, take ten and restudy the script," Rune calls out to her, and I resist the urge to whisper *You* have *done this before, right?* to her as she stalks past me in a rage. I'm not a petty person—most of the time—and as stuck-up as she might seem, I definitely don't want to be on the bad side of a Hollywood golden child like her.

By the time my next scene comes around, I'm feeling less on edge. Miles and Jamila give me whispered words of encouragement as I head back onto set, the two of them slinking off to go grab food during their break, while Dawn, wrapped for the day, heads toward the exit. Sure enough, Rune approaches me and the actress playing my mom once we've taken our marks, heavily marked-up script in hand. Only difference: I'm prepared.

There's only so much I can do in the minuscule amount of time that he gives us, but at least I know what to expect. I quickly scan the script and repeat the revised lines over and over until they start to erase the memory of the originals. I square my shoulders and bite back a smile as the lights go up. The crowd goes silent, and I prepare to completely blow them all away.

"Mom, you can't—"

"Cut!" Rune calls out before I can even finish the line, and I realize with a chilling dread that I completely skipped the first five lines of the scene.

So much for blowing them all away.

"Marisol, your first line is 'What are you doing here?'"

"Right, yes, so sorry," I apologize at a rapid clip. My fictional mom gives me an odd look, and I focus my attention on a painting on the wall opposite her shoulder because facing her will only make my panic worse.

We reset and run the scene from the top.

"Mom, what're you doing here?" I say, correctly this time.

My scene partner doesn't even get to read her first line before Rune calls cut again. I bite back a groan of frustration, putting on my best polite expression when I turn to face him.

"Don't say 'Mom,'" he says so sharply it cuts straight through me. "We adjusted this."

"O-of course." *Don't say sorry.* "So sorry."

Dammit. A jellyfish has more spine than me.

Rune doesn't respond to my apology, just twirls his hand in a gesture for us to get a move on. My partner doesn't bother to hide her annoyance now. Thankfully, it suits the scene. All the nerves I worked to put aside during the break come flooding back, my hands trembling as we start the scene yet again.

"Mom, I—"

"CUT!" Rune shouts, and it takes every bit of strength I have not to burst into tears.

"I'm sorry, I need a minute to—"

"Esther!" Rune calls out for one of his various personal assistants. A petite girl with pin-straight black hair and an all-black ensemble to match appears at his side practically out of thin air, handing him an extra-large tea. He takes a disgruntled sip, the crease in his brow slackening once he's swallowed.

Note to self: Tea calms the beast.

"Go practice lines with Marisol until she has them down perfectly." He places enough emphasis on that last part for me to know that stumbling again isn't an option.

Esther nods, gesturing for me to follow her to a back room while my scene partner rolls her eyes and heads back to her own seat. We pass the lunch setup on our way to an empty production office, and I spot Miles and Jamila sitting beside each other at a table laughing at Miles's phone. Something in me twists uncomfortably watching them shift in closer, their heads pressed together as they smile for a selfie. Something I won't let myself believe is jealousy. There's no point in being jealous. I'm not here for Miles, and he sure as hell isn't here for me.

"C'mon," Esther calls out from the nearby office, and I squash down that uneasy feeling in my gut. I'm already screwing up more than I should be. I can't let myself get distracted too.

It takes almost twenty minutes for me to get my lines to a place where I'm sure I could recite them in my sleep. In the back of my mind, I know it probably shouldn't have taken me that long to learn a handful of line adjustments, but if I'm being honest, we're lucky it didn't take longer. Embarrassment, fear, and panic are one dangerous cocktail. Thankfully, my new scene partner (Esther Cho, intern turned PA and recent NYU grad, I learn during our brief conversation) has the patience of a saint.

"Don't worry," she says after we've run through the scene for a tenth time, now well assured that I know every line perfectly. "He's a dick to everyone."

"He is?" I ask with a raised brow, shocked by her casual boldness. And because it sure doesn't feel that way so far.

She shrugs, taking a sip from her Hydro Flask. "He made half the cast cry last season. Especially Eli." Shit. If Eli Rowan—breakout star of season one, and the first-ever nonbinary performer to win an Emmy—wasn't safe from Rune's wrath, none of us is. "And don't get me started on the crew. It's pretty much a rite of passage for him to fire you at least once a month."

I gulp, the sound audible in the empty room.

"It's not so bad," Esther says when she notes the panic written all over my face. "We all get our jobs back within a day."

That does little to reassure me. I know firsthand how grueling shooting can be sometimes—long hours, very little sleep. Some days the only thing that gets you through a production is "passion and belief in the work," the mantra that keeps half of Hollywood running. But I don't know that I'd ever be passionate enough about something to put up with that kind of erratic behavior.

Then again, aren't I already?

Esther escorts me back to set before she can scare me off with any more horror stories from season one. Rune is clearly disgruntled by the time we return to set, and I tighten my grip on my script, hoping he won't take any of his frustration out on Esther instead of me. Thankfully, he accepts the apple she brings him—apparently, he needs a snack every two hours or he goes *really* off the rails—and calls everyone to attention for another set of takes.

For the second time that day, the room goes silent. But, this time, I know it's not because everyone is watching in awe, hanging on to the edges of their seats to get a glimpse of a once-in-a-lifetime performance.

It's because they want to see if I fail.

As we take our marks again, I close my eyes and inhale deeply, walking myself through one of the dozen guided-meditation ASMR videos I watch before bed. There's the click of the clapboard, the hum of the lights coming to life, the whir of the camera, and when I open my eyes, I'm not me anymore.

I'm not scared and insecure and worried about what people think of me. I'm powerful, strong, and angry as hell.

We get through the first several pages of the scene flawlessly, my confidence slowly building back up with every line I don't stumble on. Even my "mom" seems surprised by my performance, hints of it showing in the cracks in her own line readings.

"Just leave me alone!" I shout, my heart pounding wildly as we make it to the last moments of the scene, adrenaline pumping through me. "I don't—"

"CUT!" Rune shouts midway through my line, and I stop like I've been unplugged.

"Wh-what?" I stammer out, still trapped somewhere between myself and my character as I whip around to face him. "That was the line, I—"

"You should be blond," he interrupts, tapping his pen to his lower lip.

"What?" I say again, sounding like a broken record.

It's a small comfort that the rest of the crew seems startled too, an unsettling air of discomfort closing in on us. This day has been exhausting for me on multiple levels, and probably twice as exhausting for the crew who had to be here even earlier than the cast.

"Your character. She should be blond," Rune repeats, gesturing to my fictional mom's platinum blond hair. "You two should be mirrors of each other."

My scene partner and I exchange a confused look. Of course we don't immediately pass as family, with my tan skin, brown hair, and brown eyes, and her pale skin, ice-white hair, and blue eyes. But she's not that far off from Mom's complexion, and people never doubt that we're related. Plus, that's the magic of television: you don't *have* to resemble anyone to make an audience buy into the fantasy.

"But—"

"Have hair and makeup reach out," Rune interrupts again, speaking to Esther this time, and I have to bite down on my lip to not let my short temper take over. "Once that's done, we'll reshoot her scenes from today."

Wait—what?

Esther nods, shooting me a sympathetic frown before

disappearing—likely to go find the hairstylist in charge of transforming me into my fictional mom's "mirror image."

So, all of the work I did today was for nothing? I'm no stranger to reshoots, but usually I haven't busted my ass this hard to get the scenes done in the first place. I grit my teeth hard enough for my jaw to ache, unclenching my fists only for the sake of not breaking off any of the acrylic French tips I spent an hour in the salon for.

"See you bright and early, people!" Rune addresses the rest of the crew, giving a hand signal for everyone to wrap up production for the day, leaving me gobsmacked and speechless without another word. No asking if I'd be okay with completely changing my appearance for the role or negotiating whether we can try a wig instead of bleaching my hair, or an apology for making me have to start over from scratch. Nothing.

I inhale sharply, the breath coming out as a shuddered exhale. No ASMR guided meditation can calm me down, but I have no choice except to put on a brave face.

Because this is pushing myself out of my comfort zone.

This is what I wanted.

CHAPTER 8

"You're sure you're feeling okay about this?" Delia asks for what feels like the hundredth time.

"Absolutely," I reassure her yet again. "This show is really special, and the experience has been amazing so far."

If by *amazing*, I mean forcing me to completely change my physical appearance and wardrobe, getting yelled at in front of the entire cast, *and* needing actors to pay for their own car ride home to make room in the budget for Rune's script changes, then yes. This has been an absolutely *amazing* experience.

My first week shooting *The Limit* has been rough. It's definitely more intense than what I'm used to—both the environment and the content of the show—but this is a learning experience on how to memorize lines on the fly, how to handle eccentric directors, and how to deal with production budget cuts. *Avalon Grove* was my first real experience on a full-scale production. Most of the other projects I've worked on have been smaller-budget indie projects. I've had a handful of roles in bigger-budget stuff too, but those parts were so small I can barely even remember working on them. If this is the road I'm going to go down for the rest of my life, I'll have to work through some rough patches here and there.

While I'll miss the sweet driver I only got to know for two days, the ten-minute walk to the subway helps me clear my head. Plus, there probably aren't any paparazzi trolling the New York subway system. Still, I adjust the brim of the ball cap holding my hair up and out of my face. Coupled with my oversized sunglasses, it's my favorite disguise. It's not foolproof, but no one's actively seeking actors riding the subway in the middle of the day.

"I've got a few more leads on rom-com projects," Delia continues. "There's this HBO series that's shooting in Paris that would love to get a self-tape from you. And a cable sitcom about a mom-and-daughter duo who rob men for a living."

I roll my eyes as I balance my phone between my ear and my shoulder, struggling to properly swipe my MetroCard through the turnstile.

TOO FAST SWIPE AGAIN

"I'm fine, Delia. Seriously," I interject, cutting off her list of potential projects. I'd be offended by her lack of faith in me if I wasn't so overwhelmed by her throwing other possibilities at me every time we check in. It's not like I can quit now. We've already started filming. And I worked way too hard on memorizing all of these line changes to give up.

"I'm having a good time, I promise," I reassure her, putting as much emphasis on the *promise* as I can while swiping my MetroCard for a second time.

TOO SLOW SWIPE AGAIN

"C'mon," I mutter under my breath, glancing over my shoulder nervously at the line starting to form behind me.

Delia stays silent on the other end of the line, as if she's still not convinced. I'm prepared to call her out on her doubt in my acting abilities while I swipe the card (hopefully) one last time.

INSUFFICIENT FARE

"Keep it moving!" a disgruntled man at the back of the line shouts.

Fine, I haven't nailed the art of swiping a MetroCard yet, but in my defense, what subway station only has *one* turnstile?

I duck out of the way, letting the person after me go next while I rush over to the machine at the opposite end of the station to refill my card.

"If you ever feel uncomfortable on set, or worried about anything, you call me ASAP, all right?" Delia's voice is soft, light. Some might even say vulnerable. A complete one-eighty to the usual no-nonsense tone I'm used to.

It should feel comforting, knowing that my straight-to-business agent is opening up, making sure I have a safe space in her, but it only grates on my already-frayed nerves. The calls, the check-ins, the constant emails with self-tape requests and a subject line reading *Not too late to switch to this if you're interested!* Why is everyone around me treating me like I'm a ticking time bomb? Like they're waiting for me to inevitably implode?

If the person who gets 15 percent of all my earnings doesn't even want me to do a big-budget prestige drama, how the hell am I supposed to believe in myself?

Out of the corner of my eye, I spot a man walking off the platform through the emergency exit door. Meanwhile, the MetroCard machine continues its struggle to process my credit card. Double-checking over my shoulder for any roaming cops or subway employees, I quickly cancel my transaction and snatch back my subway and credit cards, then dart through the door before it can close. Less than a week in New York and I'm already a delinquent.

"Thanks, Delia. I have to hop on the train. I'll talk to you later."

"You're taking the subway?" Delia makes it sound like I told her I'm headed to the moon.

"Duh, I'm a New Yorker now," I reply with an actual note of cheeriness. Taking the subway does feel daunting, and maybe the slightest bit unsanitary, but it's a core part of New York City. This summer is about pushing myself out of my comfort zone. Which includes heading into a station alone. Right before our call, I narrowly avoided touching a suspicious brown liquid that one could only hope was soda.

Delia gives me a skeptical goodbye and one last reminder to call her if I need anything. Just in time, the A train comes rumbling into the station seconds after I tuck my phone back into my pocket. The doors open, and I step inside, only for something to yank me off the train.

"Get off!" I'm prepared to reach into my bag for the can of Mace Mom insisted I carry. I whip around to shove off my attacker only to come face-to-face with Jamila.

"It's me!" she cries out, holding her hands up in surrender. Several eyes watch us warily, a group of women idling on the staircase, until I relax and pull my hand out of my tote bag. I breathe a sigh of relief that I realized it was her before I could act. Both because I'd feel guilty as hell for pepper-spraying the only person in the cast who's been nice to me, and because I can't imagine Rune would be too happy with me almost blinding his lead actress.

"Stand clear of the closing doors," the automated subway voice announces.

"Sorry, I have to get home." I turn around, prepared to bolt onto the train and apologize for brushing off Jamila the next time I see her, when she grabs my arm again, spinning me back around like we're tangoing on the dance floor.

"That train is going farther into Brooklyn," she explains. "You're going back to Manhattan, right? You said you're staying in Washington Heights."

"Oh, yeah, right," I reply quickly, not letting myself dwell on how she remembered that small tidbit I'd mentioned briefly in passing during the read-through. "Thank you. I totally missed that."

"Happens to the best of us," she says with a shrug. "I've lived here my whole life, and I still accidentally wind up deep in Brooklyn every few months."

I shudder at the thought. We fall silent as the old-school train pulls away, the screech of the tracks making both of us wince. When the rumble settles and the platform has gone quiet again, I give her a tentative smile. "I think getting lost in Brooklyn would have broken me. You're a lifesaver."

She arches one of her well-defined brows coyly, and it takes biting down on my lip not to ask her what her brow routine is because hot *damn*. Anyone who can make something as simple as brows this attractive has major skills. "Big praise coming from someone who critiqued my cupcake-eating skills."

"Well, I never said you were perfect," I reply.

Something rattles within me when she laughs in response. Either my heart or my lungs or my stomach is doing somersaults. It's the lightest I've felt in weeks. A flutter of a feeling I haven't experienced in years.

"Thank you again," she says, changing the subject. "For the cupcakes. You're pretty much my sister's favorite person ever."

"I wish it was always that easy to win someone over," I say, more to myself than to her. If everyone was as easy to win over as Jamila's sister, I'd be the MVP of the cast like I'd planned.

"I mean she likes *you*," Jamila explains. "From the other show you were on."

"O-oh." It shouldn't feel unusual. *Avalon Grove* was the number-one teen drama on cable all four seasons. I have millions of followers, stan accounts made in my name, screaming fans at every event and season premiere. But it feels like all of that was ages ago, some far-off dream. A time when I wasn't judged by my ex for the type of role that made my career.

"That's so sweet. Tell her I said thank you," I reply, but it doesn't come close to the thanks I really want to give. To thank Jamila—well, her sister—for not making me feel ashamed of my acting career thus far, even for a few moments.

Before I can figure out how to sum that up without sounding like a weirdo, the uptown train comes barreling into the station on the opposite track, whizzing past us so quickly it almost knocks me back.

"Are you . . . ?" I ask, gesturing to the train as it slows to a stop.

"Going to Washington Heights too, yeah," she finishes for me.

We stay quiet as we let others off the train first—unlike some heathens—before boarding. I run for two seats at the end of the updated spaceship train car, prepared to offer the other to Jamila only to see her standing a safe distance away.

"We don't have to sit together," she suddenly blurts out as the train doors close. "Or talk. I know there's always this weird, awkward tension when you run into someone on the platform and don't know if you should stick together or leave each other alone the rest of the ride. Because sometimes you're not in the mood to talk. Or you want to read a book, or listen to a—"

"We can sit together."

I shift to the seat closer to the door, going to pat the one beside me, but deciding against it. I don't know what butts have sat here. Instead, I gesture to the seat like a game-show host's glamorous assistant. "If you want to?"

Jamila's cheeks flush the loveliest shade of pink, and for a few brief moments, I wonder what brand of blush she uses, or if it's another thing she's won in the genetic lottery.

The second Jamila sits down beside me, an awkward silence fills the space between us. A self-fulfilling prophecy. It's not that I don't want to keep talking to her. But I'm too caught up in the way her knee is pressed against mine, and how if I lean back a little, we'll be bare arm to bare arm, and that I can smell the perfume clinging to the collar of her T-shirt—Bloom by Gucci. Great taste.

"You were really amazing today," I say to break the silence, and because if I sit there thinking about every single place our bodies are touching, I'll lose my mind. "I know I said that yesterday too, and I probably sound like a broken record, but I'm serious. And the way you and Miles can memorize those line adjustments . . ." I pause to make a hand gesture meant to mime my brain's attempt to puzzle through memorizing lines. "Learning my regular lines makes my brain short-circuit." I finish my charade performance with a whispered explosion.

Jamila giggles, but the sound is lost beneath another screech as the train takes a hard left turn, our bodies pressed even closer together now.

"They taught us a bunch of great memorization techniques at my school. I could show you some of them if you want?"

I definitely want—I'll take what I can get—but my stomach churns at the thought. I know I shouldn't be afraid to ask for help, but a twinge of fear creeps through me like a chill. Fear that Delia and Miles are right to be so hesitant about me being here. That I'm *not* cut out to be a prestige actor if I need tips from someone so green.

Production only started this week, so of course I'm a little off my game. I haven't even shaken the jet lag yet. I'm in a new city, working on an entirely new type of show, and dealing with the emotional whiplash of a breakup *while* having to live with the dad who I barely know. I'm not easy on myself, but I can cut myself some slack. Even a seasoned professional would feel a little rattled by that much change at once. I need a little more time to get adjusted.

"You learned how to memorize lines at school?" I ask, praying Jamila doesn't notice my subtle change in topic. I'm not ready to accept her offer, but definitely don't want to turn it down either. I'll just put it on the back burner.

Thankfully, she goes along without protest. "I go to a performing arts school. Near Lincoln Center."

My brow furrows. "As in the one that a bunch of famous people went to?"

As in, the same school my *Avalon Grove* castmates wished they went to. Getting to live in New York, going to class a few blocks away from the heart of the city. It's every teen actor's wet dream.

"A few," she shrugs, ducking her face bashfully, as if she didn't casually drop the news that she goes to one of the best performing arts schools in the country. It's been clear since the day I met her that she's seriously talented. Like, once-in-a-lifetime talented. And her humility makes her that much cooler.

"So, you're still in school?" I ask. Technically, I "graduated" this past May along with the rest of the *Avalon Grove* cast, but the last time I was in a real school setting was the last few months of eighth grade. The closest I've gotten to a real high school experience was shooting our finale prom/graduation episode, and I can't imagine a normal prom would be half as dramatic as a fictional one. Or, at least I hope most real proms don't involve two fistfights, a teen mom going into labor, and a called-in bomb threat.

"Going into my senior year," she replies.

"So, have you done this before?" I ask, gesturing unhelpfully. "Like, been on a show?" I clarify.

"I did a few short films for undergrads at NYU, but . . ." She shrugs. "Nothing like this before."

"Holy shit," I blurt out, even though I already knew from her lack of IMDb page that she hadn't been in anything major before. Still, her first role before she's even out of high school is a series regular—a *lead*—in a show that swept the Emmys last year? That's next-level impressive. "Sorry, I mean, that's . . ." I trail off, unable to find a word that encapsulates how enormous that kind of achievement is.

"Holy shit," she finishes for me with a shy grin. "I said the same thing when I found out."

I struggle to think of a response and am saved from finding one when several passengers file onto the train as we barrel through the busiest stops in Manhattan. We offer up our seats to two elderly women carrying several tote bags as the rest of the car fills up quickly.

It's difficult to find a place to stand where I can keep holding on to the pole—which I definitely need unless I want to fall into someone's lap. There's barely any room to move as the door attempts to close around the throng of people, the conductor warning everyone to pack into the train as tightly as possible, but we're able to settle on the opposite side of the open doors, where a man is shoved so close to me I'm practically pinned to the wall.

Normally, this size crowd would trigger my claustrophobia. I've never done well in tight spaces, especially when other people are involved—hence, fear of planes. Throw in the possibility of a fiery death and you have a recipe for disaster. But there's a certain wonder to this closeness, to the way everyone moves and sways with the train's jerky path down the track, the hum of conversations and the turning of book pages and muffled notes of music and podcasts leaking from headphones throughout the car. The way I can glance over at Jamila, admire the dimpled curve in her chin, and pretend I'm studying an ad for a divorce attorney in Long Island over her shoulder instead.

"Does it ever get less magical?" I ask as we pull into the next stop. "Living here?"

Her brows knit together as she considers the question. "It gets frustrating sometimes," she finally answers. "Rats. Train delays. High-ass rent."

I shudder three times in quick succession. Even Dad and Jerome's rent-controlled place costs way more than anyone should pay for what's basically a bedroom and a closet.

"But those things don't outweigh the good," she continues, smiling and gazing off into the distance nostalgically. "Like getting lost in Central Park. Or trekking to Brooklyn way too early in the morning and watching the sun rise over the river. Having the best meal of your life from a food truck at midnight. Those kinds of random experiences make living here worth it."

My mouth waters, not at the thought of the food, but of letting loose in the city. I salivate over the adventures I haven't had yet, and how there could be something magical waiting for me around every corner, on any day, at every hour.

"Think I can do all of that before I head back to LA?"

Nothing about New York has been what I expected since I touched down at JFK a few days ago. The eternal optimist in me has grappled with holding on to that idea of a fun, exciting summer in the city with every single curveball thrown at me.

But now, thinking about spending a day getting lost in a park, I feel that hope again.

When Jamila readjusts her grip on the pole, her hand briefly brushing against mine, I swear she takes another step closer to me. Or maybe it was me. Or maybe it was the both of us, drawn together like gravity. Whatever the case, I can feel heat radiating from her, that familiar scent of oranges and cinnamon nestled above her perfume—autumn in summer— washing over me as she replies. "Only if you have a good tour guide."

Before my heart can lurch into my throat at what her response might mean, the train beats me to the punch. We slide into the station so abruptly it throws everyone off their rhythm. Even the seasoned natives stumble—a man curses to himself as he spills his coffee, an apple rolls toward us after it tumbles out of a woman's bag.

Jamila, pressed chest to chest against me.

She puts her hand onto the wall behind me in time to save our heads from knocking together, but she's still close enough for me to feel her breath against my lips. Our heartbeats pound in frantic unison, mine threatening to burst right out of my chest. Heat spreads down my cheeks to my collar and lower and lower until I must be as pink as half my wardrobe.

"Sorry," she mumbles under her breath, whatever she says next lost beneath the sound of the conductor announcing the stop before the doors fly open.

In a blink, she was pressed up against me. Another blink, and she's gone, swept up in the swarm of people bustling onto the platform.

"I'll see you later," she calls out, craning her neck to see me above the crowd rushing to get off the train.

"See you," I reply weakly, knowing she'll never be able to hear me over the chaos of the station.

With the sweet smell of cinnamon and oranges gone, replaced by general BO funk, I'm able to snap back to reality and examine the pillars around the station. The heat and excitement built up inside me drains away as I realize in horror-movie slow motion that I don't recognize this station or its name. And that, according to the map above my head, we just passed my stop.

"Son of a—"

"Stand clear of the closing doors."

CHAPTER 9

Why have I spent 50 percent of my first week here in New York trying to convince people that I'm not on the brink of an emotional breakdown?

"I'm fine, Mom," I say, already exhausted from how many times I've had to reassure people this week.

Today isn't my best day, though. Granted, none of my days so far has been great, but this has been a particularly rough one. Sitting in a salon for five hours to get my hair fully bleached was rough enough as it is. Throw in a bunch of subway delays, a pigeon pooping on my brand-new denim jacket—though Posie claims that's good luck—and the fact that my new hair makes me look as pale as a vampire, and you have a perfect recipe for an awful day. Learning nothing from my subway ride home with Jamila and winding up deep in Brooklyn by accident was the cherry on top of the sundae.

Thank God for time differences. If Mom had called any

earlier today, she might've heard me sobbing in the middle of a train station after I realized what I'd done wrong too little too late. The Lyft back to our place cost around a hundred dollars with tip, but it was well worth it to avoid having an emotional breakdown in the subway. After an hour of transportation hell, I'm finally walking back to my apartment building. Ego bruised, but in one piece.

"So . . . how did the appointment go?" Mom asks reluctantly, clearly still eager to convince me to give up on *The Limit* and come back home.

Apparently, I'm the only person who has confidence in myself. And even that's starting to dwindle, with everyone from Dawn Greene to my own *mom* thinking I'm out of my depth. I'm not sure how long I can keep running on spite. Obviously, I still want to prove all of them wrong, but it'd be nice to have at least one person in my corner.

"It's . . ." I trail off as I catch my reflection in the window of a barbershop next door to Dad's apartment. "Interesting."

Mom coos sympathetically. I can practically feel her pushing my hair away from my face the way she would if she were here in person. "I'm sure you're as beautiful as ever."

While her optimism is appreciated, it's definitely not true. I shudder as I sneak one last glance at myself in the shop window. I look like I'm AI-generated. Unnatural. My skin has lost its tan from the California sun, and the natural blush in my cheeks has been sucked dry to match the draining bone-white color of my hair.

Not good.

All I can do now is hope Rune feels the same way and has me change back to a more natural brunette by the end of the week. With the heavy stage lights and pounds of makeup we wear on set, I'll be pale as paper in the finished product.

"Everything going okay with your dad?" Mom continues when I don't respond, too focused on not getting hit by someone riding a bike along the sidewalk.

"For the most part," I reply once I've safely stepped out of the cyclist's path. There's nothing to update her on because . . . well, Dad and I have barely seen each other. With him pulling extra hours at the theater leading up to tech week for their next show and my erratic filming schedule, the most I've seen of him this week was the day he picked me up from the airport.

"That doesn't sound very—"

Whatever Mom says next is lost as I notice a small black shadow jump out from behind a trash can and scurry inches in front of me.

I let out a bloodcurdling scream.

"Mari?! Mari, what's happening?! Do you need me to call the police?" Mom shouts frantically. I can vaguely make out the sound of her tapping on her screen, probably already queuing up nine-one-one in case I'm in danger. I wouldn't be surprised if she was booking flights to New York as we speak.

"A rat ran in front of me," I choke out, my throat tight as I fight off an onslaught of terrified tears. "I think it touched my shoe."

Get it together, Mari. You can't cry in the middle of the street over a rat. They're nuisances, like Jamila said, but everyone knows they run this city.

But it was *huge,* and gross, and it definitely bumped against the toe of my mule before slipping into the sewer drain, and that is beyond disgusting. I whine as I glance down at the smudged tip of my shoe, stained with soot, or dirt, or whatever grime rats are coated in. I've only had these for a week, and now I'm going to have to burn them.

Mom sighs on the other end of the line, done with my dramatics. Which, fair. She's had to put up with my nonsense since the day I was born, but at least I wasn't almost giving her a heart attack. "Is it gone now?"

"Mmm-hmm," I say with a sniffle, triple checking that none of his friends are lingering beside the trash can before I break into a run, desperate to get into the building as quickly as I can. "I'll call you back later," I tell Mom as I jam the key in the door. "Love you, bye!"

I'd feel guilty about ending the call before Mom can finish telling me she loves me back if I wasn't so relieved about finally being within the confines of four walls, having avoided the wrath of any lingering rats.

Unless this building has mice . . . which are basically tiny rats that bite.

And I definitely saw mousetraps in the kitchen pantry yesterday. . . .

Ugh.

One silver lining to this day: the shelving units I bought to organize my closet-room finally arrived. I heave the large box sitting beside the wall of mailboxes into my arms, grunting from the weight of it. Lugging the box up to the fifth floor definitely covers my cardio for the day and takes my mind off the thought of mice hiding inside the walls.

I hear a snap as I set down the box beside the apartment door, the hairs on the back of my neck standing on end as I glance down at my hand, praying I didn't screw up my manicure. But, sure enough, three of my acrylics have broken off. Great. Absolutely wonderful.

Fighting back the urge to sob, I finally unlock the door and kick my package inside. Bruiser is waiting for me at the entrance, happily yipping and licking at the stain on my mule—gross—while salsa music blares from the kitchen. I can hear the distant sizzle of oil in a pan, the aroma of sautéed onions wafting toward me. Weird. Jerome is the resident chef—and only halfway decent salsa dancer—but his weekly drag show is on Friday nights. Yesterday he said he wouldn't be home until at least two in the morning, and that was assuming he didn't stick around for drinks with the rest of the queens.

On my guard, I quickly scan the room for a weapon, but the best I can find is an umbrella. Still, I arm myself with the confidence of a three-hundred-pound weightlifter with a battle axe and slowly step into the kitchen, prepared to attack.

It turns out we're not being robbed by someone who loves salsa music and leaves behind home-cooked meals. A stout older woman is at the stove, swaying to the beat of the music and humming along as she stirs something in a massive pot.

Bruiser abandons me for the unfamiliar visitor and patiently sits at the woman's feet until she notices her presence, cooing as she offers Bruiser a piece of some shredded stewed meat. Bruiser happily takes the meat and skitters away to our closet-room, leaving me to fend for myself.

"Excuse me?" I call out tentatively, unsure what to say to someone who either a) broke into our apartment to cook, or, more likely, b) is a total stranger.

The woman whips around, and her face lights up like

a Christmas tree at the sight of me. She drops the wooden spoon in her hand to bustle over to me, letting out a drawn-out "oooh" as she tosses off her Puerto Rican flag–patterned apron. "Mija, let me look at you!" she says before reaching for my hand and forcing me to twirl in a circle for her like she's my fairy godmother.

"Que bonita!" she exclaims as my head spins from both the twirl and trying to keep up with what's going on. "You have your papi's eyes," she says, patting my cheek with a wrinkled ring-clad hand. My eyes find hers—a mirror of not only my own, but Dad's too—and she gives me a wink.

"Calm down, Ma," Dad calls from somewhere down the hall. "You're gonna give the girl a heart attack."

He emerges from his room still dressed in his work attire: a white dress shirt tucked into royal blue slacks. It doesn't seem like the most comfortable ensemble to wear for his line of work, especially when most of his day involves sewing period ball gowns from scratch and mending hemlines. But as he told me earlier this week: Why would anyone trust a designer who can't dress themself?

Dad winces as he loosens his matching blue tie, stopping in his tracks when he finally spots me. "Oh" is all he can say when he takes in my new hair.

Gee, thanks.

"Pareces una . . ." The woman trails off, searching for the right word before settling on "Snow princess!"

This hair *is* giving Elsa from *Frozen* vibes but without the fabulous turquoise dress and castle made of ice.

"You look very regal," Dad agrees before crossing over to

the kitchen, inhaling deeply over the cauldron-esque pot. He goes to sneak a bite when the woman comes rushing over to him and slaps his hand away, telling him off in rapid Spanish. While the two are distracted with bickering over the wooden spoon in Dad's hand, I finally take a closer peek at the woman who, I slowly realize, is my grandmother.

Her silver hair is held back in a loose bun, and a pair of glasses that seem like something a serial killer from the eighties would wear are hanging from a chain around her neck. The rest of her outfit is the definition of overstimulation. A cheetah-print cardigan over a pink Minnie Mouse T-shirt paired with brown pants and a pair of white Crocs. Pinned to the cardigan is a gold brooch of a baby cherub playing the trumpet.

Very cursed aesthetic. Are we sure we're related?

The confusing layers of her ensemble, along with the bits and pieces of Spanish I'm struggling to string together, make my temples pulse with the first signs of a migraine. With a huff, Dad finally gives up on sneaking a piece of meat before it's ready and turns his attention to me instead.

"Munchkin, you remember your abuela, right?"

Annoyance that Dad totally ignored my request to stop calling me munchkin aside—I'm a whole legal adult now— I definitely don't remember my abuela whatsoever. Most of my memories of my time living with Dad in the city are fuzzy at best. The few times he came out to visit me in LA, she never tagged along, thanks to her intense fear of flying that she must've passed down to me. We've spoken a handful of times whenever Dad handed the phone off to her during our occasional check-ins, but the language barrier has always been a bit of a problem. Her English is solid enough to hold a short conversation, but she usually defaults back to Spanish.

I put on a smile anyway and nod. "Cómo estás?" I ask her after she pulls me in for a hug and a kiss on the cheek that leaves some red lipstick behind. I've got enough rudimentary Spanish in me to get through the basics, but anything past "how are you," "I'm hungry," and "where is the bathroom" is out of my depth.

Unfortunately, she doesn't know that, and immediately launches into an answer in Spanish so fast I can't even grab on to a single word that I recognize.

Dad must catch the panic on my face and interrupts his mom midsentence with a nervous laugh. "Ma, I don't think Marisol's had much practice speaking Spanish."

That's an understatement. The last time I got to practice my Spanish was when Miles and I got really into Duolingo for two months. Unlike me, he actually mastered Mandarin by practicing with his own grandma. I never made it past the vocabulary lesson on school supplies.

"Ah!" My abuela balks, as if she's offended. "What you mean? Of course she speaks Spanish! She's Puerto Rican!"

In this moment I've never felt *less* Puerto Rican.

Dad sighs, pinching the bridge of his nose for a moment before wrapping his arm around my shoulder. "Mari didn't grow up speaking Spanish at home."

Abuela wrinkles her nose, seemingly unconvinced, but drops the argument anyway. Then she bustles back to the stove.

"I make you dinner," she proclaims while reaching for a bowl in the overhead cabinet. "Your father"—she gestures to Dad with her wooden spoon—"not know how to cook."

Dad holds up a hand to his wounded heart, an over-the-top hurt expression on his face. Guess that's where I got my dramatics from. "I do know how to cook."

Abuela whips around to shoot him a glare.

"I just don't know how to cook *well*," he amends.

Satisfied with that answer, she turns back around and starts ladling stewed meat and rice into a bowl. "Too skinny," she says over her shoulder. I'm assuming to me. That's answered when she pushes the bowl into my hand with an "Eat" and a gesture to sit at the dining table.

"Oh, I, uh, can't eat meat," I stammer out as I see what she's served me. While the shredded meat smells fantastic, my stomach would hate me for indulging in meat this rich and savory after so long without it. Her brow furrows for a moment. "I'm a vegetarian," I add, to be safe.

Abuela nods in understanding, taking the bowl back and handing it to Dad instead before serving me another one, meat-free this time, and nudges me to sit down.

Over the past week, the kitchen table has become crowded with debris. Reams of fabric for the dress Dad is working on for Jerome. The makeup bag I didn't have enough space to store in the bathroom. New toys for Bruiser since I forgot to pack hers. There's barely enough room to sit at the table when it isn't cluttered, and now it's impossible. Dad makes quick work of clearing it off as best he can, tossing the fabric into a nearby closet—that's full to the point of bursting—and moving the rest to his bedroom.

Abuela takes the seat opposite me, waiting expectantly for me to try her food. Nerves prickle my skin as I give her a nervous smile and spoon some of the rice, sauce, and a chunk of glossy avocado onto my spoon. I've never felt so . . . watched before. And that's saying something—my face was literally on millions of people's TVs every week for four years. The pressure weighs on my shoulders like an overstuffed backpack as she doesn't take her eyes off me for even a second while I take my first bite.

I was already close to starving by the time I got here. All I had for breakfast was a protein bar. My stomach rumbled the entire subway ride home, and if I hadn't been so traumatized by my rat sighting, I probably would've picked something up from one of the shops sending intoxicating scents of fried, seared, and marinated food wafting down the block.

Still, my first bite of Abuela's food is nothing short of mind-blowing.

Fried plantains coated in a light layer of sauce that I can only describe as the garlicky goodness of the gods. Light and fluffy rice to soak up the Garlic Gods Sauce, perfectly complemented by the creamy chunks of avocado.

In short: Ten out of ten. Perfection. Possibly the best meal I've had in my life. Including the Michelin-starred restaurants Miles and I visited back when we were dating.

"Good, ah?" Abuela says with a coy smile.

"Amazing," I reply before I take an eager second bite, moaning around my fork as the flavor combo sends shivers down my spine.

"Don't tell Jerome," Dad says with a wink and a nudge to his mom's shoulder. And here I thought nothing could beat the dinners Jerome has been cooking this week.

The cliché says there's no food like a grandparent's cooking— something I never really understood. My grandparents on my mom's side both passed away when I was too young to remember them, and Mom's cooking is *definitely* not something to write home about. She regularly burns rice with the rice maker I bought her.

But now I definitely get it. A part of me aches as I demolish my food like I haven't eaten in weeks, Abuela smiling proudly and encouraging me to have seconds, and even thirds, if I want. Dad sneaking bits of meat to Bruiser under the table. Salsa music playing from the radio on top of the fridge—the song unfamiliar, but the beat making me want to shimmy in my seat.

This moment feels fun in a way I didn't think would be possible for me and Dad when I first got here. It feels . . . right.

I can't remember the last time I had a home-cooked meal before I got here. Or ate one around a real kitchen table. For the past four years, my life has been running from set to interviews to shoots before crashing on the couch because I was too exhausted to make it to bed. And I loved that life. The rush of a packed promo day. The bone-deep exhaustion when I finally got home from an all-day shoot. But I'd forgotten how much I loved this side of life too. Spending time with Mom, the only family I had back then, curled up in the living room, eating frozen pizza. Not worrying about call times or memorizing lines or rehearsing answers for interviews.

And, maybe, I miss mundanity. A little bit.

"Your nails!" Abuela exclaims as I polish off my bowl. She takes my hand in hers and runs her fingers along my jagged, broken nails.

"I know, it's horrifying," I mumble. I'll have to do a deep dive tonight to find a new go-to salon while I'm here.

"Kevin can fix," Abuela reassures me with a nod, patting my hand before nudging Dad in the ribs. "You text him."

"Kevin?" I ask.

"Your cousin," Dad explains before pulling out his phone. "He can do all that stuff. Nails. Hair. Makeup."

"Not makeup," Abuela quickly corrects him, shooting me a vaguely horrified expression. "His makeup not good. Not yet."

I stifle a laugh around my next bite of food. I can handle myself when it comes to makeup, but having a manicurist (and hairstylist, apparently) in the family is definitely convenient.

Once he's shot off a text to Cousin Kevin, Dad excuses himself and Abuela from the table.

"I'm going to drop your abuela off, then swing by the club to help out with costumes for Jerome's show," Dad explains as he grabs his keys. "We probably won't be back 'til late. Don't wait up, but don't try sneaking out. We'll know," he warns with narrowed eyes.

"Could I come to the show?" I ask eagerly, mouth full of rice. I've been dying to see Jerome live ever since he started posting clips of his performances on his socials three years ago. If he's that captivating in a thirty-second clip, I can only imagine how great he must be in person.

Dad sternly shakes his head, making an *uh-uh* sound. "No way."

"But it's an eighteen-and-up club," I protest, having already done my research.

"And I still don't want *my* kid at a club that late at night," he insists, more sternly than I thought he could be, considering he's never felt like much of an authority figure in my life. "I won't be able to keep an eye on you from backstage.

And you're a public persona. I'm not gonna let people start waltzing up to you and bothering you all night when I'm not around."

He has a point—I've never been able to exist in public spaces the way regular people can. Still, that shouldn't stop me from being able to support my family at a drag show. I pout, but don't argue, and slump back in my chair.

Abuela wipes the pout off my face as she presses a wet goodbye kiss to my cheek.

"See you soon, mama," she says before giving me one last kiss on the forehead and leaving the apartment with an armful of tote bags.

With the apartment to myself, I turn to my one source of entertainment: my phone. There's a lot to catch up on in the few days since I last checked in. It's tempting to post the selfie I took in the bathroom mirror at the salon, pouting as I tried to find an angle that didn't make me look washed out. Sadly, this hair color makes that next to impossible.

I don't mean to view Miles's story. Seriously, I don't. My feelings about him are more jumbled than ever now that we have to see each other consistently over the next three months, but the thought of him thriving in the city doesn't ignite rage in me the way it used to. Because, technically, I should be doing the same thing. Off to a bit of a rocky start, but we'll get there. Seeing Miles's story while mindlessly scrolling through photos of lattes and acai bowls and trips to the beach shouldn't upset me.

But seeing a picture of Jamila does.

It was posted an hour ago, probably during their lunch break, Jamila curled up on one of the picnic benches at a bistro a few blocks from set. Her knees are pulled to her chest, her head resting on top of them as she smiles serenely at the camera. The midafternoon sun makes her brown skin glimmer like gold, the dark brown curls spilling over her shoulder so thick and luscious she could've easily walked off the set of a conditioner commercial.

I wasn't on set today thanks to Rune not wanting to film any scenes with me until I got my hair done. With us being the youngest members of the cast by at least two decades, and Dawn acting like she's twice our age instead of nineteen, them hanging out together isn't unusual. But I still can't ignore the nerves coursing through me, making my heart race and my hands clammy.

There's no caption, just a tagged account hovering over the half-eaten caprese sandwich on the table beside her. I tap it, a flutter blossoming in my stomach as I realize it's Jamila's.

Her profile is unusually sparse for someone our age. She only has a dozen posts and around six hundred followers—though that'll change soon, once the cast announcement is up next week. The most recent photo on her account is of her and who I'm assuming are her parents and older sister, posed in front of a wooden cabin in matching shirts reading **I GOT CRABS IN LAKE ANDREAS.** The photo itself is adorable, even with the quirky shirts, and Jamila's smile stands out from the crowd. Wide and jubilant, eyes scrunched up and mouth thrown open like they caught her midlaugh.

Most of the photos on her account are of her with her family, mainly her older sister. Fatima, I learn. Photos of the two of them at a café in Morocco, having a picnic in the park, on Fatima's first day at NYU. Scrolling through strangers' social media accounts is a favorite pastime of mine, but something about going through Jamila's feels oddly intimate. Like I'm staring through a window directly into her home.

By the time I've scanned all twelve posts on her page I can easily picture her living room—the tapestries on the wall and vase of dried roses on the dining table—and the way the plant on the windowsill in her bedroom paints monster-shaped shadows on the wall at sunset. The way her eyes sparkle when they catch the light, the slight upward curve of her lips in every selfie—even when she's not trying to smile. It's easy to get lost in the photos of a life I wish I knew, family trips and nights with a sister who's more a best friend than anyone else will ever be. I can't help smiling at the selfie of Jamila before her junior prom. Her curls are pulled back into a loose bun, showing off the long, elegant expanse of her neck and the locket at the base of her throat. Whoever designed the red off-the-shoulder gown she's wearing deserves a Nobel Prize, the fabric clinging to her curves like it was made with her in mind. I tap the heart beneath the photo and move on to look at the—

Wait.

I tapped the heart button.

On an account I don't follow.

On a photo from seven months ago.

Holy mother freakin' shit.

My hands tremble as I race back to the photo, untap the heart as quickly as my shaking hand lets me, and then drop the phone like a hot potato. Everything should be fine. That like was up for barely ten seconds. By now the notification will have disappeared from her phone, and she'll never know.

My phone starts ringing.

I squeal, convinced Jamila somehow tracked down my number to tell me off for being a creep. And I wouldn't blame her. Seriously—who doesn't know not to like a photo when you're social media stalking? That's Social Media 101.

But it's just a FaceTime from Lily. Breathing a sigh of relief, I prop my phone up on a decorative vase and answer the call.

"Mari!" Lily and Posie exclaim in unison. It'd be creepy—how on each other's wavelengths they are—if I wasn't so used to it. "How's New York?"

"Smells kinda like pee, like everyone said," I say with a sigh, some of the pressure in my chest fading now that I don't feel like I have to be 100 percent positive and upbeat constantly. If Delia or Mom knew I was struggling even a tiny bit, their pressuring me into quitting *The Limit* would go into overdrive. Proof that I'm a better actor than they're giving me credit for: they still don't know I'm not having the most amazing time of my life.

"Gross," Posie says, wrinkling her nose. It's not until that moment that I realize they're seated together in what appears to be . . . an airplane?

"Are you guys flying somewhere?" I ask, scanning my memory for any texts that mentioned them going on a trip last-minute.

"We are," Lily replies with a coy smile, sharing a knowing glance with Posie before breaking out into enormous grins.

"We're going to Paris!" Posie exclaims, and Lily immediately follows with, "To film our new show!"

I nearly choke on my rice. "Wh-what?" I gasp out once I'm sure I'm not actually choking. The last time we talked, their options were seemingly as bleak as mine. It's hard enough to find opportunities that call for twins, let alone make yourself stand out when you have someone who looks exactly like you in the audition room.

"Remember that pilot we shot forever ago about the sisters who trade places at a Parisian boarding school and a dance academy?" I nod, easily remembering the two weeks they were off filming and we had to write their characters out of *Avalon Grove*. "They got a full series order! We're flying out to Paris now, but we're also going to shoot a couple of episodes in the Alps, and maybe Amsterdam too!"

They say it all so quickly, it takes my brain several seconds to process, my mouth hanging open in shock. "Oh my God, that's amazing!" I blurt out once I finally catch up, my body so unsure of what to do with my excitement that I wind up flailing my hands around. "Seriously, no one deserves this more than you two!"

And that really is true. My relationship with Miles aside, Lily and Posie are by far the best part of my time on *Avalon Grove*. Things weren't as easy for them as they were for me and Miles—playing the villains everyone was meant to love to hate. Except some fans didn't know how to separate the characters on-screen with who they were in real life. Throw in the bigots who showed up out of the woodwork when the writers chose to have Posie's character transition—matching Posie's own real-life experience transitioning two years ago—and they've had to deal with more hate from full-grown adults than anyone our age should have to.

They deserve the lead roles. The trips to Paris. The swoony love stories where they're as adored on-screen as they should be in real life. The moment to be in the spotlight and show everyone how special they are.

They deserve good things.

"Love you, Mari," Posie coos. "I wish we could've told you in person."

"And they had this amazing supporting role that you would've been *perfect* for!"

"Ugh, yes." Both of them pout. "Apparently, they begged your agent to let you read for it, but she said it wouldn't work with your schedule for *The Limit*."

My call earlier this week with Delia rings in my ear. *There's this HBO series that's shooting in Paris that would love to get a self-tape from you.*

The same one I'd shot down. "R-right. Yeah," I reply with a nervous laugh. "But you don't need me! I'm sure you'll have an amazing time."

A crackly voice cuts off the girls before they can respond, instructing all passengers to prepare for takeoff. "We have to go, but we'll send you pictures once we're settled!" Lily promises, passing the phone off to Posie.

"We miss you already! Love you, bye!"

I go to give them the most enthusiastic wave I can muster, but the call ends before I can even finish raising my hand. The screen goes black, and I'm left with a new sinking feeling. I'm happy for Lily and Posie, that hasn't changed, but I'm suddenly a lot less confident in my own life plan. Here I am with hair I hate, working with a director I'm not convinced likes me, to prove a point to my ex-boyfriend, when I could be jetting off to Paris to shoot a show with my best friends.

Suddenly, being petty doesn't feel like the best idea.

Before I can linger on that thought, a new notification lights up my phone again. An Instagram notification that I never would've expected.

Jamila El Amrani (@jamilaela) started following you.

Rune loves my new hair. Which is great news for my career and terrible news for my self-esteem.

"It's perfect," he says in a low whisper, cupping my cheeks and staring deeply into my eyes, like he's trying to communicate with me telepathically. I fight the urge to squirm, breathing a sigh of relief when Esther clears her throat and he finally releases me.

"Let's reset," he calls out to the crew, a signal to get everything prepped for the backlog of scenes I need to reshoot now that my hair is the "correct" color, and all of the new scenes I need to shoot to stay on schedule.

Just my luck, Rune changes up the script yet again. My brain feels as scrambled as a plate of eggs within the first hour of shooting after adjusting to the many curveballs he's thrown at me.

At least I don't seem alone in my annoyance. My fictional mom appears ruffled by Rune's constant tweaks to the script, even though I'm getting the brunt of the edits. By the time we reshoot everything, I'm so exhausted from the rage I have to exert while in character that I could nap for hours.

"You can break for lunch," Rune announces, waving us off absentmindedly before turning back to his marked-up-to-hell script.

The crew rushes to set up for the next scene, and I stretch my body until it starts popping like a sheet of Bubble Wrap.

"Whoa," a voice behind me says, so unexpected I can't help but gasp like a damsel in distress, whipping around with a hand pressed to my racing heart. Miles holds his arms out, as if he's ready to catch me if I faint. "My bad, I, um . . ." He trails off, his cheeks flushing. Impressive, considering the pounds of stage makeup we both have on right now. "I was caught off guard by the new hair. You . . . don't even look like you anymore."

"Yeah," I reply sheepishly, tugging at the end of a lock of hair, still unable to process that the platinum blond strands actually belong to me and not a well-styled wig. "It'll take some getting used to."

An awkward silence settles between us. There was a time when I used to marvel at how comfortable silence felt with Miles. How being with him felt so joyful on its own that I didn't need fun or adventure or excitement. He was enough.

How could so much change in so little time?

Miles's lips part when a PA appears at his side, shuffling him toward set so he can take his mark for the next scene.

"I'll talk to you later?" he calls out over his shoulder while being swept away.

"Totally," I respond.

Welp. There goes all the emotional energy I had left. Grabbing a bagel from crafty, I head out of the building and toward the row of trailers lined up on the block outside. I haven't had a chance to check out my trailer since they first set them up earlier this week, but I'm not expecting much. On *Avalon Grove,* six of us were crammed into one RV-sized space for all four seasons. It was basically a place to crash, gossip, and eat in between scenes. With all of us coming in and out like a revolving door throughout the day, and no shortage of drama on- and off-screen, it was more like a constant slumber party than a home away from home.

Delia assured me that I'd be sharing with only one other person this time around. Hopefully it's not Dawn, though. She hasn't spoken directly to me since our weird exchange the last time I was on set, but I can't imagine she'd be too thrilled about having me as her trailer-mate, even if we barely ever see each other.

I walk into the trailer at the end of the block, my name printed in block letters on the left-hand side of the door, expecting to find a similar setup to my last trailer experience.

Definitely not a half-dressed Jamila.

"Oh God, I'm so sorry," I blurt out, whipping around and covering my eyes after Jamila let out a quiet gasp. I barely saw anything other than the strap of a black bra on her otherwise bare shoulder. Our *Avalon Grove* trailer was so cramped that walking in on someone in their underwear—and sometimes less—was a regular occurrence. So much so that I've clearly forgotten the rules of common decency.

"It—it's fine," Jamila stammers out, evidently as flustered as I was by my interruption. "I'm, uh . . . dressed now."

Cautiously, I peek back at her to confirm that, yes, she's fully dressed. "Sorry, I'm used to sharing a trailer with a bunch of people. We gave up knocking after the first few weeks."

Jamila shrugs, tugging at a loose thread on the sleeve of her white cotton V-neck. "Guess that's something I should get used to," she replies, gesturing to the expanse of the trailer.

Following the path of her hand, I finally get to scan the rest of the double-wide trailer. It's twice the size of my last trailer. Beige leather seats line the wall behind a white dining table. Deep on the opposite end of the trailer I spot a flat-screen TV mounted to the wall, beside a pull-out couch with several throw pillows. Opposite the dining table is a kitchenette with a coffee maker, a basket of fruit and protein bars, and a mini fridge stocked with at least three cans each of every variation of Coke, Pepsi, and Sprite. And even a couple of Dr Peppers. Now, *that's* luxury.

"This is definitely an upgrade."

"Anything's an upgrade from nothing," Jamila says, pulling on the mustard-yellow crocheted cardigan I saw her wearing last week—one of her costume pieces. "All we got on those short films was a foldable chair with our name taped onto the back and a water bottle. But this is definitely setting me up for disappointment in the future." She collapses onto one of the beige leather sofas, throwing her feet up with a sigh. "I'm never getting a trailer this nice again."

Probably true, but she's too fresh-faced to have her dreams

crushed. "Until you win an Emmy next year. Then you can demand your own trailer." Also true. I can easily picture Jamila sweeping awards season like Eli Rowan did.

Jamila flushes beet red, hiding her blush by folding her arm across her face. "I wouldn't go that far."

"I can see it," I continue, taking a seat on the couch opposite her, having way too much fun seeing her blush to give up. "You winning an Emmy, not you demanding your own trailer. You don't strike me as the diva type. Yet, anyway."

I don't let myself linger on the possibility that something like that could be possible for me too—an Emmy nomination. A win, even. A chance to skyrocket my career and open doors I never thought I'd be able to walk through. If I give the performance I know I can, then maybe I'll let myself dream—for real—about those possibilities. For now, I'll keep them close to my chest. I've already been crushed enough this year. I have to save my heart wherever I can.

Jamila scoffs lightheartedly while I throw my hair up into a messy bun. No one warned me that bleaching my hair would turn it into hay overnight. I desperately need to do a hair mask.

"Well, you never know." Jamila leaps up from the sofa, helping herself to an iced tea from the mini fridge. "Next week, I might be demanding only green M&M's." She rips open one of the fun-sized packets of M&M's from the basket on the counter, holding up a palmful of green ones to prove her point.

"Fine by me," I reply, swiping a Diet Coke for myself. "So long as you also demand they only stock Coke Zero."

Seriously, how did they forget *the* superior Coke product?

Jamila smirks, offering up her hand to shake. "You got it."

Electricity courses through my fingertips when I slide my hand into hers to shake on it. Must be from the fuzzy sweater dress I'm wearing from my last scene—which is killing me in this heat. Neither of us reacts to the jolt, keeping our hands intertwined for what feels like a beat too long until, finally, she pulls away. Hiding her flushed cheeks, she gathers her script from the counter.

"You mentioned you had some tips for learning lines. From school," I say before she can head back to set. "Think you could still share those with me?"

It's not admitting defeat to accept that I might need some help if I want to do my best. Jamila has mastered some kind of sorcery that allows her to perfectly recite her lines, even when Rune changes them half a dozen times. Learning her secrets will improve my performance, keep production on schedule— despite the fact that we're already massively behind because of script changes—and save both Rune and me from a summer filled with headaches. Win-win on all accounts.

And getting to spend a little more time with Jamila doesn't hurt either. For cast morale. Obviously.

"Totally, yeah, for sure," she says in one rushed breath, reaching into the worn *New Yorker* tote bag on the counter. "Just give me your number. Or your email's fine too, or I can DM it to you, whatever's easiest. I can send them to you to-night."

She hesitates with her phone in her hand, not quite out-stretched, but definitely not keeping it close to her chest. Thankfully, she didn't call me out on my social media blunder from yesterday. It would probably be easiest for her to DM me, considering we already follow each other. Instead, I take the phone from her hand with a smirk, holding it up to her face to unlock it, and send a text to myself.

> my number is fine ☺

Feeling bold, I create a contact page for myself too. Marisol Polly-Rodriguez, pink flower emoji.

Rune may have crushed my spirit and blocked me from wearing outfits with any semblance of color to set, but he can't stop me from continuing to make pink my brand.

There's a pounding at the door as soon as I hand my phone back to her. "Jamila! We need you on set in five," one of the PAs shouts.

"Coming!" she calls back, briefly glancing down at her phone, which is open to our newly created text thread. A grin tugs at the corner of her lips, but she doesn't let it linger. Tossing her phone into her tote and grabbing her script, she heads for set. I settle onto the couch, prepared to treat myself to a power nap before my next scene, when she abruptly turns around at the entrance to the trailer.

"I like the hair, by the way," she says over her shoulder. "Blond suits you."

Before I can respond, she closes the door behind her, and I'm left with the sound of my rapidly beating heart.

CHAPTER 11

For the second time in less than a week, I come home to a stranger in my house. The apartment should've been empty. I'd have no reason to be on high alert as I trudged up the five flights of stairs, taking my sweet time as I processed everything that went down on set today.

And yet, I find myself screaming as soon as I open the door, because there's someone hunched over the dining table, sorting through several boxes. And this time there's no spare umbrella sitting around for me to defend myself with. Bruiser breaks into a round of barks when the intruder lets out a yelp of their own, the room a cacophony of noise.

"Jesus, give a guy a warning," the intruder says once his own screams have subsided, holding a hand against his chest.

He doesn't look any older than me, might even be younger. He has a thin frame and only a few inches of height on me. Small enough that I should be able to take him down if I have to, especially if I throw in some biting. My teeth are viciously sharp.

Plus, I'm still buzzing from exchanging numbers with Jamila, and from the jitters I always get after wrapping for the day. Worries that I didn't give enough variety in my takes, or that I didn't push myself as hard as I could've. Worries I've never had about a performance before. First there was Miles. Now *The Limit* has found a way to make me, someone who's always felt confident and assured in their talent, doubt myself at every turn. What I'm saying is, I could take out a lot of emotions on this rando.

"Who are you?!" I shout, pressing my keys between my knuckles and holding them up as a weapon, and a warning.

"Whoa, whoa." He immediately holds his hands up in surrender, backing away from the boxes until he's flat against the opposite wall. "Your dad told me to come over because you needed your nails done."

My brain—already fried from a day of learning Rune's endless line adjustments—struggles to put the pieces together. Fragments of my last conversation with Dad come back to mind—his promise that my cousin could come over and help me out with my dire nail situation.

"You're Kevin?" I ask, slowly lowering my key-weapon, but not letting my guard down yet.

The longer I stare at him, the more I can kind of see the family resemblance. His skin and hair are several shades darker than both mine and Dad's, closer to Jerome's complexion, but he has the same natural wave to his hair that I've had since birth. The same light brown eyes with subtle flecks of gold.

Even the same slight gap between his front teeth that I hated so much I begged Mom for braces for my eighth birthday.

"The one and only," he says with a flourish, resting a hand on his hip now that he's no longer on his guard. "And *you* must be the famous cousin."

I swallow hard. It's not untrue, but I'm not sure that's the name I want to make for myself with the family I'm just getting to know. "I'm not really—"

"Don't try to be humble," Kevin interrupts with a wave of his hand. "Anyone who has over a million followers is definitely famous."

I consider explaining that several people I know have bought a couple hundred thousand followers to make themselves seem more popular than they actually are, but that's gossip for another day. Instead, his nose wrinkles when he catches sight of my hand resting limply at my side, and he crosses the room to take it into his own. My cheeks flush as he examines my chewed-up nails, practically bitten down to the nubs. The hair and makeup departments were able to cover them up with some basic nude press-ons for shooting, but having my bare, unpolished nails bared to the world feels like walking around in my underwear.

"Your dad's right. You *do* need my help," Kevin says before pulling me toward the dining table.

Bruiser follows diligently at my heel, keeping a watchful eye on us as we settle down at Kevin's makeshift workstation. He definitely came prepared, his supplies laid out across the kitchen table, transforming it into a full-scale salon. As soon as we're both sitting down, Kevin gets straight to work on pushing back my wrecked cuticles.

"So, I know you probably signed a million NDAs and whatever, but I'm guessing you're here to film something fancy," he says without taking his eyes off his work.

I nod. "It's the second season of this show called *The Limit*."

While I still have to keep the details under wraps, there's no harm in telling him what I'm here to film. With the cast announcement going up this week, it's only a matter of days before the rest of the world knows why I'm here anyway.

Kevin's brows shoot up and he stalls between my ring finger and pinkie to glance up at me with his lips parted in a comically huge O. "Wait, isn't that the same show your ex is supposedly on?"

The heat in my cheeks spreads all the way down to my toes. Strangers knowing the intimate details of my life isn't unusual, but there's something different about it coming from a family member. I barely know anything about Kevin, yet he already knows I had a disastrous breakup with my ex, *and* that I'm on the same show as said ex. Like my life is the TV show everyone's tuning into every week to see.

"Y-yeah," I choke out, trying to hide how flustered the question made me by ducking my chin against my chest, hopefully hiding my reddened cheeks.

"Sorry, didn't mean to be nosy," Kevin says quickly. "It was so wild to see the breakup on the news and be like, 'Hey, that's my cousin!' Sort of. I mean, not that you're not my cousin, but—"

"But we've never met before. I get it," I finish for him, giving him a soft smile.

Kevin meets my smile with one of his own before turning back to his work, focusing on buffing and shaping my nails to prepare them for the clear polish he set aside. "So, what's it like? Filming on a set?"

I shrug, making sure not to move my hands too much. "Kind of like any other job, I guess. It can be really fun, too. Like you're having a really long sleepover with your friends. Most of the time."

He peeks up at me with a raised brow. "Most of the time?"

"This show's not as . . . fun. But it makes sense as a next step in my career. It's more intense than the other stuff I've done." I choose my words carefully. The last thing I want is to come off as ungrateful for the opportunities I've been lucky enough to have.

"Does that have to do with the fact that your ex is there?"

"No," I answer quickly, shaking my head to hammer home the sentiment. "I mean, not really. I didn't join the show to try to get back together with him or anything. It's just . . . weird. Seeing him there. Remembering everything he said when we broke up." I trail off for a moment, shaking off the memories of that night. "Makes it hard to believe in myself sometimes, I guess."

Kevin sets down the nail file to give me a wide grin, the gap between his front teeth on full, proud display. "Well, you *are* a Rodriguez. You've got star power in your blood."

"Thanks," I reply, a new kind of warmth swelling inside of me. The good kind, this time. The same warmth I felt having dinner with Abuela last week, finally filling in the empty branches on my family tree. Not feeling like a stranger to my own life anymore. When I got here, I didn't feel like much of a Rodriguez. But it's hard not to now—with people like Abuela and Kevin welcoming me with such open arms.

It's even harder not to wonder how much I've been missing out on.

I examine my nails while Kevin starts opening the polish. "You're really good at this." Not that I didn't think he would be, but I'm still pleasantly surprised by how perfectly my nails have been restored, even before the polish. I'm too uncoordinated to paint my own nails, and the few times I've asked Mom to do it she's never been able to stay within the lines, like a toddler learning how to color.

"Remember that the next time you need someone to help you get ready for the red carpet," Kevin says with a wink.

We remain silent while Kevin concentrates on applying even, smooth layers of polish. Between hands, I catch him glancing over at the boxes crowding the tables—the same ones he was rummaging through when I got here.

"You planning on stealing Jerome's new wigs?" I ask playfully. Jerome bulk-ordered a bunch of different options for an amateur drag competition he's hosting in two weeks. The forty-inch human-hair unit was the obvious choice. As beautiful as he is in and out of drag, even Jerome can't pull off a ten-dollar synthetic wig from Amazon.

"I wish," Kevin replies with a roll of his eyes. "I've been asking him for years to start teaching me about fashion and stuff so I can start developing my drag, but he always brushes me off because I'm still 'too young,'" he says in an eerily accurate impression of Jerome.

"Well, I could help you, if you want. With fashion stuff," I offer tentatively. I might not know as much about drag as Jerome does, but I definitely know how to put together a show-stopping outfit for any body type, at any budget.

Kevin stills midway through painting a second layer onto my index finger. "Really?"

"Totally!" I reply so enthusiastically I practically bounce out of my seat. Nothing makes my week better than a shopping spree, and a potential makeover is Marisol heaven. Other than shopping for more beige and neutral basics to wear to rehearsal since Rune banished anything colorful, I haven't gone on a proper shopping trip since I've gotten to the city. Which is pretty much a crime.

If anything, Kevin would be doing *me* a favor.

But Kevin's eyes shift away from me, his shoulders slumping as he gets back to finishing my nails. "It's all right. I was thinking I could try signing up for that competition Jerome is hosting, but that's not enough time to put something together. I can try again next year."

He sounds an awful lot like me on my first day of shooting—convincing myself I'm going to fail before I've even begun. I gently tug my hand out of his grip, keeping it hidden under the table until he meets my eyes.

"I do my best work on tight deadlines."

He seems hesitant, biting his lip and tapping his foot for a moment before finally replying. "You're sure?"

I pretend to hum in thought before setting my hand back down on his makeshift workstation. "Only if you promise to be my resident manicurist whenever I have red carpets or shoots."

He snorts, shaking his head slightly before slapping his hand into mine for a firm but careful-not-to-smudge-my-drying-polish shake. "It's a deal."

HOLLYWOOD TODAY

FULL CAST ANNOUNCED FOR SEASON TWO OF THE EMMY AWARD–WINNING SERIES *THE LIMIT*
BY VIVI LOAIZA

The cast announcement for the highly anticipated second season of *The Limit*, the anthology series that swept awards season last year, was exclusively shared with *Hollywood Today* this afternoon. Former *Avalon Grove* star Miles Zhao is set to lead the second season as Will, a teen boy struggling with addiction and his worsening mental health after falling asleep at the wheel, leading to a car accident that kills both his father and younger brother. Newcomer Jamila El Amrani joins the cast as Will's longtime best friend and potential love interest, alongside fellow *Avalon Grove* star Marisol Polly-Rodriguez and *Coldhearted* star Dawn Greene in supporting roles, rounding out the teenage cast.

COMMENTS

OMG MILES AND MARISOL IN ANOTHER SHOW TOGETHER?????

the dramaaaaaaaaaaaa

didn't we hear rumors about him being cast like a month ago? what if she went after the same show as him after he dumped her?? I could see her being that petty lol

yay Marisol!!!!!!!!!

Idk who Jamila is but someone needs to drop her haircare routine ASAP

Dawn's not playing the lead??? guaranteed flop

CHAPTER 12

"These words are losing meaning," I say with a groan, letting my head flop back onto the *Live, Laugh, Love* throw pillow behind me. We've quickly learned that the original owner of this trailer was a big fan of the T.J. Maxx clearance section. The **BLESS THIS MESS** plaque over the bathroom door haunts me every time I sit on the couch.

"That means it's working," Jamila says with a wink, flipping back to the first page of my script. "From the top."

While Jamila's suggestion that I ground myself in every scene by focusing on one of the senses has made a world of difference in memorizing my lines, my stomach is too empty for me to ground myself in taste again. Not unless I want to start chewing on one of the **BUT FIRST, WINE** pillows.

"Can we take a break?" I ask, hoisting myself up onto my elbows. It's one of the few days we get to shoot off-location, mainly some exterior shots in Williamsburg, along with a few interiors at a townhouse that production rented for the day. While normally I love camping out in our trailer, I wouldn't mind exploring the area a bit during our breaks between scenes. "If we keep going, my brain is going to leak out of my ears. And I really want to try that taco truck down the block."

Jamila taps her chin in thought before flipping my script closed. "For the sake of these cushions, fine."

"We do *not* need to save these cushions," I mutter to myself, but still loud enough to earn a laugh from her.

"Someone's not keeping calm and slaying the day," she responds, pointing to the framed quote on the wall beside the kitchenette with an expression so serious it makes me snort.

"Sorry, I was too busy"—I reach for the pillow behind my head—"'Carpe diem–ing this bitch.'"

This time, we both burst into giggles, finally addressing the tacky elephant in the room. It's impressive, really. How the hell did one person manage to find decor for every single cringe phrase from the last millennium?

While I can't lie and say I don't miss the chaos of sharing a trailer with a gaggle of my former castmates, having Jamila as a trailer-mate has made this latest experience significantly more bearable. There's only so much I can do to adjust to the quick changes Rune is always throwing at us, but the techniques Jamila texted me, along with the line-reading app she recommended I download, have made an enormous difference. So much so that I'm actually starting to think Rune doesn't completely hate me. Jury's still out, but I'm definitely not the cast troublemaker anymore.

At least for now.

I pull myself off the couch when someone starts pounding

on the door. They must need me back on set sooner than we thought—so much for trying that taco truck. "Coming," I call out while grabbing one of the various horrific headbands my character wears. Between this and the platinum blond hair, I look like one of those porcelain dolls whose eyes watch you wherever you go.

I throw open the door and walk directly into the very solid and sculpted chest of the PA sent to retrieve me. Since when is one of the PAs jacked?

Except it's not a PA. I've walked directly into my ex-boyfriend's very solid and sculpted chest, because of course I have.

"Hey." He's sturdy, like a brick wall. Even with the full force of my body I hardly moved him. "Jamila here?"

It takes longer than I care to admit for me to be able to put the dots together. Miles. Outside. Jamila. Inside. Memorizing those lines really *did* turn my brain into soup. Thankfully, Jamila comes to my rescue.

"Thanks again," she says, accepting the *New Yorker* tote bag she always carries around from his outstretched hand. She must've left it on set after their scene together this morning.

Miles nods in reply, our eyes catching for one too-long, too-charged second before he murmurs goodbye and finally closes the door behind him.

That's one thing that hasn't changed in the past two weeks. Me and Miles. Or, rather, the lack of me and Miles.

Again, my goal was never to rekindle the spark between us. If anything, I wanted to prove that I didn't need him as much as he didn't need me. And I'm definitely doing that. The nights are lonelier without someone to text random videos to or ask if they'd love me if I was a worm. Especially with Lily and Posie on a round-the-clock shooting schedule in an entirely different time zone. But life without Miles doesn't feel as lonely as it once did. Especially now that my days are filled with running lines with Jamila or making plans to go shopping with Kevin. Life feels fresh, and exciting, and hopeful.

Suddenly, Jamila clears her throat. I snap back to reality, pushing the trailer door open again and heading out like we originally planned. Jamila follows closely behind me as we head for the taco truck around the block, the silence making my skin prickle.

"Is there, uh . . ." She clears her throat again, avoiding meeting my gaze. "Something going on between you two?"

"Me and Miles?" I ask, even though, hello, it should be obvious. Jamila nods, something unusual building between the two of us. Tension, or maybe fear. And I'm not sure which is worse.

"We were costars, back on *Avalon Grove*," I say, unsure where to begin with our story. Since her sister is a fan of the show, it's likely Jamila already knows about that part of my and Miles's past. I'm not sure how much she knows, though, so might as well start at the beginning.

"We dated for a while. But . . ." I pause, weighing how much I'm willing to tell her. Whether it's worth pulling open a half-healed wound.

"You're not together anymore," Jamila says, finishing that thought for me, and I'm not sure if it's a question or a statement.

I nod stiffly. "It was splashed across every gossip site you can think of," I say with a roll of my eyes, not bothering to hide the bitterness in my tone.

Jamila wrinkles her nose. "I don't pay attention to those," she says quickly, as if to reassure me. And it does, strangely enough. Knowing that there's someone who hasn't seen me at my lowest moment. Who doesn't think of me as the teeny-bopper actress who got dumped and took her frustration out on paparazzi.

Someone who can know me for me.

"I'm sorry, though," she adds quietly, shifting as though she's going to reach out for me, but deciding against it. "Break-ups suck."

I do my best to shrug nonchalantly, but there's not a nonchalant bone in my body. *It was for the best* sits on the tip of my tongue, but I hold it back. Was our breakup really for the best? It got me here—to this show, to sharing a trailer with Jamila, to this moment. That's enough, right?

"It's fine," I finally settle on. "I've moved on. I'm sure he's moving on too."

"Nothing's going on between us," Jamila adds abruptly, waving her arms as if to clear the air of the idea that he's moving on with *her.*

My heart stutters, and I resist the urge to exhale sharply. The thought of Miles and Jamila falling for each other has definitely crossed my mind at least once. . . . Fine. Multiple times. But you can't blame me when their chemistry on set is so palpable, half the crew has to fan themselves off whenever we call cut. They're usually huddled close between scenes, heads pressed together as they watch videos and scroll through social media together. Occasionally, Miles drops a photo of her on his story, and I try to convince myself it doesn't hurt every time he does.

Clearly, I've been doing a terrible job.

"O-oh," I stammer out, not sure if I'm mortified or relieved by her assurance. "It—it'd be fine if you were, though," I add quickly. The last thing I want to be is the resident bitter ex. If Miles and Jamila are meant to be, they're meant to be. And their stunning babies will grace the cover of *Vogue* before they turn one.

Jamila snorts—which is definitely not the response I expected. "That won't be happening anytime soon." She ducks her head bashfully when I quirk a brow. "I'm a lesbian."

Oh.

Well, that was unexpected.

Not in a bad way, though. Not in a bad way at all.

"That's cool," I respond like the most uncool person on the planet. Jesus, I sound like a secretly homophobic mom who's hoping her kid is going through a "phase." "I . . . get it," I tack on, as if that vague mess of a reply will make any difference. If anything, it's giving "Don't worry, I'm an ally!" vibes instead of "Pretty women make me sweat," like I was going for.

This time, it's Jamila's turn to raise an eyebrow at me. She seems taken aback, hopefully with surprise at my potential queerness as opposed to potential homophobia. "Are you sapphic?"

"No, I'm Puerto Rican," I reply because my brain is incapable of forming a coherent reply before blurting out the first thought that comes to mind.

What is it about this girl that makes my brain short-circuit every time we have a conversation that lasts more than five minutes?

"I mean, yes," I choke out. "I'm bi, so, yes. I definitely like girls."

Jamila does me the grace of stifling her laugh, biting down on her lip, and I can't help but marvel at how her teeth sparkle like freshly polished diamonds. Before meeting her, I didn't even think it was possible to have teeth that white. And that's coming from someone who regularly works with people who have veneers.

"Cool," Jamila responds, but it sounds *actually* cool coming from her.

I'm saved from embarrassing myself yet again as we finally reach the row of trucks down the block from where we're shooting. Jamila insists that she doesn't want anything, but I order an extra vegetarian taco for her anyway. She grins as I hand her the red-and-white-checkered plastic basket.

"Making good progress on your bucket list," she says as we clink our tacos together in a toast.

My mouth is too full for me to respond, the intense flavors of roasted veggies and cilantro and the perfect avocado crema overwhelming me. I let out a quiet moan that I can't even be embarrassed about because the food is that damn good. Other A-listers might insist that high-quality food can never come from a truck, but this single bite would prove all of them wrong.

"At this rate I'm going to stay in the city just for the food," I muse before helping myself to another hearty bite.

Jamila beams, chewing her own taco far more delicately

than I'm chewing mine. She opens her mouth to respond but cuts herself off to pull her phone out of her pocket, her nose wrinkling at whatever the notification is.

"This is normal, right?" she asks, holding up her phone toward me to reveal a flurry of notifications coming in, making her phone buzz like it's an EDM beat. They're from the same account, going through and liking her posts and leaving multiple all-caps or all-emoji comments calling Jamila everything from "queen" to "mother."

"I have no idea who this person is," she explains as the notifications come to a brief halt, only to start back up again.

"Very normal," I reassure her. "You'll want to switch off your notifications." If I kept mine on, I'd never be able to get anything done. Especially after the cast announcement earlier this week. Even with my notifications off, I haven't been able to scroll my socials without getting smacked with hundreds of comments either congratulating me on my new role, or asking if this is some ploy to win Miles back.

Jamila shudders and sets her phone to Do Not Disturb. A wise choice. "This is so weird."

"Welcome to being a professional actor." I shrug, and we start heading back toward set.

"I didn't think it came with . . . extra stuff. Plus, now my agent's been pressuring me to go to this premiere on Friday to try to network." She pretends to gag, earning a soft giggle from me.

I haven't gotten as many premiere invites since I got to the city, but Delia did just forward me one earlier this week. "Is it for that indie movie about the guy who accidentally marries a martian?"

"Yeah?"

"I got invited to that one too!" I quickly open up my phone and scroll through my emails until I find the one Delia forwarded me. Her message reads *assume you won't want to go but passing along jic.* They must've invited the whole cast after the announcement went up. "Premieres are easy," I assure Jamila with a wave of my hand. "You do the red carpet for a few minutes, mingle, then if you're lucky the director doesn't give a huge speech at the end and you can head straight home afterward. Sometimes there's an after-party, but those are always weird. Definitely pass."

It's like going to a house party thrown by someone you barely know. The cast is their own clique, and everyone else is left in small-talk limbo. It's probably not as unbearable when you can actually drink to pass the time, but for a teenager, it's basically hell.

Jamila audibly gulps. "That . . . sounds like a lot."

"We could go together, if that'll help?" I offer tentatively, doing my best to keep my voice light and casual. The movie really doesn't sound like my kind of thing, but hey, if it helps Jamila adjust to her newfound celebrity, it'll be worth it. For cast bonding. And because I do admittedly love a good red-carpet moment. I desperately need to air out some of the dressier pieces I brought that are currently collecting dust in a bin shoved into the hall closet. As in the closet that *isn't* my bedroom.

"That'd be amazing," Jamila says with a beaming smile that falters just as quickly as it appeared. "I mean, don't change your plans or anything." She trails off, now peering down at her fingers.

Instead of replying, I open my phone again and shoot a message to Delia.

> Would love to go to that premiere you sent me last week

> RSVP yes for me, pls & thank you!

"Done," I say as the text is sent off. "Besides, I owe you for all the line tips. Let's call it a trade—you help me study my lines, and I train you in the art of celebrity."

Jamila's smile returns, and I let myself give in to its magnetic pull. In a few minutes, we'll be back on set preparing to shoot for another several hours, but for now I lean in a little closer to her, cheeks warm and aching from how often I laugh whenever we're together. Premieres are another part of being an actress that loses its meaning over time. That feels more mundane than exciting after you've done a dozen in a month. But strangely enough, I'm feeling really excited about this one.

CHAPTER 13

It takes me twenty minutes to find Jamila's apartment. When she'd texted me the address—after thanking me profusely for agreeing to meet up at her place instead of at the premiere—it hadn't seemed complicated. That was until I got to the massive building towering over the entirety of the block. My Lyft dropped me off directly in front of it, and I still don't know how to get inside.

The unit takes up the majority of this stretch of West 178th, composed of three buildings attached by a series of narrow hallways, complete with a whopping total of five separate entrances. Thankfully, Jamila guided me in the direction of the correct one. Once I got inside, though, I didn't anticipate a winding series of staircases leading to one section of the building but not the other, each floor broken up into three, or sometimes even four separate segments, each with their own staircase.

It's a logistical nightmare, and I have no idea how anyone

can order takeout without leaving the delivery person panicking like they're navigating a maze.

There are sounds of general chaos when I finally make it to the correct apartment door and ring the bell. Frantic footsteps and murmured shouts, along with what may or may not be a scream before, finally, Jamila whips the door open. She sags against the doorframe, struggling to catch her breath like she ran a mile to answer the door.

"Hey," she wheezes out. "Find the place okay?"

"Took me a second," I reply while doing my best to wipe the sweat off my forehead without making it too obvious. It's definitely an understatement, but she doesn't need to know I can barely handle navigating a New York apartment building. Fortunately, this is a low-key premiere, so I'm not running up several flights of stairs in a ball gown. And I decided to keep my makeup on the simpler side tonight—it took thirty minutes nonetheless, but it's not nearly as intense as my usual multi-hour pre-premiere routine. "But I'm here."

"You're here," Jamila replies, her eyes widening slightly as she takes in my ensemble for the night. A satin lilac slip dress paired with white heels.

"You look amazing," Jamila says with a smile that makes my cheeks go as pink as my lip gloss. "I definitely don't have anything like that in my closet."

Her frown says what she doesn't as she steps out from where she's hidden in the doorway, revealing her plain black lace top and boot-cut jeans. The outfit isn't bad for a low-key premiere like this one. With toned arms and curved hips like hers, she can pull off anything—even a shirt and jeans. A loose gold necklace with a teardrop emerald—her birthstone, I'm assuming—ties the outfit together and brings out the depth of her brown eyes. It won't be the most exciting thing on the red carpet, but there's no way it'll be the worst either.

"I like it," I reply, and it's not even my usual lying-through-my-teeth-about-a-fashion-choice response.

It's understated yet classy, pulled together in a way that feels very uniquely her. But I can understand why she might not be too eager about wearing something so understated to her first-ever movie premiere. She's lucky she's getting to dip her toes into the world of celebrity life with something lower stakes—a simple red carpet, maybe a couple of questions about *The Limit*, and nothing else. Hopefully. My first premiere was for a Marvel movie, and I spent most of the night trying not to freak out about being a few feet away from massive A-list stars and struggling not to trip in my three-inch heels.

"I can look through your closet, if you want? To try to spice things up. Your outfit, I mean," I propose, doing my best to keep my voice light, not wanting to pressure her into thinking I don't like what she's already wearing.

Jamila lights up, the worry melting from her face as she eagerly throws the door open and invites me into the apartment, beckoning for me to follow her to her bedroom.

The El Amrani apartment is full of homey touches. The long hallway off the entrance is adorned with photos of the family through the years—some as recent as last year and some stretching so far back they're stiffly posed black-and-white portraits. Oil paintings of old stone buildings and markets in Marrakech, faded postcards from friends and family in Italy, New Zealand, and Japan, and hand-painted tiles and vases hanging between the photos. So many different colors and patterns and textures that seem like they should clash, but they complement each other beautifully.

We pass through the living room, and I resist the urge to stop and breathe in the scent from the honey-and-spice candle burning on the coffee table. Like most New York apartments, the room is small, but they've made the most of the space. Handwoven throw blankets are strewn across the gray sectional surrounding a flat-screen TV that's currently displaying a painting of a woman in a garden. It's the type of room I saw myself curling up in after long days on set when I first agreed to stay with Dad over the summer—cute, cozy, and extremely New York.

Like the living room, Jamila has done a lot with the little space she has in her bedroom. "I share with my sister," she explains as we step into the room.

Immediately, it's clear which side is hers. The twin bed on the left side of the room is adorned with hot pink pillows and a dozen different types of stuffed animals, while the simple white comforter on the opposite bed is pristinely made with a single pillow. Not that her older sister Fatima's side isn't adorable—definitely more my speed—but I can't imagine Jamila sleeping in a peach patterned bedspread surrounded by Squishmallows every night. There's no candle burning in this room, but there's an aroma that still stops me in my tracks. The sharp sting of clove and sweet touch of cinnamon. Oranges and dark chocolate. An intoxicating scent that is undeniably Jamila.

"If you don't find anything, I can probably borrow something from Fatima," Jamila says as she steps over to the closet, snapping me back to reality.

The single closet is neatly split in two, the clear difference in Jamila's and Fatima's wardrobes marked by the various colors and patterns transitioning to blacks and grays. Shoes are stacked on a rack beneath the hangers, rows of Doc Martens and rag & bone Chelsea boots along with ballet flats and vibrant neon-colored pumps.

Making two almost-adult women share a closet should be a crime against humanity.

I take my time combing through my options, starting with Jamila's side of the closet. True to her word, there's not much that screams "red carpet debut" in her wardrobe. Mostly it's turtlenecks and sweaters—which I would never let her go outside in. Not on a fashion basis, but for the sake of keeping her from dying of heatstroke. I stifle a gasp when I stumble upon the perfect option, running a hand along it to make sure I didn't imagine it before pulling it out of the closet.

"How about this?" I hold up the sequined dress to Jamila's frame. It's in her signature color—black, of course—with a V neckline that isn't too scandalous but still gives her the chance to flaunt her gorgeous arms and collarbone.

Jamila's cheeks flare as she takes the hanger from me and examines the dress. "I don't even remember buying this." Her brows scrunch as she scans the label attached to the size tag. "Fatima must've gotten it for me at some point, and I never got around to wearing it."

"What better time to break it out than tonight?" I ask, both because I think the dress will look great on her, and I shamelessly want to see her in it.

Jamila nods, sheepishly excusing herself to the bathroom. I carefully perch on the edge of her bed, feeling guilty about disturbing the creaseless sheets. It's a struggle to resist the urge to scan every inch of the room to learn more about Jamila. Still, there's plenty to see from the bed. Posters of Los Angeles and Seattle. Signed *Playbill*s from more Broadway shows than I can name off the top of my head. The bookshelf beside her bed is stacked with well-loved copies of Jane Austen's entire bibliography, a worn copy of *Pride and Prejudice* sitting on the nightstand. Between the rows of books—ranging from romance to poetry to memoirs—are gold plastic trophies. Everything from Best Monologue to Actress of the Year from various competitions, both within her school and from citywide competitions.

As if she could be any more impressive.

"Oh my God," a voice says over my shoulder.

I whip around, prepared to apologize even though I've got permission to be here. The girl lingering in the doorway is unfamiliar, but not for long. Her dark-brown curls are tied up in a messy bun, held together with a strawberry hair clip that perfectly matches her light pink jumpsuit. Her lips curl into a smile that mirrors the one that makes being on set feel so much less terrifying.

Fatima.

"You're actually here," Fatima says before I can introduce myself. She dashes up to me, extending a hand as if for me to shake, only to use it to gesture wildly as she continues. "*Avalon Grove* was basically my life for three years, and I was obsessed with you and everything about your character, and—" She cuts off abruptly, her smile deflating. "Sorry. This is probably super creepy."

"It's okay," I reply, resting a hand on her arm when the

deflation seems to spread to the rest of her body. She perks up at the touch, eyeing my hand eagerly. "I'm the one who's sitting in your bedroom," I continue, releasing my hold on her arm once she's steady so I can gesture to the room. "Which is supercute."

"Why, thank you." She beams, bashfully tucking a loose curl behind her ear. "Don't listen to whatever my sister tells you—I'm the one with taste in this family."

I snort, leaning in to whisper, "I believe it."

No disrespect to Jamila—the minimalist aesthetic is totally valid. I'm just more aligned with Fatima's vision: Life is always better with a pop of color.

"I'm really sorry, by the way," Fatima continues, sitting down beside me, her voice low even though there's no reason for us to be whispering. "About all that stuff with Miles. Those articles were awful. And I'm sorry, but he was a total dick about it."

At first, I braced myself. For her to take Miles's side, for her to hint that my reaction was overdramatic. For her to say that Milesol breaking up ruined her idea of love. Not for her to say what I thought had been the truth the entire time—that Miles screwed me over. That his statement made me seem like I was some passing fling instead of a serious four-year relationship. That the media was unnecessarily cruel to me. Mom, Lily and Posie, even Jerome told me Miles was an ass for what he did, but only out of obligation. This is the first time someone who read the story told by the media has been on my side. In person, at least. My followers have, for the most part, been loyal following the breakup, but it's harder to feel the sentiment behind a comment than it is to hear it in real life.

"Oh . . . thanks. It's, uh . . . we're fine now," I say quickly. Even after everything that's happened between me and Miles, I feel the need to defend him. Our breakup felt shitty, but he's not a bad person. At the end of the day, we're two teenagers who outgrew one another.

"If you ever want to talk about it, I've been interning at *Hollywood Today*," Fatima says eagerly, her hands moving a mile a minute as she talks. "Mainly writing fluff pieces on who got divorced this week and what diet supplement influencers are shilling, but I'm allowed to pitch my own pieces, too. I'm even doing a profile on Jamila about being cast on *The Limit*. You could—"

"Fatima!" Jamila's voice cuts the conversation short as she comes barreling into the room, wielding a rolled-up *New Yorker* as a weapon. "I told you to leave her alone!"

"We were just talking!" Fatima shouts back when Jamila attempts to whack her with the magazine.

Jamila relents once Fatima stands up and retreats to her own side of the room. She crosses her arms, keeping the magazine tucked beneath one arm in case she needs to use it again. "So you didn't ask to interview her for work?"

Fatima shrugs. "I was giving her an opportunity to tell her side of the story."

"Get. Out." Jamila points the magazine at Fatima, pushing it harder into her chest with each word.

"Ah, what're you two fighting about now?" a new voice calls out.

A woman appears in the hall, bracing herself on the doorway with one hand and gripping a cane with the other. Flecks of gray are streaked through the dark brown curls held together in a loose braid down the length of her back. Her face has a map of laugh lines and the first signs of emerging wrinkles, but there's an incandescent glow beneath her brown skin.

Like her daughter, she lights up the room.

"Fatima is bothering Marisol," Jamila immediately tattles, pointing at her sister like they're toddlers bickering over a broken toy.

"Fatima," their mother warns, her voice even and measured but stern. The exact type of tone that can strike fear into any child—including me. Frightening enough to make Fatima stomp out of the room with a huff. Fatima's mom pats her on the head as she leaves, biting back a laugh when Fatima grumbles something back in reply.

Their mom steps carefully into the room, leaning heavily on her cane for balance. Jamila quickly rushes to her side, wrapping an arm around her waist to steady her. "My apologies, Marisol. It's a pleasure to meet you. Jammy has told us so much about you." She pinches Jamila's cheek, much to her daughter's annoyance. Jamila scowls, muttering "Mom!" through gritted teeth while trying to both wriggle away from her mom and maintain her grip on her.

"Thank you, Mrs. El Amrani," I say once I've suppressed my giggle, taking the attention off Jamila. "You have a beautiful home."

Mrs. El Amrani grins proudly. "I'm so glad you were able to visit. You'll have to come back again when my husband is home to make you dinner. His chebakia is award-winning."

"It was a local dessert competition thing," Jamila amends sheepishly.

"That's still award-winning!" her mom snaps back, playfully

whacking Jamila on the arm. "Don't diminish your papa's accomplishments!"

"I'm not, I'm not!" she says with a laugh when her mom plays dirty and nudges her in the ribs, a spot that must be ticklish based on the way she squirms. Good to know. "Dad's an amazing cook. And *yes*, his chebakia is . . ." She pauses to fold her fingers together and give a chef's kiss. "Usually we only make it for special occasions or around Ramadan. It's basically fried dough coated in this syrupy honey and sprinkled with sesame seeds."

Fried dough covered in anything sounds delicious to me, but the way Jamila and her mom close their eyes and lean in to each other at the thought of this dish makes my mouth water so intensely I'm worried I'll drool on my dress.

Mrs. El Amrani heads back toward the door, Jamila following along at a careful distance, keeping a careful hand braced on her mom's elbow. "Make sure you take lots of pictures," she calls out to me. "This one never remembers to take any. I want to see her first red carpet appearance."

"I will, don't worry," I promise before she leaves with a soft laugh. Whether Jamila likes it or not, I'll definitely be documenting this entire experience thoroughly. Who doesn't want to remember their first premiere?

"So," I begin once we're alone, not bothering to hide my smirk. "What have you said about me, *Jammy*?"

"Ugh," Jamila groans before face-planting onto the bed. "This is why I asked them to leave the house *before* you got here, but no one ever listens to me," she complains, her voice muffled by her bedspread.

"Your family seems nice."

Her family has that soft, familiar sort of love that I thought was only possible in sitcoms. Easy banter and teasing, family recipes and souvenirs from trips around the world. The type of family I always wanted.

"They *are* nice when they're not being embarrassing." She picks herself back up and sits beside me. "Sorry Fatima tried to pounce on you. I know fans coming up to you must be super annoying."

I shrug. Definitely not the first time someone's approached me for an inside scoop, but at least this wasn't about trying to get the dirty details behind our breakup. "It's nice to hear someone's on my side."

Jamila's brow furrows. "Why wouldn't they be on your side?"

I bite my tongue, wishing I hadn't said anything. I've spent this entire time avoiding the details of what happened between me and Miles, hoping Jamila stayed true to her hatred for tabloids and never went searching for any of the articles about us. The world knowing Miles dumped me because he thought I wasn't a "serious" choice hurt enough, but something about Jamila knowing that too hurts even worse. That the one stranger who didn't know about my past—who met me as *me*—will know what the world thinks of me.

"Lots of people said Miles was . . . out of my league. Acting-wise," I say delicately. "And that I was this . . . I dunno . . . airhead teen actress." I do my best to keep my voice level, but it's hard not to let the hurt seep in.

Jamila frowns, shaking her head and scoffing. "Well, then a lot of people have no taste."

As I meet her eyes, I am reminded that there are more important things than what strangers think of me. "You don't have to say that because I'm helping you pick out what to wear."

My voice is light and teasing, but Jamila's expression is serious when she replies. "I never just say anything."

She's close enough for me to feel her breath against my lips. To smell the coconut oil lathered into her curls. Suddenly, I'm hyperaware of the heat of the room and the cracked open door, and the fact that we're sitting on her bed in her bedroom, which smells so overpoweringly like her that it feels like I'm lost in a daydream.

"That dress looks really great on you," I say finally and lean back. If I don't put distance between us ASAP, I might do something I regret. Something that'll make my life that much messier.

Taking in her outfit doesn't do anything to steady me, though. At some point, Jamila must've grabbed a pair of heels from the closet, simple black pumps that make her bronze legs stretch on for days. As expected, the sequined dress's neckline perfectly accentuates her toned arms and the base of her neck without being too much.

In short: she's drop-dead gorgeous.

"It's not too much?" she asks sheepishly, running a hand along her bare arms. She opted for gold bangles on her wrists, the bracelets clanging whenever she moves her arms.

"Not if you feel comfortable in it. And it's your first premiere. You should go all-out."

Jamila nods, standing up and examining her reflection in the full-length mirror on Fatima's side of the room. "I don't really have the makeup skills to go with this kind of outfit, though."

"Say less." I immediately jump into action, rushing over

to the vanity in the center of the room and flicking on the lights over the mirror, gesturing to the pink fuzzy stool before it. "Take a seat."

The natural color of Jamila's cheeks is on full display as she settles down in front of the mirror, pointing out which makeup belongs to her and which belongs to Fatima. And, more importantly, which of Fatima's makeup she's allowed to use and which products are off-limits. Not surprisingly, Fatima has the more robust collection, but I've made makeup miracles happen with a single eyeliner pencil and a dream.

We start off with a basic smoky eye, using some of the shimmery eye shadow palettes on Fatima's "okay to borrow" list. It doesn't take much to make Jamila's eyes pop, but the gold glitter shade brings out the warmth in her eyes without feeling too overpowering. Her brows are already sculpted by the gods, so not much to do there. I follow her lead when it comes to eyeliner, letting her use the felt-tip pen to draw her usual cat's-eye, taking over at the end to elongate the wing. Go bold or go home.

"What're you thinking for lips?" I ask, holding up an array of lipstick tubes from both her and Fatima's collections.

Jamila shrugs as she examines her options. "I usually do a lip tint."

I nod. "Makes sense. Your lips are pretty perfect already."

Why do I speak without thinking first?

My entire body clams up as I realize what I said, panicking even more when I notice the tension in Jamila's body too. To be fair, though, her lips *are* perfect. Full and naturally pouted, with a deep Cupid's bow curve. Always the perfect shade of light pink, even without gloss.

"How about red?" I propose eagerly in a rushed attempt to move the conversation into less embarrassing territory, holding up a tube of matte wine-red lipstick from MAC. Classic.

I breathe an internal sigh of relief when Jamila nods, only for the panic to return as I swipe the color along her lower lip, my fingers gently cradling her jaw. It's more intimate than applying her eyeliner had been, our faces inches apart as I trace the natural curve of her mouth. I can feel her heartbeat beneath my fingertips, see the goose bumps blossoming on her skin when I adjust my grip to lightly cup her cheek. It'd be easier if I didn't have to hold her steady, if she wasn't trembling so lightly it risks me smearing lipstick down her chin. But asking her to stay still means acknowledging the thing we're both dodging. The rapid thrum of our hearts, our held breath. The way I haven't moved in seconds and neither of us has noticed. The way we're moving closer and closer toward one another, pulled together by gravity.

Until the door slams back open.

"Did you use my moisturizer again?!" Fatima shouts as she storms into the room, stalling when Jamila and I suddenly jump apart, Jamila almost tumbling out of her chair.

"N-no," Jamila stammers, struggling to regain her balance by gripping tightly onto the edge of the vanity. "I think Mom did."

Fatima crosses her arms, scrutinizing the two of us before ultimately backing out of the room slowly. "If I find out you used it, you're *dead*," she hisses. "That cost fifty dollars."

I know exactly which moisturizer she's holding, and I'll buy her a whole truckload if it means she'll leave before she can see that I'm flushed down to my toes and struggling to catch my breath.

Mercifully, she does. I'll have to put in a bulk order tonight.

I clear my throat in an attempt to regain my composure. At some point in the heat of the moment I must've finished applying Jamila's lipstick. Not surprising, it's absolutely stunning on her. The bold pop of color feels fresh—a switch-up from her usual more muted wardrobe—and makes a total difference. Her eyes sparkle like gemstones, the highlighter along her cheekbones making her brown skin as radiant as the sun.

"Ready to go?" I choke out, my voice hoarse from the sight of her.

"Ready," she says after a short exhale, and takes my hand in hers.

CHAPTER 14

The premiere is in full swing by the time we step out of our car. A production assistant instantly appears at our side, walking beside us without taking his eyes off his clipboard, handing us a set of wristbands as soon as he's confirmed our names on the guest list, and pointing us in the direction we should go next.

"Ready for your first red carpet?" I ask Jamila, shimmying my shoulders as I head toward the tented carpet, the buzz of photographers calling out names rumbling in the distance.

I turn around, expecting Jamila to follow, but she's stuck in place, blinking at the tent like it's a hundred-foot-tall monster.

"I—I don't think I can," she stammers out, backing away slowly even though there's nowhere else for her to go.

Seeing her without her usual easy confidence is unsettling— like she's too exposed and I should shield my eyes to give her privacy. Instead, I take a careful step toward her, waiting until I'm sure she's not going to bolt to rest my hand on her arm.

"I know it seems like a lot, but you can do this," I assure her, taking in a deep breath and gesturing for her to match my pace.

We take in several deep breaths together, inhaling and exhaling in sync until she doesn't need my hand on her arm to ground her. Once she's calm and her eyes aren't the size of saucers, I straighten my back and get into my usual red carpet pose.

"Walk out there and keep your chin up." I pause, gesturing for her to mimic my movement. "Hand on your hip. Cross the legs. Dip your head down if you need to reposition or need a break. It'll keep them from getting any wonky photos of you when you're not ready. And *always* smile."

Jamila wobbles as she tries to cross her legs like mine, but I loop my arm through hers before she can stumble. "Maybe not the leg cross. That might be too advanced."

I let go of her so she can practice the pose one more time, readjusting her slightly so her shoulders are back and making sure her emerald necklace is sitting perfectly right at the hollow of her collarbone.

"Perfect." I give her pose a thumbs-up in approval before snapping a photo with my phone. "For your mom," I explain, quickly texting the picture to her before she can snatch the phone out of my hand and delete it.

Any hesitation Jamila had about the photo—about this whole situation—softens as she glances down at my phone. Even in terrible dim lighting, with camera flashes in the distance, she shines.

"I can go first," I offer once I've tucked my phone into my purse, then hold up my pinkie. "*If* you promise you'll follow right behind me?"

Jamila grins as she loops her pinkie through mine. "Promise."

We walk together to the entrance of the tent, me double-checking that Jamila isn't about to pass out before I take a deep breath of my own and step out onto the carpet.

For the first time since that night at Capri, I'm met with a flurry of flashing lights and voices yelling my name. I've turned down a dozen different premiere invites since the breakup out of fear of this moment—that it would take me right back to one of the most humiliating moments of my life. This was something I used to love—smiling for the cameras, answering questions, signing photos for fans. An exception to my claustrophobia, because who wouldn't mind being the center of attention? One of the most thrilling parts of this overwhelming career. And as scary as facing the cameras again might've felt a few weeks ago, I can't let Miles take this away from me too.

"Marisol, over here!"

"Looking beautiful!"

"How has *The Limit* been going?"

"Can you tell us anything about the part you'll be playing?"

The voices pile on top of each other as the cameras flash, clouding my vision with dark spots and stars. I keep my smile in place as I carefully step down the carpet, every movement carefully choreographed to appear camera-ready each step of the way.

"It's going to be a great season," I tease a nearby reporter. "That's all I can say."

I'm nearly to the end of the carpet, where a doorway leads

to the screening room, when the cameras' attention shifts, some of them continuing to call out questions to me while the others focus on getting shots of the newcomer. Jamila steps hesitantly into the spotlight, holding the pose we practiced. It's a little stiff, but what matters is her smile. Soft and effortless, made that much brighter by the sequins on her dress catching the light of the camera flashes. I don't need to see the photos splashed across the internet to know she's stunning. And soon, the world will know it too.

I'm frozen in place, watching proudly as she approaches the flock of reporters, ready to sneak a candid of her for her mom, when her foot catches on a snag in the carpet. Time slows as her ankle wobbles, unsteady in her new heels, and she starts to careen to the side. Without thinking, I dash as quickly as I can toward her. I loop my arm around her waist, yanking her up and pulling her against my side in a motion so fluid I honestly didn't think I had it in me.

"Be nice to her, it's her first red carpet," I say to the crowd, which rewards me with a smattering of chuckles as Jamila leans heavily against me, her cheek practically pressed against mine. She holds on to my arm tight enough to bruise, but I don't so much as wince.

"How're you so good at this?" Jamila whispers, her breath warm against my skin, as she finally steadies herself in her heels, tugging down the hem of her dress.

"It gets easier," I whisper back, an echo of our conversation about surviving life in the city, but, this time, I'm the expert.

The clicks and flashes pick up speed as we turn to face the crowd together, pressed flush against each other despite Jamila regaining her balance.

"Let's get a group shot of the *Limit* kids!" one photographer shouts.

My brow furrows as someone steps toward us. I'm wracking my brain for any mentions of Miles or Dawn coming to this premiere when Eli Rowan steps up beside me.

Eli freaking Rowan.

Eli is as effortlessly cool in person as they are on TV, in interviews, and on magazine covers. Their brown hair has been cut into a shaggy mullet, a style that I absolutely hate but manages to be extremely chic on them. They pull off a pair of slim black sunglasses as they casually wrap their arm around me, clad in a denim jacket with patches from different countries plastered across the back and sleeves.

"Perfect!" the photographer praises, and I have to physically shake myself off to snap back to reality and go back into posing mode. Jamila seems as starstruck as I am, sneaking glances at Eli in between rounds of flashes.

"Thanks, everyone," Eli says to the crowd, giving a slight bow before heading off toward the screening room.

Quickly, Jamila and I do the same, waving to the crowd and thanking them for their time before following after Eli.

"You both on season two?" Eli asks as we step into the screening room, rocket ship–shaped tubs of popcorn and neon-purple slushies laid out across the table along with our seating assignments. Eli asks this so casually you'd think we've known each for years instead of meeting for the first time a few seconds ago.

"Yeah," I reply for both of us while Jamila nods numbly, clearly stuck in "Oh my God, a real celebrity" mode. Been there. Two years ago, Zendaya had to pick my jaw up off the floor.

"Good luck," Eli says with a humorless chuckle as they help themself to one of the rocket ship popcorns. "Rune is a dick."

It's not until I feel Jamila stiffening against my hand that I realize I never let go of her waist. I shove my hands under my armpits, trying not to linger on the chill that settles over me once we're apart.

"He's definitely eccentric," I say diplomatically, not sure how much I should say somewhere this public.

Eli nods, chewing on some popcorn. "DM me if he's ever being an ass to you. He can't keep getting away with treating his employees like shit," they say before sauntering off to find their seat in the crowded theater.

I'm not able to process that Eli Rowan casually told me to DM them, both because the production assistants start ushering us toward our seats, and because I suddenly see Delia's constant checking in on me in a new light. Does she know something I don't about Rune not being the best to his cast and crew? Was working with him what she was trying to talk me out of instead of doubting my abilities? Did she tell Mom as my manager?

"The screening will begin in five!" an assistant beside us shouts, and the crowd moves so quickly I almost lose sight of Jamila.

"C'mon," she says, slipping her hand in mine and tugging me toward our seats.

As our fingers link together, warm and slightly sweaty, I forget about Rune and *The Limit* and everything Eli said. For a few blissful moments, I get to focus on Jamila, her smile, and the way her hand fits so perfectly in mine.

CHAPTER 15

"Who ate the last banana?!" Rune shouts first thing on set Wednesday morning. He's never been the "Hello, how are you?" type, but this is the third time this week he's greeted us with some kind of accusation. Yesterday, it was aimed at Esther for not having his favorite quinoa bowl on the lunch menu. Monday, it was at one of the sound guys for having the boom mic lower than usual, even though it was at the same height it always is. Rune had him fired before he could even adjust the mic. As Esther promised, he was rehired the following day.

It's like Rune is on a mission to give me the world's longest-lasting migraine. We're clocking in at a solid nineteen hours so far. It's bad enough that today is one of our aggressively early shoot days. When I came trudging into the building, the sun hadn't even risen yet. It took hair and makeup an extra fifteen minutes to cover up my eye bags.

No one owns up to the banana situation. For all we know, there weren't even any bananas at crafty this morning, but that doesn't matter. Logic never matters when it comes to Rune.

"Fine. Guess I'll have to run out and get my own banana," Rune announces to the room, as if this is the greatest tragedy of the twenty-first century. Thankfully, one of his PAs appears out of thin air—as they often do—holding a banana she clearly took out from the tote bag on her shoulder.

Rune scrutinizes the banana's brown spots, as if he somehow knows this is her personal banana and not one sent by the gods of crafty, but ultimately decides not to fight it. Once he's taken his first bite, the tension in his shoulders slackens, but his voice isn't any less tight.

"Let's get started," he barks, not changing his "I'm angry for some absurd reason" tone.

Which is just my luck since I'm in the first scene of the day.

And it's with Miles.

I quickly set down my phone—abandoning the essay-length text I'd been writing to Kevin to try to convince him that he *has* to lip-sync to a Beyoncé song for the competition. He'd been floating around a couple of different ideas, but Queen B is always the answer.

We get to our marks in a makeshift classroom, Miles seated on the edge of a desk and me standing on the opposite end of the room. As always, Rune approaches us before we begin the scene with a handful of edits to our lines. They're not total rewrites like they have been in the past, but they're substantial enough for me to need an extra minute to study and get them down.

With Jamila's continued help with practicing my lines in

our trailer, I don't break out into a panic every time Rune flips the script on me. I've even managed to come up with my own memorization technique. Focusing on the thought of telling Jamila about all these line changes after my scene has wrapped and we're on the couch in our trailer with Diet Cokes, tossing popcorn into each other's mouths. The way her lips will curl in the corners, her soft, melodic laugh, as she fights back a snort and says, "Seriously? *That's* what he went with?"

I fan my cheeks as Rune calls for everyone to get into place, brushing off the thought of Jamila and focusing on the real subject of my attention: Miles. Or Will. My ex-boyfriend. On- and off-screen.

It's another emotionally charged scene. Possibly my most intense moment of the season—when, after months of on-and-off hookups, I finally confront Miles and his obvious feelings for Jamila.

The characters, I mean. Not the real people, obviously.

"Why are we here?" Miles, in character, asks, as he looks away and crosses his arms.

"Because we need to talk," I reply sharply, easily slipping into the new harsher exterior I've created for Zoe. "About you and . . . her."

Miles does a wonderful job of making his eyes light up at the mention of Jamila's character. Something I try not to dwell on—both in real life and in character. "What about her?"

My fingers curl into a fist. "I know what's going on. You can't keep lying to me."

"I'm not—"

"You are!" I shout, tears springing to my eyes as I give

myself over completely to the scene. I channel the rage and heartbreak and insecurity I've felt over the past few months into my performance. Zoe and I may be polar opposites, but I can understand what it's like to feel disposable. Especially to someone like Miles.

"You can't come crawling back to me at night when you want to feel better about yourself, then toss me out in the morning. I'm a fucking person, Will. And I'm tired of this. I know what you went through with your dad and brother was awful, and I *know* you're struggling, but that doesn't give you an excuse to treat me like I'm something you can throw away."

Tears stream down my cheeks as the scene ends. Miles says his last line, but it's drowned out by the noise inside my brain. I remain trapped in that anger, body trembling even after we call cut. When the overhead lights switch on again, I'm surrounded by silence, but it doesn't feel intimidating this time.

Because I know I absolutely nailed it.

Once I've composed myself, I find that Miles is staring at me, mouth agape.

"That was . . ." He shakes his head in disbelief. "That was incredible, Mari."

A compliment from my ex shouldn't light my whole body on fire, but it does. Not because I'm hoping this'll change anything between us. But because it's proof—*tangible* proof—that *I've* changed. That I did exactly what I set out to do. That I proved him wrong.

Before I can relish in the victory of crushing my scene, Rune's voice calls us to attention.

"Run it again. From the second page," he says through

gritted teeth. His eyes are closed as he massages his temples, and when his script falls off his lap and onto the ground, he lets his PAs scramble to pick it up for him.

Miles and I brace ourselves, waiting for him to give any of his usual notes on our first take, but he doesn't speak up again or even look at us. He snaps his fingers when we don't get a move-on.

Quickly wiping my cheeks and restoring the bruised confidence I have by the second page of the scene, we start again.

"Zoe, you know what she means to me," says Miles, able to easily slip back into character.

"I don't. And I don't think you do either. If you—"

"Stop!" Rune shouts yet again.

There's a general air of unease when he interrupts. Producers and PAs on the edge of their seats as he storms over, his heavy steps echoing in the dead-silent room.

Walking straight up to *me*.

I flinch, not sure what I'm bracing myself for—a shout, an insult, a tackle to the ground—but preparing myself. And yet, nothing can prepare me for Rune closing the distance, leaning down until his face is pressed inches from my neck, and inhaling deeply, sniffing me like he's a dog searching for a bone.

What. The. F—

"It's you," Rune murmurs, interrupting my confused line of thought. "That perfume you're wearing has been giving me migraines all morning."

"O-oh" is the only thing I can think to say as I reach up to cover my neck with my hand, as if that can cover up the scent of Chanel's Coco Mademoiselle. "I—I'm sor—"

"Go wash it off," Rune instructs, cutting off my apology. "Don't come back until it's gone."

His voice is as strong as a shove. Not a shout, but something somehow worse. Something laced with anger, and disgust, and worst of all: disappointment.

"Okay," I manage to choke out, unsure what else I *can* say.

Over Rune's shoulder, Esther gives me a sympathetic frown. Even Miles looks like he wants to reach out for me as I rush off set, doing what little I can to hide my face.

The room is quiet as I weave through the crowd, bodies parting for me as I rush out. When I close the door to set behind me, I hear Rune call out for them to move on to the next scene, not bothering to wait for me to come back and take it from the top.

For once, I pray that Jamila's not in our trailer, but of course she is. The universe just doesn't want to cut me a break today.

"Hey. Wasn't your scene supposed . . ." Jamila trails off once she takes me in, setting down her phone and carefully approaching me. "What happened?"

I don't realize I'm crying until her fingers brush my cheeks and come back glistening. Once I see it, the tears come harder. Jamila swims in and out of view, her image broken and jumbled like I'm seeing her through a kaleidoscope. Shaking, I sit down on the edge of the couch, trying to keep my voice from cracking as I tell her everything.

"That's fucked up," she whispers as I finish, unable to keep myself from hiccupping as I choke back sobs. "I know he's always been . . . a lot. But this is on another level." She pauses, biting her lip before continuing. "Maybe we should talk to Eli . . ."

The confirmation that I'm not overreacting is encouraging but doesn't make me feel any less like *I'm* the one who's the problem. Rune has taken shots at everyone on set, sure, but it feels like I've been the punching bag of the season. From the first day I walked on set, Rune has seemed irritated by me. Not only in my performance, but in who I am as a person. I'm left constantly wondering if I'm going to get fired mid-scene. Some days are steadier than others, but on rocky days, it feels like I'm seconds away from stumbling and falling over the edge of a cliff.

And as encouraging as it was to find out Eli went through the same thing, I know we're not the same caliber. They were the lead. Their role completely changed the trajectory of their career—made them the kind of star Miles wants to be, and I never thought I *could* be. Rune may have been awful to them too, but they were able to come out on the other side of that experience a star. And if everything goes right, that'll happen for me.

"It's . . ." I begin, but can't continue. My heart clenches as I meet Jamila's eyes and see myself reflected back in them. Tired and pale and so unlike myself that it's like staring at a stranger. "It feels like I've changed everything about myself to be here. My clothes, my hair, my . . ." *My everything,* I think, but can't say out loud. "And it's still not good enough."

I know that sometimes I'm over-the-top and dramatic and "too much," but I've never felt a need to apologize for it before or felt ashamed of the things I love most about myself. I'm willing to adapt and change, to push myself and my acting abilities for the sake of exploring new possibilities. But is it worth it if the person it makes me is someone unrecognizable? Do I really want to do this—leave my comfort zone, completely change the direction of my career—if it means I can't be myself?

Jamila shifts closer until our knees are brushing beneath the dining table. She allows me to sob until I can't anymore, runs a hand down my back until my wails have died down to ragged whispers. I know I'm supposed to be taking a shower or rubbing wet wipes down my neck so I can head back to set, but I can't find it in me to stand up yet. They've moved on without me, anyway. I doubt anyone in that room is waiting anxiously for me.

"I know this might not mean anything, but for what it's worth . . ." Jamila takes my hands in hers and, finally, they stop shaking. Tears cling to my lashes as I blink up at her, resisting the urge to hide my puffy-eyed, snot-smeared face when she's always—*always*—so beautiful. But if she thinks I'm gross, she doesn't let it show. She squeezes my hand and tucks a loose strand of hair behind my ear. "I think you're pretty perfect already. As you are."

In that moment, with her fingers brushing my neck where Rune inhaled and wrinkled his nose like I was a piece of rotten fruit, it's impossible not to believe her. And impossible to deny what I have known and fought since the first time I saw her: that I'd give anything to kiss her.

Before I can linger on that thought, she loops her fingers through mine and tugs me toward the entrance to our trailer. "C'mon," she urges when I drag my feet.

I quickly wipe off my cheeks, unsure what her plan is as

she throws the door open and guides me through the maze of trailers, crew, and crafty until we're fully away from set and walking toward the block that overlooks the water. I'm prepared to ask her if we should be straying this far from set when we turn a corner and the water comes into view, immediately silencing all my questions and protests.

The sun has finally started to rise on the edge of the horizon, painting the sky above the East River the dreamiest shade of orange, with a hint of pink. The skyscrapers in Manhattan are bathed in soft golden light, the water so serene it's easy to forget how green it actually is in regular daylight. I consider pulling out my phone to take a photo for my socials, but I know I'll never be able to capture the beauty of this moment on a screen.

"Now you can cross watching the sunrise off your bucket list," Jamila explains as she gestures to the water, reminding me of our conversation on the subway during our first week on set.

All thoughts of Rune and the way he always tears me down are gone as I smile at Jamila, torn between lingering on her or the sunset. She was right: It was worth the crack-of-dawn call time. And that she's the best tour guide in the city—because I know this view wouldn't be half as stunning if she hadn't been the one to show it to me.

CHAPTER 16

Despite my acting background, I've never been good at hiding my feelings. Even if I were, I'm too exhausted by the time I get home to act like I'm anything other than irritated about how the rest of my day went. After a thorough shower to ensure I'd washed off every trace of perfume from my skin, and another round with hair and makeup, I walked back to set and spent nearly two hours waiting around before being told we'd reshoot my scene tomorrow morning instead.

I try my best to put my annoyance at Rune for wasting my time behind me as I head straight from set to meet up with Kevin at a boutique downtown. With the amateur drag competition this weekend, we need to lock down an outfit for his performance ASAP. There's no way I'm letting my cousin make his debut in a dress he stole from the back of his mom's closet. Shopping is the cure for all wounds, but I don't feel my usual buzz as I stroll through the racks. No euphoria as I find a champagne sequin jumpsuit that would go perfectly with the wig I spotted at a beauty supply store down the block from my apartment.

"Okay, what's the matter?" Kevin snaps as he steps out of the dressing room in a green midi cling dress that I give an apathetic thumbs-down.

"It doesn't do anything for your legs," I explain, gesturing to the dress's awkward length. He already has naturally glorious legs. No point in hiding them under fabric.

Kevin crosses his arms when I hand him the next option to try. "I meant with you."

"What do you mean?"

"You've been weird since we got here. Every other time I've seen you, your energy is at a ten, but I walked out in that neon-yellow feather monstrosity that made me look like Big Bird, and you didn't even say a thing," he explains, pointing to said feather monstrosity. I shudder as I take it in properly this time. It *does* look like Big Bird.

"I'm sorry, I'm just exhausted from shooting," I apologize before burying my head in my hands, applying a gentle pressure to my temples that I hope will ease my building migraine and wake me up a little. I knew I should've gotten myself a latte before ordering my Lyft. New York seriously needs more drive-throughs.

Instead of dropping the subject and moving on to the next outfit, Kevin squeezes beside me onto the bench outside of his dressing room. "Did something happen?"

I shrug, hoping it comes off as nonchalant, but the way he keeps staring intently at me tells me he's not convinced. "The director can just be really frustrating sometimes."

"Did he say something to you?"

I snort, a humorless, bitter sound. "Not exactly. But he doesn't need to say anything to make me feel awful." My head drops, hanging limply as I run my hands along my bare arms, trying to warm them back up. "It feels like I'm never doing anything right. Even when I think I'm giving a fantastic performance, he still finds something to nitpick, like my hair, or my clothes, or the freaking perfume I'm wearing."

"He sounds like a dick."

"He's a great writer, though."

"That doesn't mean he can't also be a dick." Kevin nudges his shoulder against mine. "Regardless of whatever he tries to put you through, you got this job for a reason: because you're talented. Don't let anyone ever tell you otherwise. Including him."

"If the person who hired me doesn't think I'm any good, then how am I supposed to believe in myself?" I reply, holding back tears as I voice the fear that's been plaguing me ever since my first day on this show.

I know I've been putting my best foot forward. I know I've been giving this my all. I *know* I'm giving a really great performance—possibly the best of my career. But it feels impossible not to doubt myself when Rune seems so determined to see me fail.

"Because it shouldn't matter what anyone else thinks. It only matters what *you* think," Kevin insists, taking my hand in his and squeezing gently. "But for what it's worth, I think you're pretty damn amazing. I binged *Avalon Grove* and that one holiday rom-com you did. Phenomenal. And I'm not just saying that because you're my famous cousin."

This time, my laugh isn't bitter or hollow. It's the lightest I've felt since the premiere with Jamila. I forget about who I'm trying to be and remember who I really am. A girl who loves pink and romance and fashion. A girl who isn't afraid to be herself. "Thanks."

"Don't thank me. You're the one doing me the favors."

That might technically be true, but helping him get ready for the competition has honestly been a welcome distraction from the pressures of shooting. Plus, my nails have never looked better. Rune hasn't mentioned them once, which is honestly a great sign.

Kevin stands back up, grabbing the next option—the champagne jumpsuit I have high hopes for—from the pile beside me. "You got your ticket for this Saturday, right?"

Since Dad has been so adamant about me not going to any of Jerome's shows, I made sure to book the ticket under an alias. I'm not sure how involved Jerome is in ticket sales, but I can't risk them busting our operation before it can actually go into effect.

"Duh." I pull up my confirmation email as proof with a grin. "Would you mind if I invited a friend?" I ask tentatively, suddenly very intrigued by a loose thread on my skirt. I'd had the thought to invite Jamila the night of the premiere, but chickened out at the last minute. Not because I don't think a drag show is her scene, but because this feels . . . different. An invite to do something outside of *The Limit*, outside of showing her the ropes of celebrity life. A night to be who we are—hopefully without cameras lurking around every corner. Clearly, we're friends when we're on set, and we got along well the night of the premiere, but who are we *really* when we're off-screen?

Kevin narrows his eyes at me suspiciously but doesn't pry for any details. "The more to witness my debut, the merrier." He steps back into the dressing room, head peeking out of the curtain. "Now, I want you to give me your honest opinion on this next one. No thumbs-up or thumbs-down, okay?"

"Okay," I assure him with my last thumbs-up of the evening before quickly pulling out my phone and texting Jamila.

> Hey! So, my cousin is going to be part of an amateur drag competition Friday night—any interest in being my plus one? Give you a chance to experience the joys of going incognito in a crowd!

Yet another unfortunate lesson Jamila will have to learn sooner or later: public spaces like a nightclub aren't your friend when you're a recognizable face. The sooner she learns how to keep people from figuring out who she is so she can spend her night enjoying herself instead of fielding selfies and autographs, the better.

I hit send on the text before I can dwell too long on the wording—my plus-one, seriously? It's not like we're going to a wedding—and shove my phone back into my pocket moments before Kevin steps out in the jumpsuit.

"Oh. My. God," I say, each word its own statement.

"It's a little much, right?" Kevin shifts to face the full-length mirror nervously, tugging the V-neckline of the jumpsuit closer together.

"'Too much' isn't in my vocabulary. It's *perfect!*"

Even without padding, the cut and style of the jumpsuit

perfectly accentuate Kevin's figure, making his legs look like they go on for miles. The color pops and flawlessly complements the copper undertones of his skin. Plus, if it's already dazzling like a disco ball in the horrible dressing room fluorescent lighting, I can only imagine what it'll be like on stage.

I leap out of my seat, unable to contain my excitement as I gesture for him to give me a full twirl so I can confirm what I already knew: this is the perfect choice. "If Jerome doesn't crown you on the spot, I'll replace his coffee creamer with sour cream."

The hesitation Kevin had when he stepped out of the dressing room melts away, his laugh deep and loud and his smile brighter than the sun. Seeing someone feel comfortable in their own skin because you brought out the beauty they've had in them the entire time is the best part of any makeover. That glow gets me every time.

"Don't try to pay for this. It's on me," I insist as Kevin does another once-over in the mirror. His smile fades as he whips around to protest, but I hold up a finger before he can argue with me. "Think of it as a thank-you gift for my favorite cousin."

Slowly, his smile blossoms again. Instead of showing his appreciation with words, he pulls me into a hug that says it for him. I can't help but sniffle as I hug him back as tightly as I can. It feels really damn good to have a friend in this city, a place that once felt so unfamiliar and terrifying. But it feels even better to know that person is family.

My phone buzzes while Kevin changes back into his street clothes. New texts from Jamila.

> I'd love to 😊

> warning you now tho in case any dancing is involved: I'm a terrible dancer

I don't bother to hide my smile, lingering a beat too long on the text before tucking my phone away. Kevin stands in the doorway to the dressing room, eyebrow quirked as he watches my cheeks flush, but doesn't tease or call me out again. My smile while reading the text stays in place as we check out, and as we grab dinner at a sushi place down the block, and as a couple of overeager fans ask for photos and hit me with dozens of questions about Miles. Even as we take the subway home because Kevin insists it's part of the New York experience. The grin on my face lasts until I'm finally in bed for the night, Bruiser curled up beside me, staring at the ceiling and dreaming about spending another night with Jamila.

CHAPTER 17

Blazin' Saddles is, surprisingly, not country-themed. While there are a handful of posters of steamy cowboy kisses, the overall vibe is giving more disco than Wild West. Probably on account of the seven—yes, seven—disco balls over the dance floor. There's even a mega disco ball in the private lounge, a balcony alcove with a perfect view of the main stage.

The club is in full swing by the time Jamila and I arrive, even though it's early by New York standards. Our escort—a queen in a hot pink corset and matching tutu—whisks us through the club and up to the VIP lounge I decided to splurge on. For privacy, even though I'm in full incognito mode tonight, to be safe. Both so I don't get spotted by any potential fans, or Dad and Jerome. I made sure to give Jamila a thorough tutorial on how to stay undercover without compromising on fashion or aesthetics. While I normally wouldn't choose to wear an all-black ensemble, it's a necessary evil on a night like tonight.

Thankfully, Jamila's only watching and learning tonight. Her social following has quickly climbed into the low five digits ever since the cast announcement, but she should enjoy these last few months of being able to live somewhat under the radar. Once the show airs, privacy will be a thing of the past.

I tug on the end of my pin-straight black wig as we weave through the crowd toward the staircase leading to the lounge. It's locked in place with plenty of wig glue, but sweat broke out along my brow the second we stepped into the club. Obviously, I used a sweatproof glue, but the thought of my next paparazzi scandal being me with a crooked wig makes me shudder.

Jamila hovers close behind me, lightly gripping my arm as our escort effortlessly leads us up the stairs in six-inch heels. I watch in awe as bodies twist around each other in the packed club below us, queens and bartenders and patrons weaving around the tightly packed space without spilling a single drop of their drinks like it's a choreographed dance.

The roped-off balcony is much smaller than the floor below, but certainly not empty. Most of the black leather booths are occupied by the time we arrive—several high-profile drag queens in one corner, and a former pop star turned Oscar-winning actress in the other. The exact types of people who won't acknowledge our presence, so long as we don't acknowledge theirs.

"Can I get you dolls anything?" our escort—Kitty—asks, eyeing the large black Xs on our hands. Jamila doesn't drink and neither do I, so we don't bother trying to convince Kitty to slip us something.

"Just two lemonades, please," I reply, grateful that Jamila and I planned our order on the way here.

Moments after Kitty sets down our drinks, I spot Dad lingering at the edge of the stage.

"That's my dad."

My breath hitches, and I attempt to hide behind Jamila, even though he probably can't see me from the stage and has no reason to suspect that I might be here. He looks like he walked straight out of work, a tomato-shaped pincushion strapped to his arm and a tape measure wrapped around his neck like a designer scarf. He disappears almost as quickly as he appeared, stepping back behind the curtain with a huff. Jamila attempts to hide her giggle behind her hand when I finally emerge from where I was attempting to hide.

"It must be supercool having a dad who's a costume designer," she says after I breathe a sigh of relief. Even with her leaning in while she speaks, it's tough to hear her over the music. Not that I mind the "Single Ladies" meets "thank u, next" mashup playing, but it does make having a conversation a pain in the ass.

"I guess so," I reply with a shrug.

In theory, it *is* supercool. While I definitely don't have any more space in my wardrobe, I wouldn't mind snagging a few custom pieces from Dad's collection. Like one of the dresses he designed for Jerome tonight—a seventies-inspired lavender flower-print minidress. It's refreshing to be around someone who appreciates the fine details of fashion the same way I do, even if I don't get to explore it as much these days, thanks to my on-set uniform. Alas, that doesn't change the fact that we've been living together for weeks and I feel as distant as ever from him.

"Are you two close?" Jamila asks, hitting right on the topic I was hoping to avoid.

I shift uncomfortably. Not because of the closeness or the way my eardrums are starting to throb, but because I'm not sure how to answer. Whether to tell her the long-winded story behind my existence. That before I came here, Dad felt more like a name in my phone than a *dad*. That part of the reason I was terrified of coming here was because it meant spending time with someone I wasn't sure would like me, even though they helped bring me into the world. A drag show on a Saturday night is not the ideal place to delve into my daddy issues.

"I don't really—"

I'm saved from having to finish my vague answer by Kitty stepping up to the mic at the center of the stage.

"Welcome, ladies and gays, to Blazin' Saddles!" The crowd gives her a roar of applause, several people pushing up to the lip of the stage. "Are you ready to get this competition started?"

This time, the crowd's response is loud enough to make the floor vibrate beneath our feet. Jamila gives an impressive whistle by sticking two fingers in her mouth—I'll need to ask her how she does that later.

"Give it up for your host: the one, the only . . . Miss Anita Break!"

I didn't think it was possible for the crowd to get any rowdier, but as the lights dim and a single long, exposed leg steps into the spotlight, my eardrums feel like they're going to pop. I clap until my hands go numb, scream until my voice cracks, as Anita slowly steps into the spotlight, wearing a fire-engine-red sequined gown that twinkles in the light. The wig that's been sitting on the kitchen table all week has been transformed, luscious black locks trailing down Anita's shoulder, her dark brown skin glimmering with a mix of baby oil and glitter.

"How y'all doing tonight?" she says into the mic once she's fully stepped into the spotlight, and gets a roaring cheer in response. She laughs and demurely tosses a curl over her bare shoulder. In the sliver of space between the left-hand side of the stage and the curtain, I spot Dad beaming like he's won the lottery.

"We've got an amazing show for you tonight," Anita continues, clapping her hands together. "For any newcomers, tonight is our monthly New to the Saddle competition. I got a peek at some of our contestants earlier, and y'all are *not* ready." The crowd gives a few whoops and hollers.

I'm clinging to the edge of my seat as Anita goes over the only rule (no acts over five minutes), and the prize (five hundred dollars and a guest slot at Anita's next show) before announcing the first performer of the night.

"Please welcome to the stage: Diamond Du Jour."

"That's her!" I whisper eagerly to Jamila, gently nudging her in the ribs.

We'd strategically planned for Kevin to sign up for the first performance slot. Maybe not the best choice judgment-wise. People are always harsher on the first few acts in a competition—I know firsthand after doing that celebrity dancing show—but we figured this would prevent Kevin from potentially getting figured out backstage by Dad or Jerome between acts. While the makeup, hair, and outfit definitely transformed him into someone unrecognizable, there wasn't much we could do about the gap in his smile—a dead giveaway if Dad or Jerome paid close enough attention. With how strict they've been about not letting even *me* come to one of the shows, I wouldn't be surprised if they kicked Kevin out before he could even step on stage. And I did not spend over an hour on makeup today to not see Diamond make her stage debut.

Jamila eagerly shifts closer to me as we crane our necks to get the best view of the stage. Anita saunters off to join her fellow judges at the table set up for them at the base of the stage.

You could hear a pin drop as the crowd waits for the night's first competitor to take the stage. Slowly, almost as dramatically as Anita did earlier, Diamond steps out onto the stage with her arms up in the air, welcoming the immediate applause. As anticipated, the spotlight and disco balls hitting her jumpsuit light her up like a shooting star. She styled her caramel-colored wig perfectly—voluminous and thick with eighties-style curls. And I can see the glimmer of the highlighter along her cheekbones from the balcony.

As she steps up to the mic, I sneak a nervous glance over at Anita, prepared to see recognition slowly dawning on her, but she's living for Diamond as much as the crowd is.

Diamond knows exactly how to tease the audience, taking her time stepping up to the mic. The crowd quiets down, everyone leaning in with her as she grips the mic, closes her eyes, and snaps her fingers, bringing the music to life. She struts across the stage as the opening notes of her custom remix of Beyoncé's "Crazy in Love" begins to play, crumpled bills tossed at her before she's even uttered a single word. It's impossible to look away once Diamond takes center stage, lip-syncing each word perfectly, gliding across the stage in time to the music. Somehow, she's able to move like there's a fan following beside her, perfectly blowing her hair out of her face and over her shoulder.

What starts as a slow but powerful performance quickly kicks up a notch when she gets to the chorus, whipping her hair like a runway model yet somehow never getting any strands stuck in her gloss. Jamila and I gasp in unison as she twirls across the stage, landing a split so on beat to the song, the entire room erupts. But the split is only the beginning. Diamond kicks into high-gear, dancing and strutting across the stage with a confidence that rivals only the real Beyoncé's, coupled with dips and moves of her own that still perfectly match the song's energy. When the performance wraps up in a death drop that makes me gasp again, the audience bursts into hysterics. Screams and cries of Diamond's name ring in my ears as I bounce on my tiptoes and cheer for her as loud as I possibly can with what little of my voice is left. The stage is littered with bills, from singles to fives to even a few tens, that she gracefully sweeps into her arms as she waves to the crowd one last time.

Anita has no idea who she is, giving Diamond a full-on standing ovation. Or maybe she does know and doesn't care that we went behind her back. All that matters is Diamond's showstopping performance.

I immediately pull out my phone.

DIAMOND, CONGRATULATIONS!!!

Diamond is a tough act to follow, but the two performers lined up after her put up a good fight—a queen giving an edgy performance to a rock song I vaguely recognize, and a king who gives a steamy *Magic Mike*–inspired lap dance to one lucky audience member. Anita steps back onto the stage after the lap dance to announce that they'll be back with the next three competitors after a brief break. As soon as she snaps her fingers, the DJ turns up the music again.

With the music back, the others in the private lounge flock to the smaller dance floor in the center of the room, no one stays in their seats once the DJ shifts to a remix of a Madonna song.

"C'mon!" I say to Jamila, holding out my hand to her. Who knows how long we have left here? For all we know, Diamond's real identity will be found out any second now, and Anita will personally escort all three of us off the premises. So I want to make my time here last.

"I'm not great at dancing," she replies stiffly, tucking her hands beneath her legs.

"You don't have to be a good dancer to dance." I point my thumb over my shoulder at where a bald man in a suit is whipping his nonexistent hair to the beat.

Jamila smiles, but it's gone once she scans the crowd of dancing bodies. "I don't know. . . ."

"Well, I'm not leaving without getting in at least one dance tonight. So you can join, or you can watch." I back away from her slowly. "Your choice." I arch my brow, giving her one last chance to join before fully throwing myself into the pulsing mass of bodies.

My dance skills are nothing to write home about either, but it's easy to get lost in the music. I let my hands move above my body, my hips swaying to the beat. The others on the dance floor welcome me without a second glance, everyone too caught up in themselves or their drinks or their partners to care who's in their space because we're all safe here.

When I close my eyes, the bass lines up with my heartbeat, pounding in time to the rhythm. I'm not sure how long I spend here, letting the music guide me. Seconds, minutes, or hours until a spark makes my eyes open again. The brush of an arm against mine, a familiar smile in the crowd.

"Changed your mind?" I ask Jamila, my smile so wide it hurts to my cheeks.

Despite her protests, she's a natural on the dance floor. Her moves aren't over-the-top or energetic, but she's able to hold her own by two-stepping in time with the music—more than most of the others in the crowd can say. "You made it look fun."

I smirk, resisting the urge to twirl her over and over until I can hear that laugh again. Instead, I stop dancing long enough to stand on my tiptoes and cup my hands around my mouth. "Attention, everyone! I convinced *the* Jamila El Amrani to dance tonight!"

Before I can continue, she lunges at me, cupping a hand around my mouth as she fights back a laugh. "Don't embarrass me more than I already am."

"Only if you dance with me," I reply when her hand drops from my mouth and lingers on my shoulder.

I say it without thinking, without considering what it would mean to move in closer to her, to have her arm around my waist and her lips a breath away from mine. My lips part when she steps toward me, as she takes my arms and wraps them around her shoulders. I struggle to keep my balance when her hands grip my waist. We're swaying slowly, not at all in time with the rapid pace of the music, but the world starts to spin. All that matters is her, her touch, and the way it makes my heart race. The crowd cheers as the DJ transitions into a remix of Whitney Houston's "I Wanna Dance with Somebody," everyone around us pairing up and pushing the two of us closer.

Our foreheads rest together, the fabrics of our dresses clinging and catching on each other. I'm not sure who moves in first—her or me—but I don't care now that she's here. Close enough for me to feel every beat of her heart. Close enough that kissing her doesn't feel impossible—it feels like fate.

And who am I to deny fate?

When I lean up on my toes to brush my lips against hers, she meets me halfway, grip tightening on my waist as our mouths collide with enough force to knock me back. But she holds me tight and doesn't let go.

My fingers tangle in her curls while she cups my jaw, and at some point, I'm not sure where she ends and I begin. If I thought I was unsteady before, it's nothing compared to leaning up to kiss her again and again until my chest tightens and begs for breath—but I can't stop, never want to stop. Because her lips are as soft as her skin and she tastes like she smells, like oranges and chocolate.

We part only because we have to, both of us heaving for breath as the song finishes, and a new contestant is welcomed to the stage. The disco ball above us bathes Jamila in flashes of silver light, and I didn't think it was possible, but she's somehow even more beautiful.

Slowly, my hand travels down from her neck, my fingertips

skimming her arm, until I loop our fingers together. My cheeks ache from smiling, and my lips feel swollen, and my gloss is smudged, but I don't care. Not about anything that isn't kissing her again. I lean forward to do exactly that, tugging her toward me. First her hand slips out of mine, then her body, mine shivering from the loss of her warmth.

"I have to go," she whispers, almost lost beneath the screech of a microphone.

And before I can ask her what she means, she's gone.

CHAPTER 18

No surprise, Diamond takes first place in the competition. But the thrill of the win is short-lived.

"This is *unacceptable*!" Dad shouts backstage, flanked by Jerome, who's now half out of drag.

Thankfully, we weren't found out until the closing ceremony. After Diamond was crowned first place, accepting her bouquet of flowers and five hundred dollars cash, Dad and Jerome clocked her as Kevin seconds into her acceptance speech. They let Diamond have her moment in the spotlight, bowing for the crowd before instantly pulling her into a dressing room and demanding to know how the hell she managed to pull this off. Minutes later, they found me.

Dad's voice is a blur as I sit slumped on a stool at Jerome's/ Anita's vanity beside Kevin, still dressed as Diamond, but all the confidence that won him the competition is long gone.

"We didn't do anything wrong," Kevin protests, his grip tightening enough that his bouquet begins to crumple.

"But you know we didn't want you coming to the club for a reason. You're *teenagers*."

"It's an over-eighteen club, and we're both eighteen," Kevin snaps back instantly.

"That doesn't change that you went behind our backs."

The two of them keep at it, lobbing accusations and excuses back and forth while Jerome occasionally chimes in, but I'm numb to the world. I'd attempted to chase after Jamila, but quickly lost her in the crowd. All my worried texts to her have gone unanswered, and I know I should give her the space she clearly needs, but I want to know if she made it home all right.

"And you," Dad says, suddenly turning his attention to me. Begrudgingly, I look up to meet his scowl. "I'm not sure what your mother lets you do out in LA, but we have rules you need to follow if you're going to stay in our house. You're grounded. You go to set, you come straight back home, got it?"

His tone makes the numbness fade and anger spark at his implication that Mom lets me do whatever I want. I don't like the way he said it—and I especially don't like the backhanded jab at Mom's parenting. Which he has no right to comment on, considering he was barely a part of my life up until a few weeks ago. I debate telling him he can't ground me, that I'm eighteen and perfectly capable of finding my own place now that I'm settled, but decide against it. The last thing I need right now is a move.

So I say nothing. I nod and accept my punishment. All the

joy I felt less than an hour ago so far gone it feels like a distant memory.

And here I thought things couldn't possibly get more awkward on set. Except, this time, it's impossible to avoid my problems.

Well, *problem*.

I'm able to bypass going back to my trailer after shooting my first scene of the day—thankfully not with Miles or Jamila—by spending an extra twenty minutes deciding what fillings I want in my omelet at the crafty breakfast truck. Then I camp out in hair and makeup for another half hour between scenes since Gianna, my usual hairstylist, recently redid the deck of her house up in Westchester and has *plenty* of photos she wants to share. Who would've thought you could photograph wood from so many angles?

Avoiding Jamila may be exhausting, sure, and maybe a teeny, tiny bit immature, but it's the only choice I have. All my texts from that night at the club went unanswered, even the ones asking if she got home safely. It got to the point that I was worried something happened to her. I was convinced I'd show up to set on Monday to an announcement that Jamila had either gone missing or broken a leg heading down the subway steps, or some other travel-related catastrophe.

Instead, it's as normal a day as any. Except for my exhaustion and mega eye bags, everything is business as usual. I've basically been locked in my room since we got home on

Saturday, but sleep doesn't come easily when you have this much on your mind. Dad, Jerome, and I have done a great job of avoiding each other in an apartment that can barely fit one person comfortably.

Kevin's phone privileges were taken away by his mom—my aunt Alexia—once Dad told her the full story. While she didn't disapprove of him doing drag, she *definitely* didn't like that he'd snuck out behind her back to a place that served alcohol. My only human contact on Sunday is a video from Lily and Posie of them spread out on a beach in the South of France. A fresh reminder that I could've been with them, soaking up the sun and eating twenty-dollar cheese with fresh baguettes.

According to the call sheet, Jamila arrived an hour before me, and based on the lack of adjustments to our schedule for the day, she made it in one piece.

Not that I can confirm, since I haven't seen her.

After wrapping my last scene for the day, I make a beeline straight for the exit. No point in stopping by my trailer to wipe off my full face of makeup when I can easily do that once I'm home. While I can't avoid Jamila forever, considering we have a handful of scenes left together before we wrap next month, I can at least stay away from her until I'm able to think about the way she ran off on Saturday without feeling like I'll burst into tears.

"Marisol!" Esther calls out, chasing me down before I can slip off set unseen. "Rune made some adjustments to your scenes for tomorrow. I left the new script on the table in your trailer."

Well, there goes that plan. I give Esther a tight-lipped smile and "thank you" and head toward the trailers instead. No need to panic. Jamila's next scene isn't for another half hour, but that doesn't mean she's hanging out in the trailer. She could be grabbing lunch at the bistro she loves down the street or hanging with Miles or with the wardrobe department because one of the costumers always brings in fresh-baked cookies for Monday morning shoots.

But no. She's sitting smack in the front of the trailer when I walk in.

"Hi," she says, eyes locked on me the second I come through the door, as if she was waiting for me.

It's then that I spot the lack of a script on the dining table beside her. My brow furrows as I put the pieces together, realizing I may have walked directly into a trap. "Did you get Esther to trick me into coming here?"

"I need to talk to you," she says instead of directly answering my question, standing up but not approaching me.

I scoff, crossing my arms and leaning against the closed door behind me. The smart thing to do would be to leave, but she has this way of luring me in. "Doesn't seem like we have much to talk about."

"I'm sorry. I was an asshole on Saturday." Her eyes close as she exhales slowly, like she's doing a grounding exercise mid-conversation. "I . . . panicked."

"Because we kissed?"

That much should be obvious, but I don't understand it. I can understand if maybe I misread the vibes between us; I'd apologize for making her uncomfortable and be extremely embarrassed, but would move on nonetheless. What I can't understand is her completely ghosting me. To the point that she couldn't even tell me if she was alive. I'd spent all night lying awake in bed, waiting for her to text back.

"No. I—I mean yes. I mean . . . it's complicated."

"Are you not out?" I ask in a whisper, as if someone could overhear us, though it seems unlikely. There were several photos of her at different Pride events on her socials. Even the confidence she'd had when she told me she was a lesbian, and that there was nothing to worry about between her and Miles. Nothing about her has ever screamed "buried deep in the closet."

"No, I am. Everyone I know is well aware that I'm very, *very* gay. . . ." She collapses back onto the couch, running her hands down her face before looking back up at me. "When I first signed with my agent, I told her I really wanted to focus on queer roles. Characters that felt like me—the kind I didn't get to see growing up. And she said that was fine, we could try for those types of roles later down the road. But . . . not now."

I step farther into the trailer, though keep my guard up. "Why not now?"

"Because it's hard. Because there are barely any projects that have sapphic leads out there, and the ones that do wind up getting canceled after a season or two if they're lucky enough to get picked up."

"What does that have to do with us?"

Jamila swallows hard, avoiding my gaze to focus on her hands instead. "She said I should keep my personal life private. For a while."

"She's making you go back into the closet?!" I don't mean to say it as loud as I do. I also don't mean to launch myself

224

into the seat across from her, our knees almost touching and my hands almost grabbing hers to force her to look at me and get that this is *not* okay.

"No, I mean . . . I guess. Sort of?" Jamila groans, rubbing the back of her neck. "It's not like I can't tell anyone I'm a lesbian, but she doesn't want me shouting from the rooftop about my gayness. Or . . . dating anyone super publicly. She doesn't want me to be typecast into one role."

Then it clicks into place. Maybe if she'd kissed another girl that night, it wouldn't have been a problem. But she kissed me. A girl who couldn't even go to a nightclub without having to wear a disguise. Who has millions of followers and knows how to walk a red carpet like the back of her hand. Whose most recent breakup was splashed all over the news.

It's me. She shouldn't be dating someone like *me*.

I bristle, but don't say anything.

"That's bullshit," I mutter bitterly after several seconds of silence. Both because, duh, it is, and . . . because it sort of makes sense.

Delia is as intense an agent as they come, but my coming out didn't have much impact on the trajectory of my career. She threw a like on my post, commented a heart, and that was that. But I also already had a series regular role on one of the most successful teen dramas on cable. Plus, a longstanding relationship with one of TV's up-and-coming golden boys. My career was in its early days, but it wasn't in its infancy anymore. I had some level of clout—proof that I could play a cookie-cutter girl from the suburbs whose only experience with romance was falling for her male childhood best friend.

Jamila is starting from the bottom. *The Limit* will buy her a ton of favor in the industry, that I'm sure of, but it's impossible to say how far it will take her. With a performance like hers, she deserves every series regular role she reads for. Leads. Bigger casts, bigger buzz. But we all know this industry is fickle. Giving the best performance doesn't always guarantee you the lead roles. Especially if you're someone like Jamila—brown and (somewhat openly) queer.

"I know, but what am I supposed to do?" Jamila chokes out, her eyes glossy. A pang strikes through my heart. "She's an incredible agent. She got me this part and has lined up some serious auditions for me since then. And . . . maybe she's right." Jamila toys with her fingers again, picking at a burn on her ring finger. "It's unfair, but isn't that what everyone says about this industry? That it's unfair?"

The worst part is she's right, and we both know it.

I slide onto the couch beside her, wrap an arm around her trembling shoulders, and pull her close. She leans in until her head disappears in the curve of my neck. Her shallow breath is warm and wet against my skin, but I don't dwell on the chill that it sends down my spine. I focus on holding her, running my hand along her arm until her body relaxes into mine.

"So . . ." I pause, unsure how to continue. How to address the elephant in the room. "We shouldn't be . . . uh . . . involved. With each other."

Jamila snorts, and I'd be offended by her reaction if I wasn't so relieved to see her laugh. "Actually, I very much *do* want to be involved with you."

My hand stills above her elbow, gripping tighter than I mean to. "It feels like there's a *but* coming?"

Jamila nods, pulling away from my neck to face me. "But I'd

have to be careful. No posting about my personal life the way I usually would. No shouting from the rooftops that I kissed the most gorgeous girl I've ever met, even though I really want to. At least until people get to know me for me, not who I date." She tucks a loose lock of hair behind my ear, letting her fingers linger on my cheek. Flashes of Friday night rush through me like a riptide, igniting the same fire in my belly that pushed me to kiss her in the first place. "I know this is the norm for you. Avoiding paparazzi and fans and stuff, and I don't want you to feel like this is another part of your life that you have to hide. So . . . I get it. If you'd rather not. Y'know. Be involved with me."

For once, I listen to my body. I capture her lips with mine. There's a sharp, salty sting I don't remember from last night, and I wonder if she'd been crying before I found her. The thought makes me soften my touch, resting a hand on hers where it's laying in the space between us. She meets the force of my body with her own, entangling our fingers on the leather. It's not the same as Saturday night—slow and tender, like we want to savor every second of each other—but it still takes my breath away.

"I really, really want to be involved with you," I whisper against her lips when we part.

"Really?" I can feel the way her lips tug into a smile, and I press a kiss to the corner of her mouth before cupping her cheeks.

"Really."

When we kiss again, it's messy and off-center, and we're too distracted by laughing to fix our positioning, but we don't care because it's perfectly imperfect. It's hard to imagine a world where I don't shout about her to the world, don't sing her praises every day and post photos of her at golden hour. So much of my relationship with Miles was defined by what the world saw—the hidden glances, the way we smiled at each other from across a room, the photos we posted together after twenty minutes of careful posing.

And look where we are now.

This is a good thing, I tell myself as we pull apart to dive in for a less awkward kiss this time. Not the circumstances, but the privacy. Keeping this perfect thing to myself. Not letting the world pull it apart and dissect it and take it for themselves. We can learn who we are together at our own pace with no one watching over our shoulders. No articles, no media, no pressure. Just us and the way we make each other feel. I don't like the circumstances or the why behind it—that we have to hide ourselves so the industry we work in will accept us as blank slates.

But there can still be silver linings.

CHAPTER 19

The more my personal life thrives, the worse life on set becomes. Rune must have some kind of machine that senses whether or not I had a good night or weekend and decides how to best terrorize me the following day.

After spending the night watching a movie with Jamila over FaceTime—my saving grace now that I'm not allowed to leave the house and am avoiding Dad like the plague—I showed up to set exhausted but invigorated. Within ten minutes of stepping onto the lot, Rune declared that all phones were officially banned from set. Apparently, someone had leaked a couple pages of the first episode script, screwing the rest of us over by forcing us into total lockdown mode. By the end of the day, the PAs rolled out the new protocol: collecting our personal phones as we arrive and keeping them locked securely in a back office until we leave for the day.

The phone ban is more annoying than anything else. I've

gotten into the habit of texting Jamila whenever our shooting schedules don't overlap, sending her selfies and memes and dozens of random thoughts because she always seems to appreciate them. Unlike a certain ex of mine, who always told me off for being such an overzealous texter. Not that I'm comparing. Though it's nice to be able to text the person you're seeing to ask them if they'd like you if you were a worm and get an actual response (*only if I get to dress you up in cute little worm outfits*) instead of a dismissal (*why do you always ask such weird questions?*).

Our first day of shooting without access to our phones is boring and uneventful. Our schedules never line up, so Jamila and I can't even sneak away to our trailer for some time alone before we wrap for the day. On the few days that we're shooting on location, exploring the area surrounding our base camp isn't anywhere near as fun without her. I don't have many scenes this week, and the ones I do have are with Miles, while she has to spend most of her week with her on-screen parents and Dawn. Better her than me, though. One saving grace is how little Dawn's character interacts on-screen with mine.

Being a few feet away from Jamila but never getting to communicate, much less touch her, is frustrating—especially when we've finally admitted that we're . . . something. We're figuring out what that something is. With lots of kissing. So much kissing.

Thankfully, Jamila, bless her, is an innovator.

"This is for you." Esther hands me a folded-up piece of notebook paper.

"Who's it from?" I ask as I unfold it, bracing myself for yet another one of Rune's weird directorial habits to emerge.

Esther shrugs coyly, suddenly becoming extremely interested in the empty bottle of water on the table beside me.

Written in loopy handwriting so pristine it could easily be a font, is a short message.

Hi, you're cute :)

My cheeks flare as I glance up from the note toward the bedroom set on the opposite end of the room. Jamila and Miles are debriefing with Rune after their latest run-through of their first scene of the day. For a flash of a second, Jamila looks away from Rune, long enough to give me a blink-and-you'll-miss-it wink before turning her attention fully back to him.

I quickly scribble back a message of my own, folding the paper up again and handing it back to Esther.

"I'm not a messenger pigeon, you know," she replies while tucking the note into the breast pocket of her flannel.

"It'll be the last one, I promise," I say with my best puppy-dog pout.

Esther gives in with a grumble, stomping off to deliver my message.

It is not the last one. Sorry, Esther.

To be fair, Jamila and I spread our messenger duties among the rest of the production crew. Sometimes we even pass them ourselves, sliding notes into each other's hands as we pass by, holding back smiles and lingering touches. It becomes a running joke between us and the crew—that they're aiding the star-crossed lovers, kept apart by a lack of cell phones. Slowly, we push the boundaries. A week after we start sending the notes, Jamila's hand twitches toward mine beneath the picnic table we've settled at for lunch. I don't bother hiding my smile as we link our fingers out of view of our castmates. Subtle touches evolve into stolen kisses, quick and breathless behind closed doors. Longer when we're in the privacy of our trailer.

It's not very discreet, but Jamila assures me that she doesn't mind. Set is our own little world where we're free to be ourselves.

"We're allowed to have this," she says one afternoon as we lounge together on the pull-out bed in our trailer, trading slow kisses and careful touches. "Our little utopia."

Our little utopia quickly becomes the highlight of my day. Suddenly, I don't mind not having my phone every minute of the day anymore. Not when I can spend that time writing terrible sonnets about the way Jamila's eyes sparkle like a sunrise on the back of Chipotle receipts or letting her play with my hair while I rest my head in her lap.

This morning, I was too busy shamelessly gazing into said eyes to actually hear what she was saying to me.

"Does that work?" she asks, bringing me back to reality.

I quickly shake myself off and scan the set of questions Fatima wrote up for the senior staff writer who will be interviewing Jamila for her profile piece in *Hollywood Today*. Jamila was panicked about the idea of her first-ever professional interview, even if it had been set up by her sister, so I took up my celebrity-guru mantle once again to show her how it's done.

Except I'm obviously very distracted by her eyes. And her lips. And her everything.

"Try relaxing," I suggest, remembering how stiff she was when she started answering the first question on the list (How did you get your start in acting?). She sounded like she was reading off a teleprompter. I can definitely understand nerves getting the best of you—it happened to me plenty of times early in my career. "And be yourself. Remember that you can always stop and start over again if you have to. This isn't on camera, and these questions are all written by someone you know and trust."

I know it's easier said than done. But Jamila gives me a nod and prepares to start her answer over again when a large group of crew members wheel an enormous white wooden box onto set.

"What's that for?" I whisper out of the corner of my mouth.

"No idea. It's not in any of my scenes." She quickly flips through her script, confirming that there's no spooky box involved in anything she needs to shoot today.

I'm about to flip through my own script when Rune appears from behind the box. "Marisol!" he calls out, beckoning for me to come join him.

That can't be good.

Jamila and I exchange a worried look as I slowly slide off my director's chair. During one of our rambling trailer conversations, after she'd told me about a car accident she'd been involved in as a kid that left her still terrified of driving, I'd told her about my claustrophobia. A nervous reaction that developed over time after I accidentally got stuck in Mom's closet when I was five. Jamila reaches out before I can walk away, giving my hand a reassuring squeeze—not caring who might see. Off to our right, Dawn finally glances up from her script to watch me make my way to set. Naturally, today is the day when she wants to acknowledge our existence.

"We've made a couple changes to your scene for the day," Rune explains once I approach. Miles stands a few feet away, eyeing us curiously.

That's not surprising, but the presence of the box definitely is. I quickly scan my script again. Besides a couple of moments with Miles, Jamila, and Dawn, the only other scene I have is on my own. After an argument about my meddling in his life, Miles's character winds up locking me in his bedroom to try to slip away and meet up with Jamila's.

"We want to really emphasize the upset and terror you feel when Will abandons you. We're going for a more stylistic approach—an all-black, windowless moment. So we'll have you in here." He pauses to gesture to the box, which stands well over fifteen feet tall, nearly touching the spotlights hanging above us, but it can't be any bigger than five feet wide.

Fear rockets through my body, sweat breaking out across my forehead and hands within seconds. "O-oh, well—"

"She's claustrophobic," Miles cuts in before I can finish, saving me from having to explain myself. "Can't she do the scene in the bedroom like we originally planned?"

I didn't expect Miles to jump to my aid, but I'm grateful either way. He stands firm beside me, presenting a united front. The more I study the stark white box towering behind Rune, the woozier I feel. Having someone beside me to potentially hold for balance is reassuring. The last thing I need is to pass out in front of half the cast and crew.

Rune's rare smile falters and morphs into a frown. He

doesn't sneer at Miles the way he often does at me, his expression calmer and measured as he tightens his grip on the rolled-up script in his hand. "It'd be best if she did the scene according to our *new* plan. For the integrity of my artistic vision."

Miles's mouth opens, but no words come out. I'm not sure how to respond either, how to argue against Rune's "artistic vision."

"And you *did* agree to being locked in tight spaces," Rune adds, holding up a copy of the form I'd filled out at my audition months ago. One question pops out.

Would you feel comfortable being locked in an
enclosed space for up to ten minutes?

Goddammit. I knew I should've said no.

"Are we sure this is necessary?" Jamila chimes in, having raced over from her seat. She gently grasps my arm, standing opposite me so I'm safely squeezed in a "my ex and my current girlfriend" sandwich. Which would feel hilariously awkward if I didn't feel like I was seconds from passing out.

"Doesn't seem that complex to me," Dawn chimes in, as if we asked for her opinion.

She preens when Rune gives her an appreciative smile before he turns to us, his expression morphing into a frown. "Well, why don't we see what Marisol thinks?"

The venom in his voice makes it clear I *don't* have a choice here. I've already caused enough trouble on set with him—from my colorful outfits to my issues learning lines to my migraine-inducing perfume. I've already gotten three strikes, and I can't risk another one. Esther's words from our first week of filming echo in my ears. About how it's practically a rite of passage for him to fire you. She'd been talking about PAs, but that doesn't ease the panic swirling in my gut. What's stopping him from getting rid of me next?

I can't get kicked off the show now. Not when I busted my ass to get here, then worked even harder to stay here. It's more than a matter of pride at this point. As frustrating as this experience has been, I know I'm giving a career-best performance here. The kind that could completely change the trajectory of my career—set me up for award nominations and lead roles with the type of directors who would've scoffed at my résumé two months ago. I'm not willing to give up and have all my hard work go to waste.

Besides, I can take this as another opportunity to prove myself as a performer—as terrifying as it might feel. While my stunts on *Avalon Grove* were limited, I was always eager to take them on myself. This is simply another stunt. A much, much, much tighter and darker and eerier stunt. I'm here to push myself out of my comfort zone, though—and what better way to do that than by putting myself in the least comfortable place possible?

"I—I can do it," I stammer, doing my best to hide the tremor in my voice.

Rune either doesn't notice or doesn't care, but Jamila and Miles certainly do. While Rune whips around, calling out instructions for the crew to get everything set up for the shoot, Miles and Jamila turn to face me.

"Mari," Miles whispers, "you don't have to do this."

To my right, Jamila nods in agreement. "We can try to talk to him again. Or get one of the producers to step in, or—"

"I've got it," I interject, my voice more confident this time. I've mastered the art of learning lines on the fly. I've also learned how to harness my inner mean girl through my character. This is another thing to check off the list of my developing acting skills. "Seriously, I'll be fine."

Jamila and Miles don't seem convinced. They look at one another, having an unspoken conversation with their eyes and the twitch of their mouths before Rune shouts for everyone to clear set for shooting.

Before they leave, Jamila reaches for my hand one more time, the pressure of her fingers in mine comforting enough to ground me for a few seconds. "You'll be okay. Remember to breathe," she says, holding my gaze until I give her a nod before letting go and returning to her seat. She shoots Dawn a glare as she does.

As I approach the box, I glance over my shoulder at where Jamila and Miles are settled back down in their seats on the sidelines. There's something calming in seeing them there. Knowing they're only a few feet away.

But that peace goes out the window as I step into the dark, narrow box. The set designer carved a narrow hole for me to enter through, which casts the box in total darkness as soon as it's sealed shut again. Above me, a bright white light flicks on, bathing me in the most unflattering lighting known to man. It doesn't do much to ease the tension. Each of the walls is painted black, making the space feel more like an endless void than an enclosed space. Which is even more terrifying to think about.

"There are cameras to your left and right," Rune calls out, his voice muffled from the plywood holding the box together. I glance up, blinded by the lights above me, and spot a small blinking red light before I flinch away, black spots clouding my vision. "Don't pay attention to them, though," Rune continues. "Focus on your emotions. The rage."

I nod numbly as the voices beyond the box fade into a hum. Vague murmurs about cameras rolling, a call for quiet on the set, and finally, action.

Get it together, Marisol.

The room is silent. I can only hear my heart pounding in my ears, the blood rushing through me as I lift my hands to the wall in front of me, hitting once, then twice, to make sure it's steady. Panic travels up my throat until I worry I'll be sick, tears stinging and blurring the world in front of me. But it doesn't matter. There's nothing to see anyway.

I've got this, I've got this, I've got this.

I repeat the words to myself until they begin to lose meaning. This is just like my first day on set when I panicked about all of Rune's line adjustments. Or the time I had to pretend to fall out a window for that holiday rom-com. I'll be fine—I'm always fine. If Miles or Jamila or Dawn was asked to do this, they'd do it without any protest, so I should too.

All the confidence I work up leaks out of me the second Rune shouts that we're rolling.

I can't remember any of my lines, what this scene is about, or why I'm here. Instead, I'm reliving the choking feeling of being trapped in that closet thirteen years ago. Pounding on the doors with my tiny fists while I cried until my throat gave in.

Collapsing in a heap on the floor, holding one of Mom's dresses to my nose and letting the smell of her perfume comfort me to sleep. The way Mom wailed when she found me, cradling me to her chest as she cried that she thought she lost me.

I'm not sure when I start screaming. I'm not even sure if anyone on the other side of the box can hear me. My skin burns from my fists colliding with the walls, my throat raw as I let all of my fear pour out of me. I swear the room starts closing in on me, the space getting tighter and stuffier with every passing second. It's hard to breathe, and my chest tightens to the point that my screams turn into gasps for breath.

Every part of me is trembling as I'm pulled out of the box by a team of PAs; a flock of producers and more PAs surround me with portable fans and water bottles. My screams finally die down as my eyes adjust to the sudden burst of light. I can't make out anything among the jumbled voices talking over each other except for my own desperate gasps for breath.

"I need a minute," I manage to say, operating on instinct as I scramble to my feet. The crowd parts for me like I'm infected, no one following as I stumble my way off the set and out to the sidewalk.

Free of the building, I suck in desperate gulps of fresh summer air and collapse against the wall behind me, letting my eyes slip closed. I let my senses ground me. Cars honking, birds chirping, dishes clanking at the bistro across the street. Motor oil and car exhaust, fresh bread and something deep-fried. Cinnamon and clove.

My eyes fly open to find Jamila standing in front of me.

She runs a hand through my hair, then down my cheek,

scanning my body like she's checking for injuries. "Are you okay?"

I muster a weak "mmm-hmm" before my body collapses into hers and I weakly grip at the hem of her shirt for purchase. She has enough strength for both of us, wrapping her arms around me and holding me against her where I feel warm and soft and *safe*.

"You're okay," she whispers, this time against the crown of my head. "Esther said you can go home for the day. We'll deal with Rune."

Relief floods through me, making my body sag more than I thought was possible. I stifle a sob as I nod slowly. I've never wanted to go home to my dad's cramped apartment so badly. To curl up on my air mattress with Bruiser, letting Dad and Jerome comfort me with sliced fruit and words of affirmation.

The tenderness of Jamila's touch is suddenly gone as someone appears at her side. Miles, I realize as I quickly wipe my damp cheeks.

"H-hey," Jamila says, shoving the hands that were cradling my cheeks seconds earlier into her pockets. "I was telling Mari she can go home for the day."

But Miles doesn't hear Jamila's explanation. If he notices anything off about us or how close we were standing, he doesn't let it show as he rushes up to me, puts a hand on my shoulder, and examines me closely.

"How're you feeling?" he asks, not waiting for a response before continuing. "Were you able to do your breathing exercises? Do you need me to run through them with you?"

It's unusually touching—knowing he remembers how to calm me down after a claustrophobia-induced panic attack—

and the closest we've been in months. But my stomach doesn't flutter the way it used to whenever Miles held me tight. Now all I can do is peer over his shoulder at Jamila. She pulls her hands out of her pockets to shove them under her armpits, unsure what to do with herself, averting her gaze. As though we need privacy.

As though he's still the person who knows me best.

"I'm okay," I assure him with a nod and a tight-lipped smile. "Just gonna head home and go to bed, probably."

"You're sure?" Miles doesn't back away even after I nod again, but he does let go of my shoulder. "Text me if you need anything, okay?"

"I will," I reply, even though I know I won't. After the breakup, I'd gone off the deep end and assumed Miles didn't care about me whatsoever, which was maybe unfair to him, but I was hurt and in a delicate place. At least now I know that he is in my corner. In his own way.

"Don't let Rune get to you, okay?" he says before walking away.

Jamila's stiff posture relaxes once Miles is out of view. She glances over her shoulder, checking that no one else is coming to check in on me, before closing the distance between us, cupping my face and running her thumb across the apple of my damp cheeks.

"I've got you," she says, so quiet I almost don't hear it.

I kiss her, letting the smell of her wrap around me like a blanket that'll shield me from the fear lingering inside me. We hold on to each other for probably longer than we should. We know we're safe for now, but someone could come outside any minute. And yet we can't find it in ourselves to pull away.

She rests her forehead against mine, our noses gently brushing. "FaceTime tonight? We can watch whatever movie you want."

I nod, releasing a shaky laugh. "Okay," I reply, even though I don't want to let her go. Thankfully, she lingers for a few more minutes, waiting until I've ordered my Uber to head back inside. As much as I want to be home, even the thought of the car ride there makes my stomach ache. Because in the silence of the backseat, there won't be any escape from the worry now swirling through my mind.

That I've pissed off Rune for the final time.

CHAPTER 20

My acting skills save me from having to tell Dad and Jerome the truth. When I blame my general unease on period cramps, they immediately clam up and leave me be, returning with a hot-water bottle, dark chocolate, and an offer to bring dinner to my room. Jamila shouldn't be home for another hour, so I'm killing time watching mindless YouTube videos. I'm considering grabbing a serving of the Impossible Meat ropa vieja Abuela dropped off for us yesterday—she's convinced I've been eating rabbit food whenever she's not around to feed me herself—when Dad reappears in my doorway.

"Hey, munchkin," he singsongs after knocking on the cracked-open door, unusually chipper for someone who grounded me not that long ago. "You doing okay?"

I set aside my computer to peer up at him from my cocoon of blankets, where Bruiser's fast asleep on my lap. "I'll survive," I reply, poking out a hand from under the sheets to scratch the top of her head.

"Great, great," Dad mumbles, staring down at his shoes. "So, you have a visitor, actually."

Immediately, I perk up. I don't think it's Jamila because she was scheduled to be shooting until at least eight tonight, and it's barely past seven. Kevin, like me, is still grounded and forbidden to leave his apartment past five. Even to visit his favorite cousin.

"It's, uh . . . Miles," Dad says cautiously, interrupting my brainstorm.

Oh. Well, can't say I saw that coming.

"I can tell him you're not up to seeing anyone if you want," he continues, almost too eagerly. Like he's dying to kick Miles to the curb. "We'll let him down easy."

"N-no, it's fine. He can come in."

Dad frowns, his brows knitting together. "You're sure?" Over his shoulder, I spot Jerome peering out from their bedroom, mouthing "We can make him leave" to me.

"Yeah, I'm sure."

Dad doesn't seem convinced but doesn't argue either way. With a sigh, he heads back toward the door, and I do my best to make myself look presentable. There's not much that can be done about the Cheeto dust on my fingers and staining my comforter cocoon, but Bruiser does a very helpful job of licking up most of it once I accidentally jostle her awake. I wipe my fingers on a napkin, toss my hair into a messy bun, readjust my *Avalon Grove* hoodie, and shove my laptop beneath a pillow before Miles can see that I was considering renting *The Prince Who Saved Christmas*.

Seeing him in the doorway to my cramped bedroom is startling. His designer short-sleeve sweater and three-hundred-dollar sneakers are a stark contrast to the chipped paint on the walls and bite marks in the door from Bruiser throwing a fit last week.

"Hey," he says, giving me a wave with his free hand—a cardboard box in the other—but remaining outside of the room. "Mind if I come in?"

"If you can find space." I scoop Bruiser up, clearing enough room for Miles to cram himself onto the edge of the bed. He looks like he's been shoved into a clown car, his shoulders up to his ears and all six feet of his legs pressed up to his chest like he's trying to curl into a fetal position.

"You never texted, so I brought you these . . . in case your day got worse," he says before I can ask him why he's here. He sets the box down between us.

Bruiser leaps into action, eagerly sniffing the box with intrigue as I examine the logo printed along the lid.

"You went to Doughnut Plant?"

I don't bother waiting for an explanation before throwing the box open, unveiling six of the most beautiful doughnuts I've ever seen. Ages ago, I spent my (unemployed) nights researching places Miles and I would go to when I came to visit him in the city. Museums and coffee shops and jazz clubs and a dozen different restaurants and bakeries. Doughnut Plant was at the top of the list.

"You mentioned you hadn't tried them yet," he says with a shy smile, shoving his hands into his pockets.

Warmth rushes through me. I'm touched that he remembers something I said in passing to Esther during lunch last week. In the dim light of the sunset, I see the boy I fell in love with. The one who drove through peak LA traffic to bring me to the beach. Who learned the lyrics to every single Olivia Rodrigo song so we could belt them together on the drive home. Who grew up with me, who taught me what it means to love and be loved.

Hard as I might try to deny it, that boy hasn't gone anywhere. Changed—matured in ways that floor me—but the same, deep down.

"Thank you," I whisper, not trusting my voice not to crack before helping myself to a black-and-white doughnut, moaning around my first bite.

"As good as you thought?" he asks with a chuckle.

"Better." Instead of wolfing down the rest in two more bites, I split the doughnut in half, handing the unbitten side to him.

While Bruiser attempts to nab a piece from me, silence settles between the two of us. The question of why he's here—and with doughnuts, no less—hanging in the air.

"I'm sorry about today," he says finally, after I've finished my first doughnut and started on a second.

My hand stalls, a PB&J doughnut midway to my lips. "For what?"

"For not standing up for you."

"But you did?"

"I could've fought harder, though," he insists, frowning. "We filled out that form ages ago, and we didn't know what it was for. He can't hold you to that."

Slowly, I lower my doughnut, but make sure to keep it out of Bruiser's greedy, wet reach. "It could've been worse."

It's a half-hearted lie and we both know it. My time on

The Limit hasn't been easy, but today was by far the worst. I'll gladly never wear pink for the rest of my life if it means I don't have to be locked in that box again.

Well . . . maybe give up pink for a year.

Miles shifts closer to me, the mattress groaning and sagging beneath his weight. Bruiser quickly abandons her doughnut endeavors to crawl into his lap, pawing at his hoodie until he cradles her like a newborn baby, the way he always did whenever he came to visit. She closes her eyes, nuzzling happily into his hand when he scratches beneath her chin. Seeing her so happy and comfortable shouldn't make tears prickle the corners of my eyes, but it does. Realizing that I'm not the only one who has missed having Miles in my life.

"You can leave the show, you know," Miles says after Bruiser has had her fill of pets and has fallen back asleep in his arms. "Rune has been a dick to you, and you don't deserve to be treated like that."

"I can't leave," I protest, pulling my knees up to my chest and hugging my arms around them. "He'll blacklist me. I'll never get another role like this again."

"He can't do that. Sure, he has clout, but he doesn't own Hollywood," he says with a roll of his eyes, though I highly doubt that's true. We both know from experience that everyone knows everyone. For an industry that claims to always be welcoming in new talent, it's small as hell. And in a world this small, Rune has plenty of power behind him. "And I thought you weren't interested in these types of shows anyway?"

"Well, I wasn't," I mutter bitterly, considering biting my tongue before I say anything I'll regret. "Until *someone* called me unserious to *Stars Weekly*."

Whoops.

Actually, no. It feels good to finally call Miles out. Air it out in private instead of over text or in hushed whispers on set. Months have gone by, and I can't shake off the hurt of him going behind my back and telling the media about our breakup before I even had time to process it. Like he was orchestrating one of the lowest moments of my life behind the scenes for weeks.

"Shit . . ." he mutters, running a hand through his hair. "I'm sorry, Mari. I didn't mean it like that, I swear."

I don't say anything because I'm not sure if I believe him. As I replay that night in my mind yet again, it's impossible to figure out how he *didn't* mean it that way.

"My reps wrote up that statement for me, and I didn't know how else to say that we broke up, so I went with what they suggested," he says, and the softness of his voice convinces me that he probably is telling the truth. It's impossible to reconcile the boy who was my first love with the boy who crushed me in a matter of minutes, but I'm starting to understand now. Maybe the boy I loved was buried under that awful breakup speech after all, following orders instead of speaking from his heart.

"So your reps told you to break up with me?"

The thought feels like a gut punch. First Jamila, and now possibly Miles—the industry that's given me everything I've ever wanted, determined to get in the way of me falling for the people who make me feel light as air and warm as sunshine.

Does Hollywood have a vendetta against me? Is it because I said matcha is overrated?

"No!" he replies a bit too quickly, as if he was eagerly waiting to break up with me instead of getting nudged into it by his team. "I mean . . . we both saw it coming, didn't we?"

My gaze drops to my kneecaps, vision blurring for what feels like the hundredth time today. "No." I pause. "Did you tell anyone you were thinking about breaking up with me? An insider for that article said we'd been on the rocks for months."

Miles sighs, taking his time responding. "Maybe one of the guys from the show? I . . . I thought we were going in different directions. Me coming here. You staying back in LA. Without *Avalon Grove*, we barely saw each other, and I figured it'd be easier to do a clean break while we were on good terms before we attempted long distance and things got worse."

"What if they didn't get worse, though?" I ask, voice hoarse.

It doesn't matter now—shouldn't matter. While I've moved past him, the piece of me that loved him still has a dozen questions. The girl who showed up to Capri that night thinking she'd come home with some leftover tiramisu, not a broken heart, is curious.

He shrugs, leaning back against the cracked open window behind him, staring up at the lazily spinning ceiling fan. "I guess we'll never know."

We let that sit out in the open. The final remnants of who we used to be, finally put to rest. Something I never thought I'd say comes to the forefront of my mind as I snuggle back into my cocoon and think about everything that's happened this summer.

I'm glad Miles broke up with me. If he hadn't, maybe I would be that girl he worried I'd become. Hung up on her long-distance boyfriend, waiting around for the day she gets to visit him. Life now isn't perfect by any means, but at least I challenged myself. I came to a city I barely knew, lived with the family I knew even less, and pushed myself to tackle the type of role I never thought I was capable of performing. I pushed myself to my limits—no pun intended—and learned how strong I am in the process. I refused to let the world underestimate me.

I met a girl and kissed her on the dance floor. A girl I can't believe thinks I'm as beautiful as she is.

After everything, this breakup brought me a new life, a chance to reconnect with my family. To get to know my dad and Jerome and Abuela and Kevin.

To be with Jamila.

"We're older now, Mari," Miles continues when I don't respond. "We're different people than we were at fourteen, and that's a *good* thing. I didn't mean to make you feel ashamed because our tastes aren't the same. All I wanted was for you to be happy—to pursue whatever it is you wanted to do. Even if that didn't involve me."

I nod in understanding, wiping at the few tears that managed to slip down my cheeks. I'm not *not* pissed that he thought he got to decide that for me, but less so now that I know he wasn't throwing salt in the wound at the same time. Maybe I'll always be a little bitter about the breakup. But at least I don't feel the need to think back and wonder what we could've been anymore.

"I'm sorry for coming here," I say, wiping my cheek. "I know it was weird, but . . . I got so in my head about everything. I wanted to prove that I wasn't what you, and others, thought I was."

"I'm sorry I made you think you had anything to prove,"

he says softly, shifting closer until his hand is resting on my knee. "There's nothing wrong with *Avalon Grove*. With those rom-coms you auditioned for—and should've booked, by the way. *The Limit* isn't better because it's won a few awards."

"A lot of awards," I interject.

"Even a lot of awards." He chuckles, shoving me playfully. "What matters is what *you* want to do. And if you don't want to work on this show anymore, that's okay."

"Thanks, Miles." I sniffle, wiping at my runny nose with the sleeve of my hoodie, not dwelling on how gross I must look. "That means a lot."

Miles gives me that smile—the same one that made me fall for him four years ago. It doesn't make my heart race the way it used to, but I can't deny that it's a pretty stunning smile. His face moves in closer to mine, his eyes slowly slip closed as he goes to cup my cheek, and—

Wait, what?!

I leap out of bed, nearly tripping over my tangle of blankets in my rush to get out of the path of Miles's puckered lips. "Whoa, whoa—"

"Oh God, my bad, I'm sorry," Miles apologizes, jumping off the bed too and pressing himself to the opposite wall as he runs a frantic hand through his hair. "I—I thought we had a vibe going and—"

"I'm with Jamila," I blurt out before I can consider the consequences of telling him. Jamila asked if I wanted her to share the news with Miles on our behalf, but I told her I'd rather give it some time. Let us all move on from our nightmarish breakup before dropping the bomb that I'm dating *his* love interest.

"Oh. Wow. That's . . . wow." Miles lets out a humorless but not unkind laugh. He shakes his head, clearly struggling to deal with the whiplash of what I've told him. "Congrats?"

"Thanks?" I reply, both of us turning our statements into questions.

Miles runs both hands down his face, groaning as he pulls his blemish-free skin down like he's a melting Halloween mask.

"We're trying to keep things low-key."

"Right. Totally. Your secret's safe with me." He holds up a pair of crossed fingers. "Scout's honor."

The silence returns, and not the thoughtful kind. Miles shifts awkwardly, running a hand down his jacket as he eyes the doorway. Down the hall, I spot Jerome poking his head out from the kitchen again, backing away when he realizes I instantly spotted him.

Finally, Miles turns around to face me again instead of staring at the wall and holds out his hand. "Friends?"

I bite back a laugh when I notice how intensely his hand is shaking. Like he's settling a deal with the devil instead of asking his ex to be friends again. I pull him into a hug. "Only if you keep bringing me doughnuts."

STARS WEEKLY

EXCLUSIVE: *AVALON GROVE* STAR MARISOL POLLY-RODRIGUEZ SPOTTED KISSING MYSTERY WOMAN
BY EMERALD ROWE

It seems Marisol Polly-Rodriguez has *definitely* moved on from costar Miles Zhao. In new photos submitted by an anonymous source to *Stars Weekly*, Polly-Rodriguez is seen tenderly embracing an unknown woman. The photos came just a few weeks after Polly-Rodriguez and Zhao announced the end of their nearly four-year-long relationship. With Zhao and Polly-Rodriguez both starring in the second season of *The Limit* together, this is certain to stir things up between the two—if it hasn't already.

"She's there to win him back for sure," says an anonymous source who claims to have worked on set of *The Limit* season two.

Well, one thing is for certain—she's definitely not kissing Zhao in these new photos. Is this a post-breakup fling? Or a plot to make Zhao jealous?

COMMENTS

Lol well that was fast

NOOOOOOOO MY MILESOL HEART

How is this news???

Girl slow down you've been single for like 2 minutes

good for her!!!!! miles treated her terribly, she deserves
someone new

GO OFF MY SAPPHIC QUEEN

Why does that girl she's kissing seem so familiar??

CHAPTER 21

I wake up the next morning to a stomachache and three missed calls and a text from Delia.

> Call me ASAP

That was from ten minutes ago. I don't bother scrolling through the rest of my notifications; I immediately sit up and call her. Whatever this is about, it must be seriously important for her to be calling me at four in the morning LA time.

"You're in the news again," Delia says in lieu of a greeting, back to business as usual.

"Is that a good thing?" I ask, even though, based on her tone, it isn't. Though the rest of my team isn't with her this time. So at least it isn't catastrophically bad. Or good, for that matter.

"You tell me."

Before I can ask what she means, my phone buzzes with a new text from her. A link to an article on *Stars Weekly*. Dread rushes through me, along with a sense of déjà vu. The last time I opened one of these links, it led me to an article plastered with photos of me mid–emotional breakdown.

This article is no different. A photo is the focal point—blurry this time, at least. No HD close-ups of the snot on my upper lip. It's hard to make out the details at first, but the site does me the courtesy of zooming in about a hundred times until the blocky pixels start to take on a more recognizable shape.

Me, kissing Jamila outside of set yesterday.

"Shit."

"Good shit or bad shit?" Delia asks, already typing at top speed.

"Bad shit," I mumble, scanning the article to confirm there aren't any more pictures. Luckily, it's only the one.

Even luckier, Jamila isn't visible.

My mind goes straight to her. All you can make out from the photo is the back of her head, her curls tied up in a messy bun instead of down her back like usual. She's not so public a persona that people can immediately identify her—not yet, at least. But it wouldn't be hard to connect the dots. Our head shots side by side in the cast announcement. Her thick dark brown curls woven through my fingers. It's only a matter of time before someone figures it out, if they haven't already. . . .

What also strikes me as odd is the angle. The photo is blurry, thanks to it being taken through a pane of glass, but there's no denying that it was taken from inside the building where we were shooting. Most likely from the doorway a few inches away from where we were standing.

Which means someone from *The Limit* took this. Someone who had a way to get access to our phones.

"I can try to get this taken down, but no guarantees," Delia says with a sigh. "*Stars Weekly* would rather eat their own asses than retract an article."

She reassures me that this isn't the end of the world, making a promise to call me back if she can get the article taken down. As soon as we hang up, I immediately text Jamila.

> We need to talk

In retrospect, I definitely could've worded that text better.

"I thought you were breaking up with me," she hisses once we find each other on set later that morning.

"Sorry, sorry," I mutter, doing my best to keep my voice to a whisper despite the panic coursing through me. I'd made sure to follow up my text with a link to the article, but apparently, I didn't do it fast enough.

Jamila leads me to a darkened corner on the opposite end of the room, behind a stack of ten-foot-high plywood, shielding us from view. We don't have enough time to make it back to our trailer before she's needed for her first scene of the day, but we can't wait around to talk about this. The PAs haven't come around to collect our phones yet, so I pull up the article where it's already open in my search tab and hand it to Jamila. She sighs and toys with her curls as she scans the headline.

"At least they can't tell it's you," I offer, but my voice doesn't sound very convincing. "My agent's working to get it taken down," I add, leaving off the part about her not making any promises.

Jamila remains quiet, eyes glued to the blown-up photo of an unfamiliar hand cradling my jaw, running their thumb across my lip.

"Someone from the crew must've taken this," she says, noting the same thing I did when I first saw the photo.

"Or the cast," I add. I'd like to think our castmates would understand the value of privacy, but we can't rule anyone out. "But I have no idea who."

Jamila bites her lips, glancing past my shoulder where everyone is buzzing to set up for the first scene of the day. The thought that someone here—anyone—could've set us up for disaster sets me on edge. I already struggled to feel comfortable here. Now there's no shot of that.

"I think—"

"Marisol! Jamila!" Rune cuts Jamila off.

Despite being hidden, we jump apart and keep our hands to ourselves. We exchange a worried look, and I wish I could loop our fingers together again, give hers a reassuring squeeze the way she did for me, as we step out from our hiding spot.

Rune is in the center of the room, holding a stack of papers in his clenched fist. A circle clears around him, the crew backing out of his warpath as he scans the room for his targets—for *us*. When he finally spots us in the crowd, my body tenses, freezes as he starts storming toward us like a heat-seeking missile.

"Care to explain *this?*" he spits, throwing down the stack of papers onto a table to our left. It's a printed-out copy of the article—the paper so crumpled you can hardly make out the headline.

"We—"

Rune doesn't let me finish, snatching the papers back off the table before Jamila can even begin. Apparently, the question was rhetorical.

"We assembled this cast the way we did for a reason," Rune announces to the room like he's delivering a speech. "Chemistry. Dynamics. *This*"—he points to the grainy photo— "interrupts those dynamics. *No* dating between castmates, between crewmates, between *anyone* on this set. Do you understand?!" he shouts, spit flying from his mouth and onto a nearby camera.

The room is so silent you can hear a pin drop. My mind races, unsure what this means. Is he demanding Jamila and I break up? Is he even allowed to do that? Rules on set are one thing, but dictating what we do with our personal lives doesn't seem fair, even for Hollywood.

A throat clears tentatively, and the entire room turns in the direction of the sound, every eye suddenly on Miles. He fumbles under the rapid influx of attention, his cheeks flushing when Rune fixes his gaze on him next.

"Actually," he says diplomatically, clearing his throat again and speaking louder this time, his voice echoing through the room. "Marisol and I dated before we were cast on the show, and our relationship hasn't ever caused any issue with the 'dynamics' of the cast. Now or then."

God bless Miles for being the voice of reason. I'd bear-hug him if I wasn't too terrified to move.

"Why do you think I cast her?" Rune replies, brushing him off with a wave of his hand. "She's the primary antagonist of the series. What better way to bring that to life than with two people with *real* tension?" he says as if that's a totally normal way to cast a show—to use our personal lives as fuel for our on-screen relationship.

I swallow hard, realizing what this means. That maybe I didn't get this role after all. Or at least not the way I thought I did. Based on merit and my performance ability. I got it because I was Miles's ex-girlfriend.

Rune has never operated logically—that much has been clear since day one. But this takes things to a whole new level. We're fighting a losing battle. There's no way we'll ever be able to convince him to change his mind, because he never wants to admit that he's wrong.

And no one ever tries to stop him.

"This seems a bit intense, though, doesn't it?" another voice says, to my surprise. It's one of the adult actors—Miles's character's dad—who chimes in, sitting up from his own director's chair, cup of coffee still in hand. He says it casually, the way only a seasoned pro can. Someone who's seen their fair share of overly demanding directors.

"They're kids," the actress who plays my mom adds. Coming to my defense like she's my off-screen mom too.

"And they've been together for weeks," a PA chimes in, someone who ran our notes back and forth for us. "No one has noticed anything off about the dynamic."

There's a general murmur of agreement throughout the room, both from our castmates and the crew. Esther, to Rune's left, nods hard enough to make her topknot come loose. Hope swells through me as I take in the dozens of nodding heads, finally turning to Jamila. Her attention is still so focused on Rune that she startles when I reach for her hand. For a moment, I expect her to pull away, but she doesn't. She smiles and steps closer to me, our linked fingers pressed between us. We can stand up to him, put an end to his tyranny for good. Together.

But not everyone stands in support of us.

"It's incredibly unprofessional," Dawn interjects, hopping off her director's chair to step between us and Rune. "We should be focused on our performances. Making sure we have our lines memorized and ready to go. Not making out between scenes."

She doesn't direct this at me, but her target is clear. It's a not-at-all subtle jab at my struggles to keep up with Rune's line adjustments. My nails dig into my palm as I clench my fists to keep myself from screaming. What the hell is her problem? What did we ever do to her to make her think she's so much better than us? All we've ever done is be nice to her—even when she clearly didn't deserve it.

Suddenly, a thought hits me. An accusation that I wouldn't make out loud but that my gut tells me must be true. That *Dawn* is the one who took the photo. I wouldn't put it past her to insist on getting her phone back. Or even having more than one on her.

"I know my script back to front," she preens before I can

figure out a way to voice my thought without outright accusing her. "Everyone's lines. Not just mine. *That's* professionalism."

Well, hooray for her, but that doesn't change anything.

Except, apparently, it does.

"On the grounds of unprofessionalism"—Rune claps his hands together before turning to me—"Marisol, you're fired."

Everyone gasps collectively, disgruntled whispers surrounding me like the buzzing of insects as I stammer out a choked "Wh-what?"

"You can't do that!" Jamila protests, never letting go of my hand, tightening her grip.

Rune shrugs and folds his arms across his chest. "I can, and I have. Read your contracts."

There's no doubt in my mind that he's right. That somehow, we missed some loophole in my agreement that allows him to do exactly this. Or maybe we let it slide, didn't bother fighting it. Because we never thought it would come to this.

"Dawn, you'll step in for Marisol," Rune commands, and she looks like she won the lottery. "We'll reshoot your scenes once we've brought someone else in."

"You did this, didn't you?" I shout at Dawn this time, not bothering to think of tact or a subtle way to go about accusing her. "You took the picture of us?"

Clearly, there's only one person who stands to gain something if I'm kicked off the show. It's the same person who's acted like I have no right to be here since day one, and she just got exactly what she wanted. Dawn gasps, glaring me down, but she can't shake me. Not anymore.

"I had nothing to do with it. We're not even allowed to

have our phones," she snaps back, and I see it. The veneer that separates the real Dawn from who she becomes whenever she performs. A strange lilt to her voice, a subtle tilt of her head.

She's lying. And she's not even doing a good job at it.

"Next time you want to land a part, you should try doing a better job at your audition," I spit back, whipping around on my heels before I can see her reaction. All hell breaks loose throughout the room, PAs and producers clamoring to get Rune to see some sense, cast members shaking their heads in confusion and disappointment. Dawn yells something back at me that I don't quite hear, but I flip her off anyway. Screw having her on my good side. I don't need to be associated with someone like her to advance my career when she's trying to tank it. Jamila stands in front of me, blocking an escape route, and she cups my face.

"We'll figure this out, okay?" she says, her voice nervous and borderline frantic. "He can't do this."

Except he can. Esther already warned me of that. I've seen it with my own eyes—crew members fired one morning and back the next. And why would he change his mind when he has Dawn, the Hollywood golden child, ready and willing to take over my role at the drop of a hat? We can fight and claw our way into forcing him to let me stay, but is it really worth the effort?

All I've done since the table read is try to be the person Rune so desperately wants me to be in the name of trying to prove myself as an actor. But what do the color of my hair, what clothes I wear, or my perfume have to do with who I am as a performer? I know I've given the best performance I possibly can, and if that's not enough for him, then what else is there left for me to give? He can try to strip me of everything that makes me *me*, and I can keep telling myself it's worth it to change my career, but I'm done.

I'm Marisol Polly-Rodriguez. *That's* who I am as an actor. And Rune can never take that away from me.

"It's fine," I say, my voice lost under the general chaos of the room. My hand rests on top of Jamila's, pulling gently until she lets go of my face. I give her hand one last squeeze and back away slowly, the fight seeping out of me like sand through my fingers. "I don't want to be a part of this show anymore."

With that, I let go of her hand and finally walk away from the thing I thought I wanted most.

CHAPTER 22

Like a burn, the pain doesn't hit until later. Not until I'm home, curled up on the couch sobbing into a pillow while Bruiser gives me sympathetic licks on my arm. Walking away was easy. Facing reality is hard.

I can't bring myself to tell Delia yet. I'm not sure if she'll be pissed or relieved or vindicated. All of her and Mom's worrying was warranted. I couldn't handle this show—it was never meant for me. What felt like strength an hour ago feels like weakness once I'm alone with nothing but my thoughts and Bruiser's occasional grunts.

Months ago, I'd thought getting dumped by Miles was my lowest point, but I was wrong. Once again, I'm not even granted the luxury of privacy to grieve the upheaval of my life. Dad comes stumbling in through the door, muttering under his breath about pain-in-the-ass actors, already tugging his tie loose when he spots me on the couch.

"Munch, what's the matter?" he asks, racing to my side, checking me for any signs of injury or illness.

Instead of bottling my feelings up, pretending everything is fine the way I have been for weeks, I tell him everything— about Rune, about Jamila, about how horrible my experience on the show has been—in between hiccupped sobs. His anger grows with every passing word, wrinkles lining his forehead as his brows knit tighter and tighter together. Red trickles through his cheeks down to his neck, and the hand running circles along my back gets more forceful with every passing second.

"This is ridiculous," he says when I finally finish my story, culminating in my firing. "You should have told us from day one how this director was treating you."

"I—I'm sorry. I thought I could handle it," I apologize meekly, flinching at his tone.

Quickly, he softens. "It's not your fault, munchkin. None of this is your fault."

It's such a simple phrase and yet so soothing. Reassuring after weeks of thinking I was to blame for everything going wrong with the perfect life I'd planned out, because I wasn't talented or strong-willed enough. *None of this is my fault.*

Dad stands up and paces the narrow length of the room as he massages his forehead until the wrinkles start to recede. "We can sue the guy for harassment, maybe. Get a lawyer involved." He stops in his tracks and groans, rubbing his eyes like he's trying to massage all the tension out of his body. "I'll talk to your mother and see if we can get your agent on the phone. She'll know more about this than either of us does."

At the mention of Mom, he hardens again, the anger he

worked out of his body coming rushing back. "I *told* her getting you involved in acting so young was a mistake. God, you're barely eighteen. You should be going on college tours and picking out a dress for prom, not dealing with this. She never listened to me and look what happened." He gestures to my crumpled form like I'm something to be ashamed of.

"Hey," I snap, even startling myself at the force in my voice. "You don't get to talk about her like that."

Dad steps back, blinking up at me like he doesn't recognize me. And I don't either—this new, forceful part of me that isn't willing to stand by and let someone, not even my biological father, talk about my mom.

"Mom did everything for me. She worked three jobs to make sure the lights stayed on and still found time to drive me to dance practice, and playdates, and all my auditions. Acting was *my* idea. Not hers. And I'll never regret doing it because it gave us stability for the first time in years. Not that you would know—since you were never there." It's a low blow, I know, and I'll probably regret it in the morning, but I can't help it now. "I wouldn't even be here right now if she didn't suggest it. You don't get to step up now and decide Mom was in the wrong. You don't get to judge how I was raised eighteen years later."

Everything I've ever wanted to say to Dad is out in the air. The progress we've made this summer goes swirling down the drain as the color leaves his face. I'm too frustrated to feel guilty for taking out my anger on him. He doesn't deserve to get the sharp end of my emotions, but he's not innocent either. While I could've phrased it more gently, he doesn't get to bad-mouth Mom. Not when he pops into my life whenever he wants to, like I'm a plant he waters sporadically instead of a child.

"Mari, I—"

I don't let him finish. Turning on my heels, I stomp back toward my room, waiting for Bruiser to catch up before slamming the door behind me. Tomorrow I can pick the pieces back up, put my life back together again like I did when Miles dumped me. But not tonight. Tonight, I bury my face in my pillow and stare out my window at the skyline of a city I thought held so much promise, and cry. I cry because I came here for a job I ended up hating. I cry because I hurt my dad. I cry because everything is falling apart.

Never mind what I said earlier. *This* is my lowest moment.

CHAPTER 23

I've never been hungover before, but I imagine it must feel like this. Mouth dry as if I swallowed a handful of cotton. Bones sore and aching. Neck twisted at an awkward angle. Dried drool streaked down my chin.

"Cut it out, Bruiser," I grumble when I feel her paw insistent against my back, probably asking for breakfast.

"I'm offended that you can't tell your own mother from your dog."

I sit up faster than I should. The world spins so fast I have to brace myself against the wall until my vision clears. I'm convinced I'm still dreaming as the world slowly comes into view, but she really is here, even when the fog finally lifts.

Mom.

"I missed you too," Mom says with a chuckle when I launch myself into her arms so hard she lets out a quiet "oof." She cups the back of my head, tangling her fingers in my hair and scratching gently at my scalp the way she always used to when I came crawling into her bed after nightmares or thunderstorms. Calm washes over me, my body relaxing in a way it hasn't since I left California.

Finally, I'm somewhere safe.

"Your dad told me everything," she whispers against my head, pressing a soft kiss to the top of it. "I flew out last night."

Apologies sit on the tip of my tongue, for making her drop everything to fly out here, but I can't bring myself to say them. Not when the feeling of her arms wrapped around me brings on the sense of comfort I've been yearning for since I got here. I've missed her so much. More than I'll ever be able to put into words—so I hold her tighter instead.

We lie like that, hugging on my bed with Bruiser squished between us, for what feels like hours. Until the rumble of my stomach breaks the silence. We let out quiet laughs as we pull apart, my stomach betraying me again with an even louder roar.

There's a knock at the open door and Dad's head appears cautiously in the doorway. My stomach sinks at the sight of him, not out of anger but embarrassment. Guilt over how I went off on him last night.

"You ladies doing okay?" he asks as he takes a tentative step forward.

We both nod, my cheeks growing hot as he finally enters the room, a plate of waffles in hand.

"Jerome figured you might be hungry since you missed dinner last night," he explains as he sets the plate down on the nightstand jammed between my air mattress and the wall.

Bruiser leaps to attention, but Mom swiftly catches her before she can eat our breakfast.

"Your abuela dropped off some food for you last night too, if you want that."

My stomach does the talking for me, letting out its loudest roar yet. This time, we all laugh together at my insatiable hunger. But when the laughter dies down, my eyes drift toward the floor.

"I'm sorry, Dad," I say, unable to get my voice above a whisper. "I didn't mean to lash out at you yesterday."

"It's all right, munch," he replies, squeezing onto the opposite side of the bed, my mattress groaning from the unexpected weight of three humans and a dog. "We both said some things we regret. You were right, I never should've spoken about your mom the way I did." He looks past me over at Mom, reaching out to take her hand in his. "She's one of the strongest women I know."

Mom wipes at the corner of her eye, sniffling as she squeezes his hand and wraps an arm around me. "And we're *both* so proud of you and the woman you're becoming."

Dad's arms wrap around me too and they both envelop me in their combined warmth. Mom's perfume, Dad's cologne. The smell of Abuela's sofrito wafting in the air. The ever-present smell of sunscreen I associate with California. For the first time I can remember, we hug as a family.

"Things are going to change from here on," Mom promises as we pull apart.

"You can come visit us whenever you want," Dad continues, gesturing toward my cramped room. "Consider this your room permanently now."

Before I can let that news sink in—the thought of coming back here, of creating a real, concrete life here—Mom clasps my hands and frowns.

"I'm sorry we let you think your dad wasn't interested in being involved in your life growing up, because he wanted to be. He wanted to be there for you so, so badly. But we both knew we didn't want the same thing. I had dreams of moving out to LA. His dream was to stay here, with his family."

Dad nods in agreement, resting an encouraging hand on Mom's shoulder as she continues.

"We thought it'd be easier if you stayed with me full-time. Shuttling back and forth across the country every couple of months would be disorienting and confusing, and we thought that was best for you." Mom exhales sharply, and I finally see the exhaustion written all over her. Swollen purple bruises beneath her eyes, gray hairs streaked between her pristine blond strands. "When things got difficult for us, I . . . I never told your dad. Not because I didn't want his help, but because I felt . . . ashamed. I'd spent so long talking about this dream, of becoming an actress, and none of it was panning out the way I'd hoped."

My grip tightens on her hand as her voice trembles. The thought of Mom in my position, alone and terrified of failure, doesn't seem possible. Like Dad said, she's the strongest woman I know. We both knew things were hard, but she never let it show. How she juggled all of it—multiple jobs, a crumbling dream, and me—by herself is something I'll never understand, but will always be grateful for. Especially now.

"But I should've told him," Mom continues, steadier as she

smiles at Dad. "Because your dad is my best friend. And he has *always* been there for me."

Again, we hold each other close. Stay quiet as Mom struggles to catch her breath and hold back her tears. We don't need words—we say it the way we grip each other like we'll float away if we don't hold tight enough. I'm not sure how long we spend sitting there, curled into one another, but I don't care. This is all I've ever wanted, really. A family united.

When we finally pull apart, Mom does her best to wipe the smudged mascara beneath her eyes and morph into business Momager.

"C'mon," she instructs as she stands up. "We have work to do."

"We do?" I ask, blinking around in confusion. I'd sorta been hoping we could do brunch or something. Maybe go for a walk in Central Park with Bruiser.

She turns to me with a beaming smile, Dad joining her at her side with a grin of his own. "We've got a director to deal with."

True to her word, Mom gets straight to business. Once it's a more acceptable hour on the West Coast, she hops on the phone with Delia to explain the situation while Dad and Jerome comb through the various contracts I signed for the show. I realize with a sinking feeling in my gut that Joanna *did* warn me about the exact clause that let Rune fire me. She flagged it as a concern, but we agreed to wave it off due to the super-tight shooting schedule. If we hadn't come to an agreement within a week, I wouldn't have been allowed on set. At the time, we couldn't have imagined that the "we can fire you for whatever we want whenever we want" clause would actually be used. Yet, lo and behold.

We take the video-call debrief with my entire team from the kitchen/dining/living room, the only space that can accommodate the four of us comfortably. Joanna, as expected, reminds us that she did, in fact, tell us this could happen. Slightly off-screen, I hang my head in shame. That's the last time I ignore a red flag from my lawyer. Once I've swallowed my guilt, I shift back into frame. For the second time in twenty-four hours, Delia assures me she'll do the best she can but can't make any promises.

"You're not the first person to have issues with him," she says with a roll of her eyes.

That I'm well aware of. I messaged Eli this morning to tell them what happened but haven't heard back yet. I'm not sure what they would be able to do to help with this situation, but it's at least comforting to know I'm not the only person who's clashed with Rune. Maybe that means there'll be more we can do, somehow. Or they'll have their own ideas. Delia ends the call with a promise to keep us updated.

Mom, Dad, and Jerome move on to more pressing tasks— combing the internet for any proof of others who have worked with Rune, then bashed him or talked about their negative experiences on set. There's a lot they're able to find on production message boards and Reddit threads about life on Hollywood sets. We're not sure what exactly we can do with this information, but it's helpful for building my case, so we save everything.

Abuela shows up midway through us combing the internet for dirt with what she deems a very necessary delivery of food.

"You need food to focus!" she explains as she ladles each of us a bowl of rice.

Who am I to argue with free lunch? While Dad and Abuela bicker in the kitchen about her letting him wash the dishes, I reach for my phone, holding my breath for a text from Jamila, but the screen is as blank as it was when I woke up this morning.

It doesn't hurt that she hasn't texted me since yesterday—or at least, that's what I tell myself. Maybe she was exhausted by the time she got home or forgot to charge her phone.

Or maybe she doesn't *want* to talk to me.

The last thing I remember before leaving was the hurt in her eyes, how crushed she'd seemed when I walked away. What if leaving her behind to deal with the aftermath of Rune's blowup felt like a betrayal? She promised me that we could do something about this together, but I was the one who walked away and gave up before we could even try fighting.

I open up our text chain, my fingers hovering over the keyboard, searching for the right thing to say. *What's up* feels too blasé and *hey so are we okay?* feels too loaded. I linger on the last text she sent me—a behind-the-scenes video Fatima shot of the interview she set up for her at *Hollywood Today*—which Jamila, of course, absolutely crushed. In small part thanks to my coaching her, but mostly because she relaxed enough to let her personality shine through.

Suddenly, an idea comes to me.

As if on cue, my phone lights up with an incoming call from Jamila—exactly the person I needed to hear from. I answer immediately, and Jamila launches into what must be a prepared speech as soon as I pick up.

"I'm sorry I didn't call or text," she says breathlessly, as if she just ran up a flight of stairs. "Rune kept everyone on set way late because he wants to reshoot everything now that you're gone. And he said if any of us tries to leave or argue with him, we're out of the show too. By the time we got our phones back after we wrapped, it was almost four."

I pull back enough to glance at the time. "Shouldn't you be sleeping?" It's not super early in the morning, but if I had to stay on set until four in the morning, I'd be sleeping in until well past noon.

"I wanted to make sure you were okay," she replies quietly, sounding more exhausted than out of breath now.

"I'm fine," I assure her, heart swelling from the confirmation that we're okay—that *she's* okay. Tired, but okay. As much as I'd like to relax on the couch and let the sound of her voice soothe all the worries weighing on my shoulders, I have an asshole to take down. "And I have an idea."

CHAPTER 24

The *Hollywood Today* office is a lot posher than I expected. Sleek marble floors, alternating between red and black cubicles in the company's signature brand colors. Floor-to-ceiling windows in the corner offices with a perfect view of bustling Bryant Park. Glossy framed photos of past covers along the walls—complete with signatures. *Hollywood Today* isn't a gossip mag, but I wasn't sure what to expect from a company that regularly puts out articles like WHICH K-POP GIRL GROUP YOU SHOULD STAN BASED ON YOUR ZODIAC SIGN.

Annaleigh Small, editor-in-chief of the Celebrity News column, meets us in the large conference room off the main waiting area. Bowls of M&M's and fresh fruit are spread out along the sleek glass table that stretches the length of the room, the *Hollywood Today* logo displayed on the flat-screen TV mounted on the wall behind Annaleigh's seat at the head of the table.

"It's a pleasure to meet you, Marisol," Annaleigh says as she shakes my hand before turning her attention to Jamila. "And I've heard a lot about you, Jamila."

Off in the corner, Fatima beams before eagerly pulling out chairs for us at the conference table. Like most interns, she flutters around Annaleigh, handing her papers, clipboards, and pens before she can request them.

With introductions and pleasantries out of the way, Annaleigh gets straight to business. "I've read your proposal." She flips open the folder sitting in front of her. "We're obviously very interested in pursuing this further."

Jamila, Fatima, and I worked late into the night all week to put together this proposal for a tell-all piece where I reveal everything about my horrendous experience working with Rune on *The Limit*. Normally, my ironclad NDA would force me to keep the dirty details to myself, but Joanna worked overtime scanning every single line of my various agreements until she found the exact clause we needed. Now that Rune fired me, the NDA is technically null and void. You'd think he would've addressed that, considering how often he fires his employees, but unless he rehires me, which I definitely wouldn't agree to, I'm free to say whatever I want. Looks like he's not the only one who can take advantage of his weird, predatory contract.

Jamila gives me an encouraging shoulder nudge at Annaleigh's clear interest in telling our story, but all I can give her back is a nod before turning to check my phone again. No new texts. Yet.

"Our only concern is credibility," Annaleigh continues. "Not that we don't believe you or your experiences, Marisol," she says delicately. "We want to be sure that we have multiple sources confirming everything you'll be discussing."

"I can confirm everything," Jamila chimes in eagerly. "Miles Zhao can come on as a source, too. As long as we can be kept anonymous. We also have three PAs who are willing to be anonymous sources as well."

Annaleigh gives us a tight-lipped smile. Beside me, Jamila's shoulders deflate—that's definitely not the overjoyed reaction we were hoping for. "We appreciate you all coming forward, but ideally, we'd have at least one other source besides Marisol who's willing to identify themselves. Someone from last season or one of Rune's other productions would be even better, to prove that this has been an ongoing pattern."

Suddenly, my phone buzzes.

Sorry, im here

"We can do that," I announce to the room, already halfway out of my seat. "I have someone waiting downstairs to be checked in," I tell Fatima, who leaps out of her seat and rushes to the reception desk.

Jamila's lips are parted in quiet shock beside me, and I swallow down the guilt of not telling her about my backup plan sooner. The only reason I hadn't was to not get our hopes up. There was no guarantee this was going to work, and I figured it'd be easier to deal with just my own disappointment rather than hers too.

"We didn't want to share any details until they confirmed they'd be willing to come forward as a source, but we just heard back. They're in," I explain.

Before either Jamila or Annaleigh can ask who the new source is, Fatima busts open the door, and Esther steps into the room.

Followed by Eli Rowan.

"Holy shit," Jamila mutters under her breath.

"Eli Rowan. Sorry we're late," they say with a polite smile, offering their hand up to Annaleigh to shake before returning to Esther's side. "We hit some traffic on the way."

I stifle a laugh as I watch the cogs in Jamila's brain work overtime to process everything in front of us. It shouldn't be surprising that Esther and Eli know each other—Esther did say that she worked on *The Limit*'s first season. But what is surprising is Eli sliding their fingers through Esther's, pressing a quick, subtle kiss to her knuckles.

Esther definitely left *that* part out of the story.

"Thank you so much for joining us," Annaleigh replies, gesturing for Eli and Esther to take a seat at the table. Fatima eagerly pulls out their chairs, offering them water and snacks, which they both politely decline. She returns to her corner of the room, not bothering to hide her elation, practically vibrating in her seat as we get back to business.

"So, Eli, you're willing to be a second source for the article?" Annaleigh asks with a raised brow.

"For sure. Working with that prick was one of the worst experiences of my life," they say without a care in the world, and I wish I could be even an ounce as cool as them.

Annaleigh smirks, glancing back down at the proposal. "And you're willing to be a named source?"

Eli nods. "Fuck that guy and his NDAs."

My heart swells, every part of me vibrating with excitement as Jamila reaches for my hand, gripping it so tight it feels like the bones could snap, but I don't care because we're doing the damn thing. When I meet her gaze, tears glossing her vision, it takes every ounce of strength I have not to kiss her then and there.

"Fabulous," Annaleigh says with a grin, flipping the folder shut and pulling a laptop toward her instead, typing at top speed. "We'll have our production management team reach out to coordinate interview times—we're happy to do it either here in our office, or we can come to you. Whichever you prefer. We haven't discussed this at our assignments weekly yet, but I'm sure several of our senior writers would be interested in tackling this piece."

"Actually," I interject before Annaleigh can continue, "I want Fatima to be assigned to the article."

We knew they'd pull something like this—take Fatima's work and pass it off to a more seasoned writer instead. She'd even prepared me before we submitted the proposal that I'd have to speak with one of the senior writers instead of her, assuring me that they were top-notch journalists, and I shouldn't worry about trusting them. But it's not a matter of trust; I'll gladly tell my story to anyone who'll listen. It's about fairness. Fatima is the entire reason we're here. Fatima's the one who stayed up until three in the morning helping us put together this proposal.

Fatima deserves to be credited for this interview.

Annaleigh is frozen for several seconds before she finally speaks again. "We don't typically allow interns full-scale pieces like this," she says carefully, keeping her tone controlled, but not covering up the passive-aggressive bite.

"This piece was Fatima's idea," I continue, ignoring the concerned looks both Jamila and Fatima are sending my way. "And I only feel comfortable talking to someone I trust."

Not technically true, but whatever I have to say to make sure Fatima gets the job she deserves.

Eli does a terrible job of hiding their snort behind their hand, and Esther nudges them playfully in the ribs.

"Fine," Annaleigh says through gritted teeth. "But she has to work closely with a senior writer who will be present at every interview and oversee all drafts before she submits them to me."

"Deal," I reply eagerly before she can take back the offer, shooting a smile at Fatima as we shake on the agreement.

"Thank you," she mouths as she clutches her clipboard to her chest. I settle back in my seat, tuning out Annaleigh as she continues going over the logistics, and reach out to take Jamila's hand, running my thumb over her knuckles.

I'm the one who should be thanking them.

CHAPTER 25

I've done hundreds of photo shoots over the years, but none has ever made me feel as terrified as this one. Not even the time I was dangled twenty feet in the air over a dam in Vancouver for *Teen Vogue*.

As far as shoots go, it's pretty straightforward. Annaleigh insisted on a shoot so we'd have a set of photos to go along with the piece—a cover feature, she assured me. A modest crew is assembled on the roof of the loft in Brooklyn they've rented for the day, fluttering around the cramped space while I readjust the pink cotton sundress I've chosen for the occasion.

"Stop it." Jamila bats playfully at my hands while I readjust the bow holding the bodice top together yet again. "You look perfect," she reassures me, pushing the glossy curtain of my hair over my shoulder, exposing my mostly bare shoulder.

One silver lining of no longer being under Rune's rule, aside from being able to relax for the first time in months, is no longer having to abide by his wardrobe rules. Within days of my firing, I went straight back to the salon that made me platinum and had them restore the life to my hair that Rune sucked dry. It's not a perfect match to my original rich brunette, but it's close enough to make me feel like myself again. Along with finally getting to break out the pinks and buttercream-yellow ensembles I'd shoved to the back of my closet, and spritzing Coco Mademoiselle on my wrists and neck, I'm finally starting to feel like myself again.

My phone buzzes with a new text as I'm double-checking my makeup in the selfie camera.

Lily
You're going to crush it today!!!

A few seconds later . . .

Posie
We love you!!!

I don't need to put on a smile as I snap a quick selfie to send to them—laughing as they immediately spam the chat with praise for my makeup and outfit. Only a few more weeks until they're finally wrapped with filming and can head out on their weeklong trip to New York to visit moi. My skin thrums every time I think about finally getting to see them again, and all of the shopping we're going to do the second they get here. Our bank accounts are *not* ready.

On the opposite side of the roof, Fatima barks out orders left and right, running the photo shoot like a pro.

"She's perfect for this job," Jamila says as we watch her go over the shot list with the director. "People actually *like* that she's being bossy."

I snort. Admittedly, I do like how in control Fatima has been throughout this process. Knowing that what is possibly the most important interview of my life—that'll either make or break my career—is in her hands has been calming, to say the least. I may still be waking up in the middle of the night panicking about Rune showing up at my door with a pitchfork-wielding angry mob, but now that I'm here, I'm able to remind myself that this is the right decision.

"We're talking about the photo leak today . . ." I say cautiously, avoiding Jamila's eyes and focusing instead on the design on my ring fingernail. Kevin made sure to go all-out for the occasion, giving me a fresh set of acrylics complete with intricate floral designs on each nail. Last night's catch-up session/nail appointment was the perfect way to celebrate his finally being ungrounded.

The photo leak is a topic I've been dancing around, not sure how to broach with Jamila quite yet. She's been there for each of my two interview sessions so far, going in chronological order starting with my audition experience, but this is the first that directly involves her.

My firing is the heart of this story, something I know I can't avoid talking about. But it means delving into my personal life—revealing that I was dating someone on set. There's only so much I can do to cover my tracks, with the photo of me and Jamila kissing already out in the open. People came to their own conclusions after the article was out—throwing the shots of us together on the red carpet side by side with the blurry kiss photo and drawing comparisons. Still, there's plausible deniability. I can keep the details as vague as possible, maybe even fudge them a little bit to try to hide Jamila's identity. I can't help feeling guilty for getting her caught in the crosshairs. She's done more than enough to help me through this summer—I don't need to drag her down with me.

"I can try to keep things vague. Maybe make them think it was someone else," I go on, listing all the options I've already thought of. Anything to keep Jamila as anonymous as possible. "Or I can—"

"You can tell the truth," Jamila interrupts before I can finish. Her palm cradles my cheek, turning me to face her. "You can tell them it was me."

Something about her touch always makes my heart race, but this is on a whole new level. Heat surrounds me like a mist, my heart beating so fast I can feel it in my fingertips as I rest my hand on top of hers. "But your agent—"

"Is fired," she interjects again, shaking her head slightly, making her curls bounce in the midsummer breeze. "I'm not going to start my career lying about who I am."

She laces our fingers together, lowering them until they're linked in the small bit of space between us. "I want to do this with you. Together."

"Together," I whisper back, the words almost lost to the wind and the clatter of equipment and Fatima's shouts to get this show on the road.

When I came to this city, I had no idea what to expect. Whether I'd crash and burn or soar and become the person I hoped I could be. Success doesn't look like what I originally envisioned. Fired from the show I busted my ass to book. Being sorta-friends with the ex who broke my heart. Adjusting to living in a walk-in closet. Calling the most beautiful girl I've ever met mine.

Nothing about this summer has been what I expected because it's better than anything I could've ever imagined. Meeting Kevin and helping him transform into Diamond, watching him destroy his first-ever performance. Getting to eat my abuela's incredible cooking every other night. Kissing Jamila on a packed dance floor.

It's a terrifying thought, letting people in. Especially after my history with Miles and an intensely public relationship. But this time will be different. I know that for sure. Suddenly, I don't feel the need to post the selfies we take curled up in our blanket forts—even though they *are* cute as hell. I want to keep this beautiful thing close to my chest. Learn who we are together privately before the world can decide for us. And even though we may be afraid for our own reasons of what going public might mean, I know we'll be okay. Anything feels possible when her fingers are laced through mine. We'll brave the world, the critics, the fans—everyone.

Together.

HOLLYWOOD TODAY

AVALON GROVE STAR MARISOL POLLY-RODRIGUEZ TEASES NEW PROJECT AT *THE LIMIT* SEASON TWO PREMIERE

BY FATIMA EL AMRANI

Marisol Polly-Rodriguez has kept a low profile following her bombshell interview with *Hollywood Today* earlier this year, exposing Rune, director of the Emmy Award–winning anthology series *The Limit*, for inappropriate and abusive on-set behavior. Polly-Rodriguez's account, along with information revealed by season one's breakout star, Eli Rowan, drastically shifted public perception of the highly acclaimed director. While *The Limit*'s future was left uncertain after the director was quietly replaced midway through production for season two, shortly after the article's release, early reviews praised the show's bold new direction, a departure from Rune's directorial style, as well as newcomer (and Polly-Rodriguez's current flame) Jamila El Amrani's performance.

El Amrani isn't the only one receiving positive buzz about her performance. Despite initially being released from the show midway through production, Polly-Rodriguez was invited to rejoin the cast after Rune's dismissal from the show. It was a decision that, according to insiders, was extremely controversial, as former costar Dawn Greene, who was slated to take over Polly-Rodriguez's role after her firing, decided to leave the show upon her return. "She was pissed that someone she thought had 'less experience' got a bigger part than her," our source says. Less experienced or not, it's clear that Polly-Rodriguez is going to be making a splash this season, with several early reviews praising her performance as oil heiress Zoe as "raw," "real," and "career-defining."

Polly-Rodriguez stunned on the red carpet for the second season's premiere in a gown she revealed was designed by her father, Carlos Rodriguez, with hair and makeup styling by her cousin Kevin Rodriguez, the nail tech behind social media drag sensation Diamond Du Jour, making the night a true family affair. When asked about her thoughts on the season, Polly-Rodriguez gushed about her former and current flames—Miles Zhao and El Amrani, respectively—calling their performances "electric" and "once-in-a-lifetime." When asked about her own career path post-*The Limit*, Polly-Rodriguez emphasized a return to her roots. "I'm working on a new sapphic rom-com that I absolutely adore with my best friend Posie Butler," she teased, but remained coy on details of the title and official release.

It's clear that, for Polly-Rodriguez, this night was all about El Amrani. Quickly flocking back to each other's sides, the couple exchanged several kisses throughout the night, never letting go of each other's hands as they made their way through the room. "They're amazing," costar Zhao said of the couple. "But nothing ever makes me feel as single as watching those two together."

Season two of *The Limit* premieres January 17.

COMMENTS

my mothers looking stunning as always!!!!

pls can they adopt me

JAMISOL NATION WE WON TONIGHT

manifesting I find a girl who looks at me the way Marisol
Polly-Rodriguez looks at Jamila El Amrani

EPILOGUE

Normally I thrive at parties—especially ones I've organized. I knew from the minute *The Limit* was nominated for the Best Limited Series Emmy that I wanted to host an after-party to celebrate, no matter what the outcome was. I just hadn't anticipated the emotions that would come with attending my first major award ceremony. The high of seeing your face on screen in a room filled with dozens of actors you only ever dreamed of meeting. The panic as you wait for your name to be called. The crashing low as you realize it wasn't your time. Not yet, at least.

I step out onto the patio at Capri, sliding the door closed behind me until the chatter from the dining area dulls to a hum. The irony of having an after-party at the same place where Miles dumped me almost two years ago isn't lost on me. I'd originally booked a different venue—a bistro right on the water in Santa Monica—but they'd double-booked us with a wedding and I scrambled to find a replacement last-minute.

The universe works in cruel and mysterious ways.

I'm careful to keep the hem of my dress from dragging on the ground. Dad already warned me that the delicate pink fabric would stain easily, and there's no way I'm going to be photographed throughout the night with a stained dress. With the bottom of my dress and my heels in hand, I sit down on one of the tables on the patio overlooking the city. The sky is alight with stars, and there's a peacefulness in the distant music playing in the dining room and the rumble of conversation. Every crew member and castmate I've come to love gathered in one place after months apart.

"You okay?" a familiar voice calls from the doorway.

I extend my hand to Jamila as soon as I see her, a smile tugging at my lips as she strolls toward me and slides her fingers through mine. I'm still not over how stunning she looks. The rich lilac silk of her evening gown is the perfect complement to her radiant brown skin and full, free curls. She's always made my heart beat at triple speed, but tonight she takes my breath away.

"I'm good," I reply, resting our linked fingers in my lap. "Needed a break."

"I get that," she says with a sigh as she leans back in her seat and looks up at the sky.

Jamila had more to lose tonight than I did, with her individual nomination for Best Supporting Actress. She's been pinching herself ever since Delia called and told her the news, worried that it might've been a mistake, but I've assured her tonight, and every day since then, that it was more than deserved. Still, she'd taken her loss in stride, smiling throughout the ceremony even after her category. Her mom blew up the group chat we're in with her and Fatima with a very colorful series of insults for the winning actress, which Jamila politely shut down. She didn't even have to learn that bit of etiquette from me—she has natural grace and poise.

I *can* take credit for her red carpet walk, though. She can walk in five-inch heels without clinging to me for balance now. They grow up so fast.

"Is it weird that I'm glad we didn't win?" I ask as we gaze at the stars together, my thumb running along the back of her hand.

Jamila glances over at me, brows furrowed. "You are?"

Of course I was excited when we were nominated for Best Limited Series—even more so when Jamila snagged her own individual nomination. All the pipe dreams I wouldn't let myself believe in when I was pushing through those difficult first few weeks of shooting *The Limit* had come through. The nominations—not just the Emmy, but a dozen different nominations, including a Golden Globe. The job offers rolled in shortly after my profile in *Hollywood Today*.

Suddenly, the highbrow directors and showrunners who wouldn't look my way were sending me scripts and requests for lunch or coffee left and right. For once, I had choices. I could wade through the dozens of scripts I'd been sent and decide what my next project should be. Noir crime thrillers and gritty historical dramas and high-fantasy series, all with plenty of promise. Jamila quickly accepted another series regular role in a new fantasy series about several talented thieves competing against each other to pull off a high-stakes heist, but I took my time picking my next role.

In the end, I listened to my heart. As soon as Posie sent me the script for *Everything Comes Back to You*—a sapphic rom-com about rival cheerleaders who are stuck in a time loop together—I knew it was the perfect next step. The writing is smart and swoony and hilarious, and most importantly, my character loved pink. What more could you ask for?

I'm sure some people will say it was a mistake—that I should've taken *The Limit*'s push and stacked my résumé with prestige roles. But I'm done pretending to be someone I'm not.

And I think that's why I was afraid of the win. As proud as I am of my performance in *The Limit*, I haven't been able to watch the footage since we wrapped. Even now, well over a year later, I'm still brought back to those grueling days on set. All the ways I changed myself to be who Rune wanted me to be. How I almost let him convince me that I wasn't enough.

I don't want that performance to be the one my career is defined by. The first credit listed in my Wikipedia bio. The top title on my IMDb page. The role everyone cites when they try to think of where they know me from. I'm grateful for the opportunities *The Limit* has given me, and that I still got to be in the final cut of the show after everything that happened with Rune, but I want to be remembered for a role that I didn't take to prove a point. If this was the biggest moment of my career, it would prove right what everyone said about me back then—that I wasn't a "serious" actor until I got that role.

"I guess I'm glad this isn't going to be the biggest moment of my career," I say eventually, struggling to summarize all my disappointment and relief and gratitude and guilt in one succinct sentence. I turn to her with a smile, holding our linked hands up to press a kiss to the back of hers. "Meeting you was the best part, though."

"Obviously." She snorts, giving my hand a squeeze.

"I wouldn't mind if we won for *Vida and Priya*, though," I add with a raised brow. There's no guarantee that the pilot script Jamila and Fatima cowrote together last summer will be picked up anywhere, or even if it does, that we'll star in it together. Two years ago, I didn't think any of this would be possible, though, and look where we are now.

"That doesn't sound so bad," Jamila teases with a raised brow. "Think we could share a trailer again?"

"You? An Emmy-nominated actress *sharing* a trailer?" I scoff, playfully shoving her shoulder. "As if."

Jamila giggles, grabbing the arm I shoved her with and slinging it across her shoulders so she can lean her head against mine. "I'm willing to make an exception for my *very* cute costar."

She punctuates the statement with a kiss on my cheek, but it's not enough. I cup her cheek and close the little bit of distance between us, kissing her until I can taste the subtle raspberry cheesecake flavor of her lip gloss.

As frustrating as *The Limit* was, I'll never be able to regret the experience. Because it brought me Jamila, the one person who has never made me feel guilty for being myself. Who helped me take charge of my life. Who held my hand as I learned to love myself again, only for me to fall in love with her along the way.

No matter if we won or lost, no matter if we never get

nominated again, I still got my happy ending. Family in New York City who always welcome me home with open arms and a plate of tostones. Roles that let me be exactly who I am—no adjustments necessary. And a love story like the ones I was meant to star in, with the most Ridiculously Beautiful Girl.

ACKNOWLEDGMENTS

I keep bracing myself for the day acknowledgments don't feel exhilarating and intimidating, but today is not that day, and I hope that day never comes.

I've been writing stories my entire life, and I'm constantly amazed that I get to share them with the world now. All of the thank-yous to the amazing team at Joy Revolution—Bria Ragin and David and Nicola Yoon—for giving me a safe space to tell these stories. I'm beyond honored to be able to grow my career with this incredible team!

Thank you to my agent, Uwe Stender, for guiding me with grace, and always answering my rambling questions.

I'm incredibly lucky to have not one, not two, but *three* beautiful covers designed by the fabulous Casey Moses! And even luckier to have Marisol brought to life by Natalie Shaw, whose work I've long admired. Many, many additional thanks to Ken Crossland, Colleen Fellingham, Tamar Schwartz, and Shameiza Ally for all their work in turning *Marisol Acts the Part* into an actual book.

Thank you to the most amazing publicist, Kim Small, for your work in sharing my stories with the world.

This novel wouldn't exist without Scott Shigeoka's kindness and generosity. The two weeks I spent working on this story in Joshua Tree were some of the most fun I've ever had when it comes to writing, and I'll cherish those memories forever. I'd always dreamed of returning to the desert to write, and it was nothing short of a dream come true to make that a reality. Thank you, thank you, thank you for all you've done for me and other writers.

Thank you to my mentor extraordinaire, Justine Pucella Winans, who read a very early sample of this book, and who continues to share their infinite wisdom even now, four books into my career!

Thank you to GILWCTI for being such a constant source of light in this industry.

Thank you to Zach Humphrey, my dog's favorite person, for introducing me to hot pot. I've been forever changed by our friendship.

Marisol's story is very different from mine—and a lot more glamorous—but we both care deeply for our families. Thank you, Mami, for your unending support, and for always reminding me that this is the path I was meant to be on. Daddy, I think you saw all this coming long before I did. I wish you were here to see it, but I know you've been with me every step of the way.

To my own family: I love you endlessly. Your support means everything to me.

And last, but never least, Duncan. The only person I'd make the transfer at Atlantic-Barclays for.

ABOUT THE AUTHOR

Elle Gonzalez Rose is a television producer from New York who's better at writing love stories than she is at writing bios. Her dog thinks she's okay. She is also the author of *Caught in a Bad Fauxmance* and *10 Things I Hate About Prom*. Elle, not the dog.

ellegonzalezrose.com

10 Things I Hate About Prom excerpt text copyright © 2024 by Assemble Media, LLC.
Cover art copyright © 2024 by Rebeca Alvarez, bouquet icon by
Muhammad/stock.adobe.com, hands showing heart shape icon by
Pixel-Shot/stock.adobe.com, smile emoji by Vadymstock/stock.adobe.com, bee drawing
by nenilkime/stock.adobe.com. Published by Joy Revolution, an imprint of
Random House Children's Books, a division of Penguin Random House LLC, New York.

TURN THE PAGE FOR A PEEK AT...

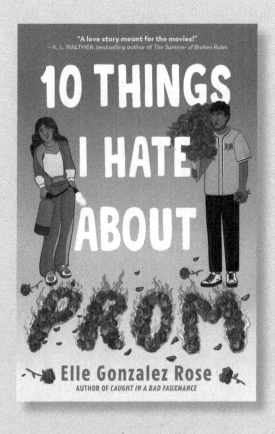

"A must-read!" —Alex Light, author of
The Upside of Falling

"Full of the humor, hijinks and heart of high school."
—Emily Wibberley and Austin Siegemund-Broka,
coauthors of *If I'm Being Honest*

"This absolute gem of a book is destined to
sweep you off your feet." —Brian D. Kennedy,
author of *My Fair Brady*

CHAPTER ONE

THERE'S NOTHING WORSE THAN working a double shift on the last day of spring break.

Except turning around to find a guy you barely know holding up a sign that says *PROM?*

My jaw locked the second the bell over the door chimed. Most weekends I don't get a moment to breathe. The rush at Casa Y Cocina is constant from brunch all the way through dinner, the hours passing by in a mad flurry of fritura samplers, piña colada mimosas, and crumpled dollar bills. But today was unusually slow. Like, keep-an-eye-out-for-tumbleweeds slow. Tío Tony even gave me the green light to head home at two if no one else came in after I finished wiping down my tables. The last time he let me dip early was when I chipped my tooth nose-diving to save a plate before it hit the ground. *Nepotism* isn't a word in the Santos family dictionary.

I can feel Tío Tony's glare on the back of my head as my

gentleman caller, Chris Pavlenko, sets the box under his arm on a table so he can get down on one knee.

Chris's brow quirks, his hot-pink duct tape sign halfway into the air when he pauses. "You're Ivelisse, right?"

Wow. A promposal from a guy who isn't even sure who I am. Shakespeare could never.

The temptation to say no is strong. Chris is usually stoned on days that end in *y*, and last month he almost drank a beaker of liquid iron because he thought it was green-apple Gatorade. But even if he doesn't immediately smell the lie, roll call in chem tomorrow will be a pretty big giveaway.

I take my time replying. Opening my mouth too soon could lead to (a) projectile vomiting, (b) saying something I'll regret, or (c) saying something I regret while projectile vomiting. So I take a deep breath, decide to use the rational part of my brain, and nod instead.

Chris grins, his eyes half open and tinged pink. "Sweet."

The smell of weed and stale tortilla chips comes with him as he shifts closer to me, overpowering the usual smell of sautéed onions and cilantro wafting from the kitchen.

"So, you down?" Chris asks as he holds the sign up over his head.

"To go to prom?"

"Yeah," he says in the same tone one might say, "Duh" or "No shit, I'm holding a sign that says *PROM?*"

My cheeks flush as I choke out a laugh, scratching the back of my neck just to give my hands something to do. It's not like he walked in here to ask Tío Tony or one of the fry cooks to prom but asking me makes just as little sense. In the four years we've known each other, Chris has said maybe ten words to me. Five of which were *Did you do the homework?* You can't blame me for being shocked that *prom?* is the eleventh.

"Ivelisse," Tío Tony barks, wiping down his knife as he slowly approaches us. "You good?"

"Yep, fine," I reply to keep the peace. Tío Tony's heart may be made of marshmallow fluff, but he definitely gets a kick out of leaning into his "bulging muscles and intimidating tattoos" exterior. I wouldn't put it past him to lift Chris up by the scruff of his neck and toss him onto the street like a rag doll.

"Oh!" Chris exclaims with a grin, as if there isn't a six-foot-five man with a meat cleaver glaring at him. "I brought these."

He gets up off his knees to grab the box he set aside. My nose wrinkles as he pulls up the lid with a lazy wave of his hand, the hairs along my arms rocketing to attention as a familiar scent wafts over me.

The peanut butter cookies make me recoil like a vampire would at garlic. Any hope I had of getting through this interaction without throwing up is long gone. I'm not afraid to admit that a box of cookies can strike the fear of God into me—not when one wrong move could land me in the emergency room with anaphylactic shock.

I jump back as Chris takes a tentative step toward me, nearly tripping over a broom. He frowns, glancing from me to the box. "I guess you don't like peanut butter?"

At this point, expecting him to remember my nut allergy would've been too much to ask.

"I'm allergic." I take another step back for good measure. "Really allergic."

"My bad," he replies as he closes the box. "Anna likes these, so I figured you might like them too."

All the nerves that calmed within me when Chris put the cookies away come again. "Anna?"

He nods, picking his PROM sign back up and wiping some dirt off the *R*. "I asked her yesterday." He wrinkles his nose, picking at a dust clump that's now stuck to the tape. "But she said no."

Finally, this bizarro situation starts to make some sense. Chris spends more time sighing over Anna Adebayo's perfume than he does taking notes. If he spent that time actually listening to her or paying attention to the pins on her backpack instead of trolling "How to Get Girls" subreddits, he'd know she's a lesbian.

"So . . . you decided to ask me instead?"

Anna and I don't have many other friends at Cordero High besides each other, which *is* how we prefer it, but that doesn't make us interchangeable. I guess proximity makes me his runner-up.

He shrugs, giving up on the dust clump and flipping the sign around to face me once more. In the new light, I spot the patches where tape has been pulled off. Sticky residue spells out *Anna*.

"You seem chill."

At least I have that going for me.

The silence goes from awkward to strained to painful as excuses sit on the tip of my tongue and die when I open my mouth. If Chris wasn't actively stoned, he might call out my hesitance. Instead, he grabs a cookie for himself, not noticing when I put a safe distance between us. Even a crumb could send me down a dangerous spiral. Though breaking out into hives *would* be a very effective way of getting myself out of this situation.

Maybe I can sneak off and camp out in the kitchen. Hiding from my problems isn't the solution I need, but I do my best thinking after a long, cathartic scream into a bag of frozen corn. There's a reason freezer screams are the backbone of the service industry. Plus, it'll give me time to think of an excuse or, better yet, an escape plan.

"I actually—"

"Chris!" another voice cuts in before I can finish.

My heart leaps from the pit of my stomach as my best friend and saving grace, Joaquin, sweeps Chris into the bro-iest of bro hugs.

"I thought you lived up in Anchor Heights?" Joaquin asks without missing a beat.

"Y-yeah, I do." Chris gives Joaquin a bleary once-over before glancing at the front door, as if to confirm he didn't materialize out of thin air. "I was just—"

"Oh, I meant to ask you," Joaquin interrupts, wrapping an arm around Chris's shoulders and guiding him toward the door. "I had this issue with my bike last week, and one of the guys mentioned you might know what the deal is."

Their voices trail off as Joaquin leads them to where his bike is locked up out front, letting the door shut behind him. I collapse onto the chair beside me, heaving a sigh with every bit of breath I have left in me.

"Ivelisse," Tío Tony calls out yet again, hovering by the entrance to the kitchen. "No more boys allowed unless they pay for food." As if I had any choice in the matter. His thick gray mustache bristles as he peeks through the front window, jutting his chin toward Joaquin. "Except for El Conejito."

Over a decade of friendship and Joaquin still can't shake off the nickname my abuela gave him when we were six. My family watched in awe as Joaquin happily nibbled on his carrot sticks instead of begging for more cake like the other sugar-high six-year-olds at my birthday party.

In our defense, he *does* have rabbit teeth.

I give Tío Tony a nod and sink back into my chair, massaging my temples in hopes of fighting off the steadily building headache. The smart thing to do would be to haul ass and slip out the rear exit while Chris is distracted, but I never make smart decisions when I'm under extreme duress.

Thankfully, Joaquin was smart enough for the both of us in that moment. My heart has stopped pounding and my headache has subsided to a dull throb by the time he returns, sans Chris Pavlenko, wearing a cocky smirk that tells me I'm never going to live this down.

"So," he singsongs as he drops into the chair across from me. "Seems like you had fun while I was gone."

I'm still too mortified to do anything other than groan and let my head fall onto the table with a thump.

"Gotta say, I didn't see this relationship coming but it makes sense. Y'know, since you two have"—he pauses to do a drum roll on the table—"chemistry."

His corniness is enough to bring me back from the dead. "Shut *up*," I snap as I lean across the table to smack his shoulder.

He tries to appear wounded, holding a hand over his heart, but he can't hold in his giggles. "Don't fight your feelings anymore, Ive. This could be the beginning of a very beautiful romance."

I roll my eyes as I slump back into my seat. "I'm sure my grandkids would love to hear about how their grandpa only asked me to prom because the girl he asked first said no."

Joaquin lets out a hiss. "Oof. Okay, never mind, that's harsh."

That's an understatement, and I didn't even tell him about the peanut butter cookies. As sad as it is, having a close brush with death the first time a guy asked me out since freshman year is a very appropriate metaphor for my love life: dead on arrival.

Using a dishrag to protect myself from any stray crumbs, I take the box Chris left behind to the kitchen and write out a note for the line cooks to help themselves.

"He did say I was chill, though," I add. Joaquin snorts, immediately trying to cover it up when I turn to glare at him. "What? You don't think I'm chill?"

He scrunches up his nose in thought, waving his hand from side to side. "On a scale of one to ten, I'd say you're like a . . . four?"

Great, so I *don't* have that going for me.

I go to whack him with the dishrag—a very chill response—except he catches the tail end of it before it can hit him. "Jesus, you're fast," I mumble as he lets go of the towel with a shit-eating grin. "Did you get any radioactive spider bites over break?

Because you can't get a tan *and* superpowers in the same week. That's just not fair."

"I wish." He leans back in his chair, one hand coming up behind his head while the other gestures down the front of his shirt. "But I did get this."

His new shirt is . . . loud. Somewhere between a Hawaiian shirt and a bowling jersey, complete with orange, blue, and white palm fronds. Paired with black jeans, it's definitely a switch from his usual wardrobe of hoodies with gray sweatpants or basketball shorts and slides.

"Interesting choice," I reply delicately as I slide back into my seat across from him.

He quirks an eyebrow. "The good kind of interesting?"

I take my time replying, rubbing my chin as I take in the full ensemble. "You look like my abuelo."

His smirk falls into a frown. "Well, then, I'll just have to give your souvenir to someone who appreciates my fashion sense." With a *humph*, he stands up from the table and heads for the door.

Roasting Joaquin Romero is by far my favorite hobby, but I'm a material girl at heart. I bolt from my seat, racing to cut him off before he can get to the exit. "Souvenir?" I ask with a raised brow.

A smirk plays at the corner of his lips for a brief moment before he slips back into his role, lifting his nose high in the air and crossing his arms as he turns his back to me. "I have nothing more to say to you."

The man plays a dirty game. Then again, he learned it from

the best: me. And the hours of telenovelas we watched in middle school. But mostly me.

I give it a few seconds before finally admitting defeat. "You're a fashion genius. An icon. Your invite to the Met Gala will arrive any day now."

He tries and fails to hold in his amusement. "You're forgiven." He holds up a warning finger as he faces me. "Just know you're on thin ice."

If that was true, the ice would've cracked five years ago when I told him his new haircut made him look like an egg. But I give him an overly gracious smile and hold out my hands like the greedy gremlin he knows and adores. "The souvenir . . . ?"

"Is at my place," he finishes, nudging past me to open the door. "Come over after your shift's done?"

"Actually, I get to cut out early today."

Joaquin gasps dramatically, bracing himself against the doorframe. "Did hell freeze over?"

I untie my apron and let my hair down from its oppressively tight bun. "No, but I did see some pigs flying around this afternoon."

After I promise to be ready in five, I head to the storage closet and grab my stuff. I rush through pulling on my sneakers and storing my apron in my designated cubby. With my luck, a party of fifteen will come strolling in any minute now and keep me here past closing.

"Bye, Tío!" I call out as I hurry across the dining room, backpack in hand, and close the door behind me before he can change his mind.

Joaquin's waiting for me on the curb, his bike propped against a fire hydrant. Before we do our usual dance to squeeze onto the seat together, I pause on the sidewalk to breathe in a deep lungful of the cool spring air. "Sweet, sweet freedom."

Joaquin takes a sniff of his own, his face crumpling into a grimace. "Freedom smells like car exhaust."

It does, but that doesn't make it any less sweet.

CHOOSE LOVE.

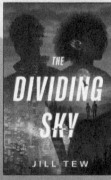

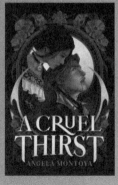

JOIN THE JOY REVOLUTION!
Swoony romances written by and starring people of color

Learn more at GetUnderlined.com